OF LOVE AND LOYALTY

AN IMMIGRANT'S JOURNEY

BARRY L. PFANSTIEL

Dedicated to Janine, my wife of fifty years, my love, my confidante, and my best friend

To Ann & Otto

Happy Reading

Hope you enjoy

[illegible]

Of Love and Loyalty:
An Immigrant's Journey

This book is a work of fiction. References to real people, events, establishments, organizations, or locales are intended only to provide a sense of authenticity and are used fictitiously. All other characters and all incidents and dialogue are drawn from the author's imagination and are not construed as real.

Cover and interior design by Raney Day Creative, LLC.

Printed in the United States of America.

Created with Vellum

Mendorf Family Tree

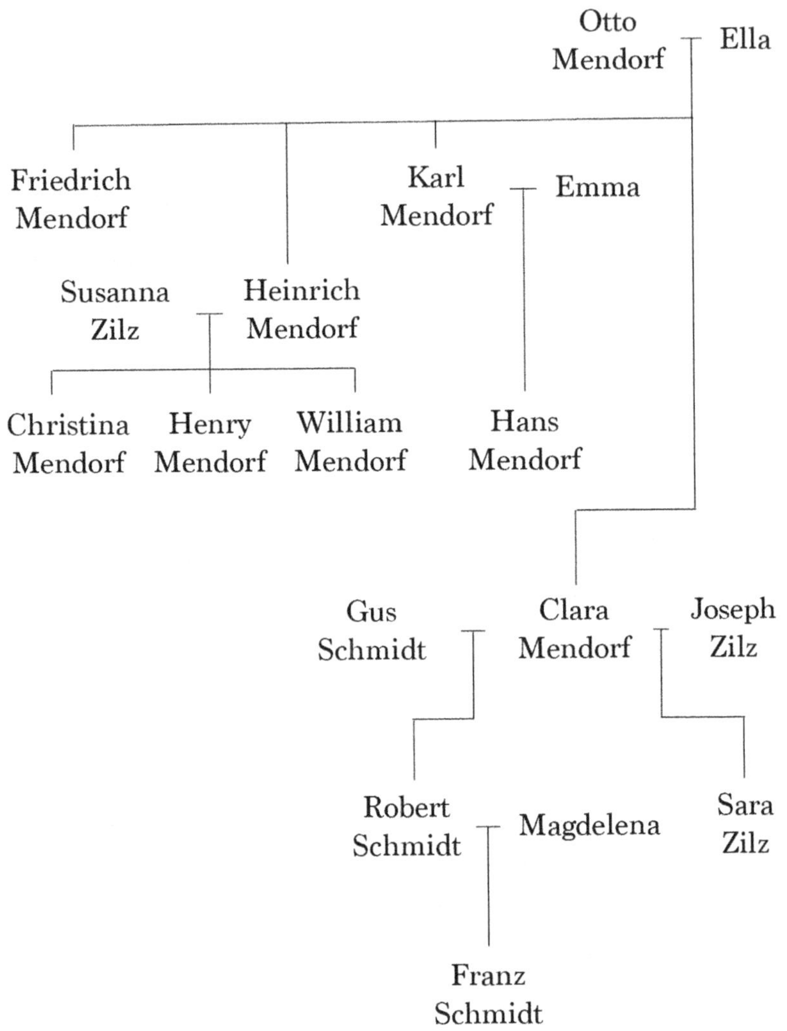

Zilz Family Tree

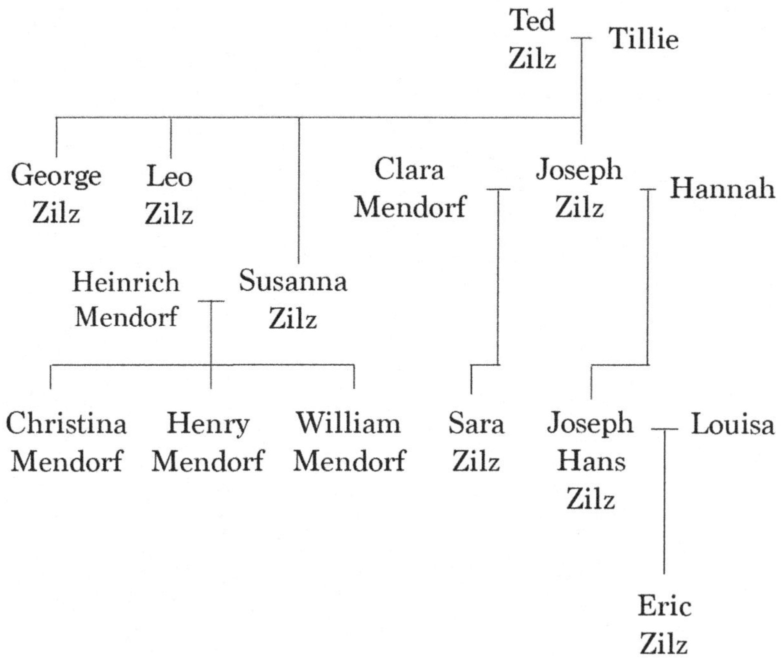

CHAPTER 1

October 1870 ... Near Schwabach, 10 miles from Nurnberg in Bavaria, Southern Germany in the home of the Otto and Ella Mendorf family

I'm standing looking out the back window of the main room of our simple house. I'm looking out, but not really seeing anything. All I see are mental images of my brother, Friedrich. I close my eyes but he's still there ... a jumble of disconnected pictures, thoughts, and feelings. My brother is dead! I can't believe it. It can't be.

Our neighbor, Ervin, brought us the news. He had seen his body … in France … six weeks ago ... the Battle of Sedan ... lying in the cold mud. Did Ervin really say that his body was lying in the cold mud or was that just how I imagined it? Confusion … it can't be, but it is. I am empty … my stomach churns ... I gag ... I run outside and throw up.

I come back in and see Mama. She sits sobbing, tears rolling down her face and onto the torn shirt that she had been mending. Trembling, she looks up at me with red eyes of desperation, as if to say, "O dear God, no ... make it not be so." She's shivering.

She wraps the shirt around her as best she can to find warmth, but it offers none.

Breaking down, she cries out for me, “Heinrich, come here so that I can hold you. I need you here with me ... please, hold me. I can’t stop shaking.” I kneel on the dirt floor and put my arms around her as she continues to shiver ... I feel her uncontrollable spasms of anguish run through her. I continue to embrace her and pull her close for warmth.

Papa is outside splitting wood. I hear the rhythm of the ax coming down on the end of the log and the thump of the wood hitting the ground. Over and over again ... four, five, six clean cuts ... and then a pause as he places another log on top of the stump. With one swing he splits the heavy oak ... always with just one swing. He is strong, but today he is also angry. This is what Papa does when he’s angry ... strikes out ... hits things.

My younger sister, Clara, lies on her bed curled into a fetal position ... whimpering and shaking, covered by a heavy blanket, and quietly speaking inarticulately to herself.

My baby brother, Karl, lies in his cradle beside Mama, crying for attention. He cries, but Mama doesn’t hear him. She is lost in her private world.

As Papa opens the door with an armful of wood for the fireplace, the mountain wind blows in, announcing an early cold winter.

Mama cries out for Papa, “Otto, I can’t take this. I refuse to believe it. I don’t know what to do! I am lost. What more do they want ... what more can they take from us? We pledged them our loyalty, and it’s cost us our son.”

Slamming the wood onto the floor, the logs scattering and bouncing off the hearth and wall, Papa erupts in grief-fed anger. Pounding his fist on the mantel, he shouts, “Damn Bismarck! Well, now he’s done it … for what it’s worth! He’ll get his dream of uniting Germany … But at what cost? Yes, Ella, it’s cost our son, my Friedrich!”

Both are now talking ... but not to each other ... just rambling, crying, sobbing ... to themselves.

Mama whimpers, "Did he suffer? Please, God, no, don't let him suffer! All little Ervin reported was that he saw him ... his body lying there ... dead."

Papa's soliloquy continues, "Where is his body? We don't know ... somewhere in France ... but I don't know where."

Still, in disbelief Mama utters, "Friedrich is," sobbing and facing the truth, "was only eighteen years old ... just a boy."

Papa, struggling to face the reality, mutters, "I'll never see him again, never talk with him again. He's gone, the one I have such high hopes for ... who showed so much promise."

Mama, continuing her inner dialogue with herself, "I sensed that something was wrong. I felt it. Woke up one night and just knew ... 'God,' I prayed, 'make it not so', but somehow, I just knew."

Fortunately, Mama's older sister, Margarete, opens the door and in one glance, assesses the desperate situation, runs to comfort Mama. Margarete enfolds her and tries to soothe her younger sister.

I return to the window, where once again, I get lost in my emptiness and memories. I relive the day… the last time I saw Friedrich. I envision him proudly marching off to fight under the blue and white Bavarian flag led by Prince Leopold, commander of the Bavarian forces.

I think back to just four years ago, how Prussia had defeated the Bavarian and Austrian armies. But now our Bavaria fights alongside Prussia. We all know that our King Ludwig II has been forced into this alliance. Prussian Chancellor Bismarck is consolidating our Bavaria and other independent states and territories to form a new German empire and is at war with France.

France has feared this unification, lest it dramatically change the political power structure of Europe. And so, France fought to maintain its dominance. But with France's defeat, the long-hoped-for unification will finally happen. I find myself silently reflecting, "But at what price? It cost me my brother!"

I see my sister stir, sitting up, her blanket wrapped closely around her as she continues to shiver. I go to hug her, to give her warmth ... and, I realize, to receive warmth and support from her as well. Holding her as our faces touch and her tears spread over my cheek, I can no longer hold back tears.

My family is dazed with disbelief at the loss of Friedrich. Especially my parents. Papa seethes with anger and strikes out in blame, and Mama withdraws into herself and clings to her sister for support. But we move on. Don't stop and feel. Don't look back. Bury your grief.

It's spring, 1871. My name is Heinrich; I am sixteen, soon to be seventeen. In springtime, each of us has his or her assigned duties. It's planting time. Papa and I hitch up the horses beginning the annual routine of preparing the ground and planting. Clara, my fourteen-year-old sister also pitches in. Mama, who is nursing my six-month-old baby brother, Karl, also needs Clara to help take care of the house. With Friedrich gone, the burden of farming falls on Papa and me. I know what I'm doing ... I know how to farm ... but Papa never seems to think I do. He's constantly telling me to do it his way.

I can tell Papa's heart isn't in it. He's just going through the motions. He's angry and takes it out on me, the horses, and Mama. Mama escapes into her world. Clara stays away from Papa lest he takes it out on her, too.

Just yesterday, Papa couldn't find his hammer and a wrench. In his frustration, he yelled at me and cussed me out, accusing me of losing it. It rankled me, and I shouted back at him that I had no idea what he was talking about. His anger spilled over, souring the mood of last night's dinner. He barked at Clara who left the room in tears. When Mama almost begged him to settle down, he stormed out the door and spent at least an hour outside. I don't know what he did, but this morning, the missing hammer and wrench were back in the toolbox. I wanted to ask how they got there but decided to let it go. Why stir him up again?

Papa and Mama are struggling, drowning in their sadness. We all are. But neither Clara's nor my grief seem to matter. Especially for Papa ... all he thinks about is his loss. He mulls on it continually. Something died that day when word came about Friedrich.

But now, there's big news. Otto von Bismarck has, at long last, brought all twenty-six German princes and rulers into a new unity under the leadership of Prussia. Kaiser Wilhelm of Prussia is now Emperor of Germany. Sixty-five years ago, Napoleon dissolved our weak unity as the Holy Roman Empire, defeating our armies and placing us under the harsh thumb of France as he built a new German state and putting into place new German princes. Though we broke Napoleon's hold during our Wars of Liberation, we were never able to unite. Instead, we remained distinct regions and territories, each having its prince, most of whom were selfish and petty and only continued our misery.

But now, we are united into a nation. Our Bavarian forces fought alongside the Prussian army, decisively defeating the hated French at the Battle of Sedan, where my brother was killed. There we had captured over 60,000 soldiers and had even taken as hostage their king, Napoleon III. Our fellow Germans now think of September 2, 1870, as "Sedan Day", to commemorate the battle that would ensure a new German Empire.

Our German forces then besieged Paris to starve the citizens of food and supplies as the winter approached. The animals of the Paris Zoo were slaughtered and eaten as were the city's dogs and cats … even rats. In January of this year, our army began shelling the city into surrender.

The French have been humiliated. France has been forced to

pay Germany five billion francs. Then on January 18, on French soil, in the Hall of Mirrors at the Palace of Versailles outside Paris, Kaiser Wilhelm of Prussia was declared Kaiser of the new united Germany Empire. Thus, it is now Germany, not France, that is THE power in Europe to be reckoned with. And finally, for the first time since 1648, Germany has also regained control of the coveted territory of Alsace-Lorraine. Indeed, France has been disgraced!

It's the talk of the village! It's a new day! Germany is in power! We are now part of a German Empire, the Second Reich, what so many had for so long striven to achieve ... and now it has come to pass. They say that life is good now.

But for our family, life is not good. That new holiday, September 2, Sedan Day, will not be remembered as a day of celebration but as the day that Friedrich died. It has cost us too much. Faced with compulsory military service for every young man, my parents are fretting about the possibility of losing me to the military. At least, I know Mama is.

As Papa and I plant our crop, I can tell that something is germinating in Papa's mind, an idea, a plan. As the crops grow during the summer, that idea is growing too.

In mid-September, he lets us in on his decision. He has made up his mind. He announces that we can no longer remain in Bavaria. He decrees what we all must now do! Though this is the first time I've heard of it, he claims that for years he's been hearing about the opportunities in America that await all who have the courage to go ... to pick up and leave ... to emigrate ... to go to America.

"But Otto," Mama objects, "Are you sure? To say goodbye to our relatives and our friends ... never seeing them again? Have you really, completely thought this through?"

"We can make new friends," counters Papa, curt and defensive.

Mama continues, "Never seeing my sister, Margarete,

again?! I can't fathom living without her." Papa wisely doesn't respond. Mama resumes, "It means leaving our beautiful beloved Bavaria. All our work on the farm, all our memories ... memories, too, of Friedrich." Biting her lower lip, as the reality sinks in, she breaks down sobbing. Papa lets her cry. He shows no sympathy or consideration. He is wooden, stern, implacable.

Finally, in desperation, Mama pleads, "Please Otto, don't you think that maybe we need to wait a little longer and then decide, to give us time to put our lives back together. Maybe wait another year? Maybe things will work out, and we'll decide to stay."

"No!" he snaps. Shaking his head and blinking back tears, "It's the memories of Friedrich that haunt me, now! He's still here, everywhere I turn. I have to get away from them!" Regaining his composure, "All summer, I've been thinking about it long and hard. I'm tired of thinking. I'm ready to go ... ready to leave here." Then, with a tinge of cruel sarcasm, he adds, "Besides, Ella, you're the one always talking about having faith ... so now, you have to have faith!" Mama stares at him in sick disbelief and leaves the room.

That's where the pronouncement, ends ... there is nothing more to talk about … no conversation. Not by Mama, not by me, not by Clara. Our opinion has no weight. This is so typical. We don't count. What will it take for Papa to rethink this?

In the meantime, Papa writes to his uncle, Georg, who emigrated to America fifteen years ago. He lives in a community of other Bavarian immigrants in Michigan. Papa writes to him in the hope that Georg will be glad to receive us and help get us settled. I don't remember Georg. All I know is that there was some kind of family argument. It had something to do with inheritance. Georg took his family and left the country.

A couple of sullen weeks pass ... weeks of tension, everyone "walking on eggshells". We're hoping that Papa will reconsider now that some time has passed. Maybe within himself, he'll come to a different decision. Maybe, he will see how unhappy we all are about the prospect of leaving. But will that matter to him? Our last hope: maybe some friends will be able to talk him out of it. But he remains resolute. He has dug in.

Mama finally, reluctantly, and grudgingly, gives up. "Ok, Otto, you win! Whatever you want, Otto ... if you think that this will make you happy. But …."

She doesn't finish the "But." She doesn't have to. I know what she means. She wants to say, "But this is all on you. Don't blame me if it doesn't work out. If we lose everything, it's all on you. If the ship sinks, it's all on you. Whatever goes wrong, it's all on you." But she doesn't say that. She only thinks it, but it's there under the surface. And she will keep it ready, just in case.

Papa has spoken. It's his decision! It's absolute!

THAT FALL, WE HARVEST OUR CROP, KEEPING ALL THE MONEY WE can from the sale. Prices are good this year. The economy is doing very well. We sell most everything else we own. We agree to sell our farm and animals to Aunt Margarete and Uncle Charles. We begin to say our goodbyes.

Mama is still numb. She forces her smiles and feigns acceptance. But those who truly know her see it for what it is. "It's all Otto's decision," they say. Everybody can see that, inside, Mama is just worn out and sad. Some are worried about her health. "After all, the birth of baby Karl was particularly hard on her, and she's still run down." But our neighbors and Mama's family agree among themselves, "What else can she do?" She has no choice; that's what marriage means, especially for the woman ... the wife ... the mother.

I look at Papa and, I think that, deep down, he wonders, too. "Am I making the right choice?", he seems to be asking in those moments when he thinks no one is watching him. But I see. It seems that, without Friedrich, he has lost much resolve. Friedrich really was his right arm. I see him talking to himself ... deliberating ... or maybe he's talking things over with Friedrich.

He is a stubborn man. As I have come to know him in my sixteen years, he thinks he must keep on going with the plan. It has come this far, and he must go on. No turning back! Turning back would make him look foolish.

But maybe it would make him look wise. But he won't see it.

All I know is that I have to leave ... and so does Mama and so does Clara. That's what it means to be family. We walk together and remain loyal.

Clara's just afraid. At fourteen, she's leaving everything that's familiar. She has never been one for adventure, for taking chances. She feels safe when she's home. And leaving our home is a huge gamble, fraught with danger and good reasons to fear. But Mama finally just tells her, "Clara, we have to do what Papa wants on this. And that's the final word ... just accept it." But her words sound hollow, even to herself.

Aunt Margarete is Mama's sister. But she's more than a sister; she's Mama's reflection … confidante, advisor, shoulder to cry on, person to laugh with ... inseparable. The months after Papa's edict have become long days of gloom. It's like, I suppose, knowing that a loved one is dying, and you can't do anything to stop it, except pray.

At first, Mama and Aunt Margarete were together whenever possible. But as the day of our leaving is growing closer, it seems that Mama and Margarete are beginning to grow apart. It's like each is starting to realize and adjust to the inevitable separation. I suppose that's healthy, but it is hard to watch as Mama turns even more inward. Her once cheerful face is now drawn with sadness and worry. I think that Mama is now more alone than ever.

Aunt Margarete has not wanted to be around Papa. She has avoided him and comes over only when she knows he won't be in the house. At the same time, Papa hasn't wanted to be near her either. He wants to avoid feeling the cold wrath emanating from her presence.

One day, they happened upon each other as Margarete was leaving our house. I watched from the barn as they both went out of their way not to come face to face. Not a single word was spoken between them. But their behavior told it all.

Margarete's husband, my Uncle Charles, is in a bind. He's always been close friends with Papa but now he's caught between his wife and his brother-in-law/friend. He is a mild man and hates the undercurrent. Lately, he's begun to drink more than his usual two mugs of beer a day.

Their son, my cousin, Lorenz, has told me that he'll be glad when we leave so that maybe his own home and family can get back to normal. He isn't being spiteful, just anxious about his own peace and tranquility.

FOURTEEN MONTHS AFTER FRIEDRICH'S DEATH, WE HAVE SOLD OR given away just about everything. These have been the most anxiety-ridden months of my family's life. But the long-dreaded day is quickly approaching when we must leave.

Papa and Mama retrieve the gold that they had squirreled away over the years to be used in case of an emergency. They exchange much of their German paper money for gold and silver. They also secure a large amount of American paper money. Mama sews most of our gold and silver and much of the American money into the linings or her and Papa's heavy coats for safekeeping.

We pack all our essential belongings into a wooden trunk that Papa has meticulously designed and crafted. Its hinged top is shaped like a camel-like hump, intended to ensure that no luggage can be placed on top of it, lest it should be cracked or even crushed. Nor can it be put at the bottom of a stack where water might otherwise damage it. The inner walls are made of two-layered sheets of wood in which Papa has chiseled spaces for concealing most of the American paper money. He then carefully has joined the layered sheets together and finishes the edges so that they appear to be single pieces of wood.

Papa has purchased an Austrian-built Gasser M1870 revolver along with twenty-four 11.25 mm cartridges. He explains to me that this is a very fine pistol, and these very lethal cartridges were designed for a military rifle. But they also fit this revolver. He removes the hammer spring from the pistol to disable it in case someone breaks into the trunk and steals it. Mama sews this spring into the hem of his coat as well.

And now, we face our final night here; we leave tomorrow at dawn. The atmosphere of our final supper is one of deafening silence. No one looks happy, certainly not Mama, Clara, or me. If Papa is, he knows better than to express it.

TONIGHT, I SAY GOODBYE TO MY GIRLFRIEND, AMELIA DILGER, who has been my girlfriend ever since I can remember! I love her. She's my age, and she says she loves me, too. Two weeks ago, I asked her to come along, and she sort of wanted to, too. But her parents said, "No, definitely not." Last week, she hesitated to tell me, but she divulged that her father had added, "Otto is on a fool's errand. He's still grief-stricken, and he doesn't have the sense God gave a bitch in heat."

We both laughed. But her father may be right.

If only she were a little older, we could get married. But I must leave because I'm now the oldest son. Papa needs me ... and I think my sister, Clara, does too. I know Mama needs me. Like it or not, I feel like the glue that is holding this family together. I have no real choice. It's all about family loyalty.

But Amelia needs me, too, and I need her and want her ... especially so, since Friedrich died. Amelia and I grew up together. I can't imagine not having her close by. I don't think I can live without her. We promise to keep in touch, to write but, inside, we both know that the mail is unpredictable and unreliable. But still, we promise.

And so, on this last night, we embrace and hug and kiss and kiss and inwardly struggle to restrain ourselves. We both have such yearning to be ... closer and never have to separate. Through tears, our parting words are the familiar *Auf Wiedersehen*, but we both know it's not true. *Auf Wiedersehen* means "See you again, soon" but we won't. Deep down we both know that. When I get home, I feel so empty and alone. And I am angry … but helpless.

WE LEAVE AT DAWN, SEEING FOR THE LAST TIME OUR FARM, OUR land, the house where I was born. I leave behind all my memories … the tree I fell from and was knocked unconscious, the barn where we used to play, and, just last year, the place where I first kissed Amelia … seeing for the last time our familiar and simple life.

Aunt Margarete and Uncle Charles take us in their wagon. Clara and I sit in the rear, feet hanging over, facing backward, seeing all that is familiar slowly recede. I glance at Clara, and she looks at me with sad teary eyes. I put my arm around her to comfort her. Mama and her sister sit on the hard seat in the middle, eyes downcast, both brokenhearted. So many memories and now, so much emptiness ... tainted with resentment and bitterness. Papa sits in the front next to Uncle Charles. Both are silent. Papa is looking forward. He sees where we're headed. I hope he is happy about what he sees. No one else is.

We say our goodbyes at the train station in Nurnberg. Mama and Aunt Margarete embrace and weep and cannot pull themselves apart. Papa just stands and stares at the ground, and Uncle Charles turns and walks about twenty feet away. Neither Papa nor Uncle Charles is going to intrude in this final goodbye. Finally, after what seems like an eternity, they separate. Aunt Margarete won't look at Papa, as she comes and gives Clara a warm hug of goodbye. Clara is crying, clutching a blanket to keep from shivering.

Aunt Margarete embraces me, and I fight back tears. Finally, she does look at Papa with a hard angry stare, and spits out, "Well, I hope this makes you happy." Not responding, Papa turns away and goes to the wagon and calls Uncle Charles to help unload the heavy trunk and lug it into the train station. Then, Uncle Charles, glancing at Papa, looks down and away, weakly extending his hand to Papa for the last time. He says goodbye to Clara and me gives a quick hug to Mama and then walks away, back toward his wagon. That's it.

With as little talking as necessary, Papa buys the tickets, and we board the train. It is a sullen journey, the air thick with tension. Papa, obviously uneasy being around us, attempts to make conversation with others on the train. He meets one other man, and they begin to pass the time together. I'm personally glad to see Papa disassociate himself from Mama, Clara, and me. I don't want to be around him right now.

We travel a great distance to the port of Hamburg. Papa books third-class passage on the *SS Westphalia*, an iron ship that combines both steam power as well as two masts for sails. We join the mass of passengers boarding: 90 in first class, 130 in second class, and 520 with us in third class.

The captain expects the trip to New York will take two

weeks. From New York, we plan to make our way to Michigan. We still have received no reply to the letter Papa had written to his Uncle Georg. Maybe he never received it. "It doesn't matter," Papa assures us, "Uncle Georg will be delighted to see us and help get us settled." That's not reassuring.

Those of us in third class will stay in the lowest level on the ship, along with all the cargo and animals that are being transported. We will be cramped, and we worry about sickness that is easily spread. Some ocean voyages have had an alarming number of deaths due to cholera and dysentery. But hopefully, because this ship is only four years old, the newer ventilation systems now being used will provide better conditions for health and comfort.

Before we get on board, Mama buys a supply of bread and other items in case there is a shortage of food.

Onboard, we must always stay together to help each other and for protection. We are constantly vigilant against theft, especially since the German government is encouraging the poor to emigrate to America, as Germany no longer wants to care for them.

CHAPTER 2

On February 22, 1872, we set sail on this voyage that will take us away from our beloved homeland, most likely never to return.

Third-class conditions are wretched. We are crammed together like animals, having straw mattresses but no blankets. Rows of bunks, stacked three to four high, serve as sleeping platforms. There is little privacy.

The toilets are mounted out in the open against the wall. At first, I felt awkward and uncomfortable letting down my pants for all to see, but really, no one pays much attention. We're all in the same boat, literally and figuratively.

Each passenger has been provided a single plate and utensils for the entire journey. The food is served from large pots, and the roughest and strongest passengers butt and bully their way ahead of the weak and elderly. It can be bedlam just to get to eat, let alone find enough to eat.

When the weather cooperates, we are allowed up to the outside deck during the day, but our third-class deck space is crowded. At least there is some fresh air. But at night and when the weather turns rainy and stormy, we are forced to go back down into the stench and close quarters of our miserable accommodations.

The noise of the engine and propellor is relentless, making it almost impossible to sleep or even talk loud enough to be heard. Plus, the vibration caused by the steam engine and the steering mechanism is frightening. At first, I worry that the ship must be sinking, but then after a while, I get used to it.

There is a constant tension in the air. Arguments and fights are common. Just a little while ago, two men almost came to blows in the food line. Luckily, early in the trip, we met other immigrant families, and together we have formed an informal alliance to watch out for one another. With all of us together, this makes us a formidable force against anyone who might try to take advantage of us or try to steal from us or perhaps even rape a young girl or woman. This comradeship and support will be essential if some of us get sick.

I'M CONCERNED ABOUT CLARA. SHE'S ALMOST THREE YEARS younger than I am and just doesn't know how to handle all this. She just wants to stay in that bug-infested bed and not venture out anywhere. She's afraid. Last night she cried herself to sleep … again. She's not eating, either. I'm afraid she'll get sick.

Mama isn't very supportive of her because Mama is dealing with her own struggles. She misses Aunt Margarete already. Clara and I know that she has gone along with Papa just because she realizes that's what it means to be married … to stay loyal no matter what. What else could she have done? But the resentment shows in her face and eyes, in her attitude toward Papa, and her snapping at Clara and me. Even almost two-year-old Karl, I think, notices things are not normal, even though he cannot understand why.

As I think about Mama, I wonder how a person can remain

loyal under such conditions without losing her mind? At some point, you can't force loyalty, can you? At least not an allegiance that comes from the heart. I hope that, if someday I can marry Amelia … or someone else, I guess … that she will not feel her loyalty to me will be forced. That would break my heart.

Speaking of Amelia, I miss her. We've known each other our whole lives … as children, school mates and attending the same church. As we grew older, we believed we were meant for each other. I'll never forget that last night together … the way she felt in my arms, her wonderful delicate smell, the tone of her voice, the affectionate words she spoke, her body pressed close to mine, the yearning and desire in her ... and in me ... the tears and the final lingering kiss and the embrace goodbye that we never wanted to end. It hurt so much to say goodbye.

This is all Papa's fault ... taking our family away from our home and relatives and friends. But I'm stuck, like a mouse in a cage, and I see no way out.

I refuse to believe that my brother Friedrich would want our family to end up like this. I'm sure he'd want us to grieve for him and remember him but then continue on with our lives. But as it is now, his loss is almost like a ghost that haunts us, that plagues our family, that sucks away our joy and love. Everywhere we look, Friedrich is there. Every step we take is a step into grief ... grief no longer for just Friedrich but, for myself, anguish for having left everything I love behind. I deeply resent Papa.

Speaking of Papa, he puts on a strong front ... displays a lot of bravado and assuredness with others we've gotten to know.

This afternoon, though, something very interesting and telling happened. Several of the men in our informal alliance were up on deck in the fresh air discussing conditions back in Germany. Most of them are from Prussia. Many of them have been forced off their farms and into the large cities because of overpopulation and falling prices. They spoke about how the rapid industrialization of Germany has created housing shortages in the cities, making housing unaffordable. The result is that people are being pressed into overcrowded, unhealthy, and dangerous living and work conditions. The rich industrialists are becoming wealthier while the laborers are fighting just to survive. These men long to return to the simple rural life and farming, to get away from the large dirty overcrowded cities and slums. Thus, they are sailing for America.

A couple of them speak of Bismarck's "cultural struggle" to rein in the Catholic Church. This movement includes dissolving religious orders, forcing Church bishop and clergy appointments to be approved by the government, purging Catholic clergy from the Prussian government, and even, on occasion, the confiscation of church property. This, they say, is intolerable, and so they too are leaving, emigrating.

As they speak, it is clear they all have very legitimate reasons for emigrating. For years, they have been hearing about the promise that America held. Most of them had relatives there already who have enticed them to come over as well. These are issues of life or death, hope or despair, freedom or repression.

But as they have spoken, Papa seems strangely quiet for a change, kind of pacing and acting antsy, anxious, nervous. I can tell he's not comfortable. And then, someone inquires why he has led his family on this journey. As he tries to tell them his reasons, several men look at him quizzically and others just stare down on the deck. It's obvious that we weren't desperate, that we weren't losing our land or our farm. It's clear to them that we weren't being swept up in the dirty, smelly, and dangerous industrialization of Germany, having to face the slums. Nor were we being forced to accept government interference in our faith. To top it all, we had lived in the beautiful state of Bavaria. So why did we leave? Why are we emigrating? Why? This seems to be their unspoken question.

It's a good question. Papa's half-baked answers don't make

sense to them. I think I know why: Papa is lost; he's on the run. Now, part of me is beginning to feel sorry for him. Resentment and compassion ... for the same person ... at the same time ... it's strange but true.

MAMA HAS MADE A NEW FRIEND ON THE SHIP, GERTRUDE HEINS. She and her husband and four children are also emigrating, headed to a town in Missouri. Gertrude is perceptive. I'm sure she can tell that Mama is miserable and sad. Since the day we set sail, she has taken time to befriend Mama. Surprisingly and, for me, happily, Mama has begun to open up to her.

We have seen a change in Mama. I've been able to tell when I look at her after she has been talking with Gertrude, that she has often been crying. These are tears of sadness, yet she seems to be becoming more accepting of this venture. All things considered, strangely enough, Mama's becoming much more like she was two years ago when Friedrich was still living. Clara and I remember when we were happy on our Bavarian farm. I have no idea what Gertrude and Mama have been talking about, but I think it's good for Mama and I know it's better for Clara and me. All Mama has volunteered to us is that she has found a new friend.

But now I'm worried because, once we disembark in New York, she and Mama will again go their separate ways. But I do enjoy this brief time of seeing Mama a little happier.

Tonight, though, something is up. Mama has insisted that we have a private meeting of our family. I've never seen my mother like she is this evening.

This family meeting has been called and is being led by Mama. Papa just stands there, obviously confused and wondering. Mama begins, "I apologize for being so unhappy, and I confess that I still am." Then, her eyes turning to Papa, she frankly states, "Otto, I have something I must say, and I want you to hear me. I want you to listen well and consider what I'm saying."

Papa looks shocked; he purses his lips, looks around like a scared rabbit, and fidgets. Mama launches into her well-thought-through presentation. "Otto, you have not been at all considerate to your family in this decision and in uprooting our lives. You have taken me away from my sister." She pauses to fight back tears and then, regaining control, "You have taken Heinrich away from Amelia and Clara away from the place where she felt safe." When he tries to argue, she shushes him, saying, "This is my turn to talk, and I want you to hear me out." I am speechless and amazed at how Mama is asserting herself.

"Otto, you have no idea whether or not we are even welcome in Michigan, since you never heard back from Uncle Georg. Maybe your only letter to him got lost, or maybe he doesn't want us there. Or maybe he's dead by now." She continues, "You remember the big argument that your father had with Georg, back in the 50s ... about inheritance. He emigrated after that. Remember?" Papa, reluctantly but honestly, admits that he too wonders whether Michigan is a good idea.

And then she proceeds to come straight out and excitingly state, "Look, we have been invited to come to Missouri with the Heins." I practically faint in disbelief. "Gertrude says that her husband, Albert, thinks that would be a good idea ... that he likes our family and believes we would be hard workers. He understands that it must be especially hard for you, Otto, to have lost Friedrich. Albert has a brother in Missouri already. He and his family have been there fifteen years, and he is constantly encouraging more immigrants to come and join them."

She then proceeds to tell Papa, "You know I didn't want to do this. I thought then that you were jumping too fast. I finally agreed because that's what a loyal wife should do, and you had given me no other choice. But now I want and need security. If our life in America is going to work, I'll have to come on board with you, and that's what I want to do." And looking at both Clara and me, she continues, "Really, we all have to come on board." Again, addressing Papa directly, "But I want you to be honest with yourself and realistic. We are in deep water, here, Otto. We have only one shot at this. The prospect in Michigan is not at all certain, and Missouri seems to me like a better future.

"Plus, this community in Missouri is made up of Lutherans." This has always been important to us. We've been staunch Lutherans, even in very Catholic Bavaria. "And to top it off," she concludes, "In Gertrude Heins, I have found a new friend, and I don't want to lose another one."

Her well-rehearsed speech climaxes as she reminds us, "Our ship will be docking in New York in two days, so we have two days to decide. But I vote for Missouri." She bobs her head in an emphatic nod, bites her lower lip, turns, and walks a few steps away.

I am dumbfounded ... to see the strength of my mother and to have Papa be willing to listen! There is now nothing but silence. Then Clara sniffles, trying to hold back tears. I can't help but go to my mother and give her a big hug. Mama is shaking and tears swim in her eyes. I invite her to keep crying. Papa, too, is moved, and I see tears in his eyes, and maybe even a sense of relief and perhaps even admiration.

Later tonight, Papa visits with Albert Heins for well over two hours. When he comes back, he announces that we're headed to Missouri!

CHAPTER 3

Two days later, even though we can see New York City off in a distance, the anchor has been dropped and we're moored several miles out. Legally entering America is not an easy process. Even before our ship reaches the shore, it is boarded by inspectors. Then, we and all the others carry our baggage off the ship and board barges. Papa and I carry the heavy trunk, and Mama and Clara carry the bedding. We are taken to a place called Castle Garden. The name sounds like a wonderland, but it is anything but that.

Herded like cattle, it's a grueling experience. Processing all of us takes many hours, and we are all exhausted. There is no place to sleep except on the floor. Each of us is medically examined and interviewed. We must be on constant alert for imposters who pose as government agents but who want to steal our money or do us harm. Some are especially interested in finding young attractive women to first "befriend" and "help", but then kidnap them and force them into prostitution.

But Castle Garden does offer some important conveniences. Our baggage is kept safe, we can book railroad passage to St. Louis, and we can exchange some gold and silver and German paper money for United States currency.

Finally, on March 18, 1872, we are allowed to freely step foot on American soil, thankful to God that we are all declared healthy and fit to be future citizens of the United States.

The Heins' family has also made it through the landing ordeal.

STILL EXHAUSTED FROM THE CROSSING, WE AND OUR BAGGAGE are taken to the Grand Central train station. We are all exhausted and now, deprived of sleep, trudging alongside the train toward the front to find our third-class accommodations.

We pass the Pullman luxury passenger cars. The folks who can afford these fares travel with the comforts of opulence. We see black men called porters serving their clientele with diligence, helping them get settled in their private rooms. We pass the dining car, already emitting the aroma of rich and expensive food. Inhaling just a whiff only serves to torture our hungry empty stomachs. Through these windows, once again, we see black porters busily setting tables with the finest china, crystal, and silverware of the Pennsylvania Railroad.

We pass the second-class cars where, peering through the windows, we see upholstered seats. At least they look comfortable, although plain compared to first class.

Then, closer to the noisy locomotive we come to third class. As we board the already crowded car, I see that our accommodations consist of narrow wooden benches attached to the floor. I sit next to Mama, and Clara sits next to Papa. Over the next three days, we get very little sleep. The benches are hard and cramped. The air is cold. The locomotive is noisy. Soot from the burning coal of the engine covers everything. It flies in whenever the door is momentarily open as the conductor makes his way through the passenger cars or a window is opened for ventilation to air out the stench of the passengers. The soot somehow manages to seep in through the tiny cracks of the car as the vibration and wind push its fine particles through.

Occasional arguments erupt as people fight for space and some degree of comfort. The smell of unwashed people and the stench of human gas is sickening. My legs get cramped by the hard bench cutting off circulation. I have to get up and stretch and just move around, but it causes so much ruckus whenever I do. All in all, we are miserable, irritable, hungry, and just angry. Inside, I am livid that Papa would do this to us.

Finally, after three days, having also suffered through delays and changing trains in Chicago, we are approaching St. Louis, Missouri. We are now on the Illinois side of the Mississippi River. There is no bridge across this wide river, so we pull into East St. Louis and disembark. We can finally get off the train.

Even though we are stopped, I feel like I'm still moving. It doesn't take long before that sensation goes away, and I realize I'm on firm ground. It feels so good. It is a cold day, and the wind snatches away any sleepiness that I had felt. I stretch my legs and cramped body. I run a short distance away … back and forth, just to take in deep breaths of clean air, feel the blood flowing and my cramped joints released. And I no longer hear the constant clacking and clanking and screeching from the movement of the train. The silence … I close my eyes and let it bathe my ears … feels so good!

We are shocked when we first glimpse the Mississippi River. It is terrifying as we look out, mouths agape, at the raging current. By German standards, this river is beyond belief. No one back in Bavaria would believe this sight! It is out of its natural banks, and debris and even large tree limbs are floating downstream. We see chunks of ice also moving down with the rapid current. We see only the tops of them and imagine how large these must be under the surface.

How are we to get across? Are we to be stuck here on the wrong side of the river until the river is more navigable?

Eventually, we are told to gather our belongings from the train. Passengers' baggage has been moved onto a ferry boat. We are relieved to see that our large trunk is there. We join the other passengers on board the ferry.

We can't help but wonder how this boat can endure the current, the debris, and especially the ice? We are told that this is a specially built boat, made of iron so that it can break through the ice and safely make its way across through the floating ice and debris. Even its name, the *Icelandic*, helps calm our nerves a little.

The trip across is stressful. The boat rocks as large debris and chunks of ice ram its sides, sending cold spray up onto our faces and clothing. One elderly woman loses her footing on the slick icy deck and falls hard. She must be helped up, but I can tell by the tears in her eyes and her labored steps that she is hurting badly. The icy wind off the river turns the spray into ice that peppers and stings my face.

At last, we arrive on the other side, in St. Louis, Missouri.

German immigrants have been flocking into St. Louis for many years. Thankfully, we make a connection with Trinity Lutheran Church near the market district, and we see some friendly faces who even speak our language. A family from the Church graciously invites us into their home for two nights so we can rest, clean up and get ready for the next leg of our journey.

Papa opens the trunk for the first time since leaving Bavaria. We are relieved to find that it had not been tampered with nor had water caused any damage. What a relief to find clean clothes!

To be clean again! To eat some tasty food … German food! To be able to sleep … lying down … not freezing … not cramped … uninterrupted! And to hear our language … and only our language … spoken! This is like heaven on earth!

Digging deeper into the trunk, Papa is especially glad to find the pistol that he had purchased before leaving Germany. He digs through the sewn thread of his coat hem to retrieve the hammer spring, inserting it back in the gun. He loads six cartridges into the cylinder, and He puts it back into the trunk until we head south.

The Heins family has also been shown the same assistance and care.

After having seen and experienced the raging Mississippi River as we made that frightening crossing, we are not surprised to find out that we must adjust our travel plans. We had hoped to be able to take a steamboat south, but we're told that that won't happen until late spring. Steamboats do not venture out until then because of river conditions. No one in his right mind would dare go out there in any kind of wooden boat. The current is treacherous, the gusting wind unpredictable and the floating debris can tear the bottom out of any sized boat.

We are now forced to spend much of our money getting ready to travel south overland in our new country. We purchase supplies, including some cookware, plates, utensils, a lantern and coal oil, an oilcloth tarp, a double-bladed ax, sufficient food supplies to last for two weeks, and some additional heavy bedding. We also buy a used John Deere wagon, two horses along with the needed harnesses, and other equipment to pull the wagon. For added protection, we purchase a Sharps military carbine that had been used in the Civil War as well as a supply of cartridges. Knowing we'll have to hunt for rabbits and squirrels and other small animals, we also buy a twelve-gauge shotgun and a supply of shells.

The Heins' do much the same as they are ready to move south. Mr. Heins also buys a shotgun, but since they are going to be received by extended family, he thinks that this should be sufficient for now.

As we are making all these preparations, a big mongrel dog begins to follow us around. Clara, overjoyed for once, takes to the dog and begins to pet it and talk to it. The dog runs around and barks with enthusiasm, coming back to lick her hand and her face. He is a young, though full-grown, dog. Papa gruffly tells her, "Clara, it's not our dog. Don't feed it and quit petting it. It's not ours." Clara grudgingly obeys, but still, when she looks at the dog, she smiles.

The dog continues to follow us.

After getting directions from other Germans who had settled in St. Louis, the Heins and our family head out toward Cape Girardeau about 125 miles south, our destination being a small settlement named Wilsons Bend. The "road" is little more than a wide, icy, muddy, rutted path.

Thankfully, as we travel, even though it is still quite cold, the game is abundant. We have little trouble shooting squirrel and rabbit for dinner. Dinner that first night is simple but filling. And yes, the dog has followed us; he thinks he's found his new family. Papa now figures that since we and the dog have traveled a full day from St. Louis, it must mean that the dog intends to stay with us. Clara calls him, "Fritz." Fritz gets to eat the scraps and the bones.

Not long after dark, Mama, Clara, and baby Karl are sleeping soundly in the back of the wagon, while Papa and I sleep underneath, along with the dog. It's a cold night, but our blankets keep us warm. It feels good to have Fritz lying next to me also offering me warmth. The Heins are sleeping in the same arrangement with Gertrude and three children in their wagon and Albert and their oldest son underneath.

Sometime during the night, Papa and I are awakened by a soft but persistent growl from Fritz. Papa nudges me and whispers that he can make out movement in the dark. In the moonlight, we detect two figures sneaking from the brush moving toward the horses. Papa draws out the loaded pistol from within his blanket and, in one motion, sits up and fires a shot, creating a god-awful retort, not to kill or maim but to frighten. He immediately cocks the revolver again, just in case.

The single shot is all it takes. The two intruders are gone in a flash. Fritz takes off running after them. A few seconds later, we hear horses galloping off into the distance.

The frightening shot has sent both families into a panic. Papa's and my ears are ringing from the blast. I've never heard such a shot; it sounded like a cannon. No wonder the intruders ran like rabbits. It takes ten minutes for us all to settle down … including the horses … but, not surprisingly, that spelled the end of sleep for the night.

Fritz comes panting back, receiving hugs from Clara, and even, a "Good boy" from Papa. It's hard to tell if Fritz now belongs to Clara or Papa.

A couple of days later, we happen upon another family of Germans headed south as well. They are the Stegers: Oscar, Theodora, and their five children. Having emigrated fifteen years ago, they are now settled in America and are now traveling home from the town of St. Genevieve where they have been sworn in at the courthouse as full-fledged American citizens. They proudly show us their documents of citizenship.

Their wagon has broken an axle in a pothole. Papa fetches our ax and off they go: Papa, Oscar, and Albert, into the woods alongside the road to look for a suitable tree to cut for a new axle. The other two oldest boys and I grab our shotguns and go looking to shoot our supper. A rabbit scampers away and is quickly blown apart when two of us fire our 12-gauge shotguns at the same time. Not much left to eat, but we pick up what's left of it … just in case.

While Mr. Steger, Albert, and Papa find and begin cutting down a tree that'll work for a new axle, we hear the chattering of squirrels and off we go. We have no trouble getting supper. The wildlife is plentiful.

Within a short time, when we return with ten squirrels and three rabbits, the men are working on the new axle. My two new friends and I gut and skin our supper-kill while the women work together preparing the rest. We three German families now in America enjoy dinner together.

After dinner, we sit and talk.

The Steger family is from Hannover. Their story is like others we had heard. The blight of industrialization had also prompted them to say farewell to the homeland.

Home for them now is a few miles on the other side of the town of Cape Girardeau with a different group of German immigrants who have settled and farm there.

We are inquisitive and ask the Stegers many questions. They explain conditions in America, particularly in Missouri. They tell us details of the War between the States about which we newcomers have only an inkling.

Mr. Steger begins by explaining, "It was about the slaves, black people forced to come here, and it was also about the rights of states to make their own decisions and not to be ruled by the federal government." He pauses to think of what he will say next.

Mrs. Steger continues, "Here in America, the relationship between the individual states and the federal government is confusing. States have rights that cannot be taken over by the government. But it's not clear to me how this works. It's not clear to Americans either, it seems. People are still not sure about what individual states can decide about what goes on in their state and what the government in Washington D.C. can do."

Mr. Steger interrupts, "Yes, but I think the federal government did what was needed to be done. Slavery is a dark stain on our new country. It is not who and what America is. America is about freedom and opportunity for all, no matter what race or religion. That's why we came over."

All of us agree that buying and owning another person and working men and women as slaves is just plain wrong. And loading them like animals onto ships and bringing them here to sell is atrocious. And then, after hearing how slave families were separated, how women were treated, and the ordeals that they endured, we are all aghast.

"But in Missouri", Mr. Steger continues, "our state was badly divided. Were the people wanting to remain part of the United States and get rid of slavery and set all men free? Or were they in favor of having and allowing slavery? You see, there were many slave-owners in Missouri. And slave owners thought that that was their right as a state. There were even some who didn't want slavery but insisted on their state having the right to choose … just a sad mess."

His wife interjects, "Missouri even had a governor, Claiborne Jackson, who wanted to separate from the United States and join the southern states. He was one of those who thought that Missouri had the right to make its own decision. He was sure that the state lawmakers would agree. But he was wrong about that."

"St. Louis," continues Mr. Steger, "became the center of concern. Honestly, if it hadn't been for all the German immigrants in the city, then the governor probably would have had his way. The largest stockpile of military supplies in all the western states was stored at the arsenal in St. Louis. It was a massive trove of rifles, muskets, gun powder, ammunition … you name it. It might well have been seized by those who were separating, who called themselves the Confederate States of America."

As Papa and Mama are listening to all of this, I see strange expressions creep across their faces. I think this must remind them of the time when my brother, Friedrich, and the Bavarian forces joined with Prussia to create a united Germany. Our individual states and territories were supposed to keep many of their rights and culture, but the feeling was that Bismarck coerced them into a union, rather than invited them. There's a difference.

I think, too, that Papa might be wondering if, perhaps by coming here, they had jumped "from the frying pan into the fire" … that perhaps it was a mistake. He looks sick to his stomach, but he won't tell Mama. And I wonder what Mama is feeling. The wounds are still open, just beginning to heal a little.

But the sound of Mr. Steger's voice refocuses my parents' attention back to the subject at hand. Mr. Steger continues, "There were four very successful German leaders who had emigrated from the fatherland after the failed rebellion of 1848." Speaking proudly, he continued, "Those four were able to convince enough Germans in St. Louis to volunteer and completely fill four of the five regiments from Missouri initially called for by President Lincoln. Think about that … four of the first five regiments formed in English-speaking St. Louis spoke German! They all volunteered."

Continuing his litany of praise, "It was a dreadful war. It lasted four years, ending in 1865. Near the end, it was like what the Thirty Years War must have been like in Germany back in the 1600s: killing, and stealing, burning, doing unspeakable things" … his voice drops to a whisper … "even to women." Speaking loudly again, "destroying crops and houses, taking our animals to eat. It was lawlessness … nothing but lawlessness. I'll tell you, there were times when we wished we'd never come here."

Breaking into the conversation, Papa inquires, "Do you still feel that way … wish you'd never come?"

"Hell no!" Mr. Steger exclaims. "Wouldn't trade it now for anything. Nothing in Germany holds a candle to the promise of what we have here. As God is my witness, if I would die today, it would still have been worth it"

His wife interrupts, "Don't take the name of the Lord in vain."

"I'm not", he says emphatically. "As God is my witness, I mean that!"

The Steger children are now giggling at their parents' little spat, and Clara and I can't help but also join in. Mama gives us a stern look. It just feels good to see that other families have their problems too.

The parents all decide it's time to go to bed and get some sleep. Of course, all three families by now have assumed we will continue the journey south together. We all feel safer now, and we will be able to pool our efforts and enjoy the company. As two new families, of course, we want to find out all we can about the Stegers' experience in this new and still-frightening land.

CHAPTER 4

After a few days, we come to a crossroads. To the left a few miles away, lies the community of Wilsons Bend, our destination. We part company with the Stegers' who continue toward their home.

Our family continues with the Heins' to Mr. Heins' brother's farm and hope we are well received. It's a little scary. By late afternoon, we arrive at Wilsons Bend and, after asking directions, Mr. Heins finds his way to his brother, Gilbert's, farm. Gilbert Heins and his two sons and one daughter are out in the fields sowing oats. But his wife, Ruth, greets us graciously and invites us all to stay for dinner.

She says that it will be a couple more hours before her husband and the children come in because they are trying to get the oats in before the next rain, which they can already feel in the air. All of us, being farmers, understand. Mr. Heins and his sons, along with Papa and myself go outside to unhitch the horses and take them to the barn to be fed. We also unload the wagons and put everything in the barn as well.

Ruth invites us all to make ourselves at home and clean up if we'd like. She says the quickest way of doing that is to use the creek. Sounds like home, already.

Ruth sends the men and older boys to go first. The air is brisk and so is the creek. It doesn't take long before we're back in the house, dry but still shivering, seated in front of the fire. But we are clean, having scrubbed away the muck and manure from the road trip. Plus, we're wearing clean clothes fetched from the trunk. It's all worth the temporary shivering.

But while the men are out in the creek, Ruth has been heating water for the women and children. They fill the metal bathtub with water, add hot water from the kettle and, one by one, they're scrubbed clean as well.

It has taken well over an hour to get all this done when through the door come Gil along with his two sons and daughter. Gil's face beams with joy at the sight of Albert and his family. He greets them with hearty handshakes and hugs. After introductions, Gil offers all of us a glass of beer. It is delicious.

After a tasty dinner, Gil asks his brother, Albert, about conditions in the homeland. Hearing firsthand about the heavy-handedness of Bismarck and his forced unity, he shakes his head in dismay and disbelief. He is further saddened to hear about how so many are having to give up farming to move to overcrowded cities and work in the emerging but dirty industrialization of Germany. Gil simply says, "That's no life." Yet he also knows that part of the farm problem in Germany is that the price of grain has fallen there because of the abundant productivity of America's farms. Such abundance of grain has driven down grain prices all over the world. Why buy German wheat for two American dollars per bushel when you can buy American wheat for one American dollar a bushel?

Looking at his brother Albert and Papa, and then at Gertrude and my Mama, he says, "But that's the promise of America. I'm glad you have come, and I think that someday you will agree." But he goes on to say, "We also remember, don't we Ruth, the early days when we came over and how unsure we were. We'd hoped we had made the smart decision, but we needed to be convinced. It didn't take long."

Gil then asks about our family. Papa and Mama tell their side of Bismarck's German Unification from our Bavarian perspective. And Papa tells them about the death of Friedrich, which, for him, was the final straw. Gil is sympathetic and tells us that we will get to meet families in the area who have lost sons and brothers and husbands in the Civil War.

Most importantly for us all, Gil says that there is land available, and he welcomes us. He says, too, that in the meantime, he knows of at least one farmer who could use immediate good farmhands, and that will help get us settled and provide us a place to lay our heads. He smiles and looks at my sister, Clara, and says, "I'm sure the young boys will love to see a pretty young girl like you wearing a dirndl. I hope you brought one from your homeland." Clara cannot but smile with a little embarrassment and says that she's brought one. And he says, *Sehr gut* ("very good").

All our anxiety about being welcome seems to have been for nothing. Gil and his family have made us feel welcome.

That night we all sleep in the barn, enjoying soft hay under our bedding. We sleep soundly. No fear of being robbed; no unbearably loud ship engines; no rocking bumpy railroad car, and no hard ground. I sleep like I haven't slept in weeks! I dream about Amelia and can't wait to write her to tell her all the news.

When I awaken the next morning, it's lightly raining. Even so, we have a good daylight tour of the farm. After looking at his farm, Papa asks, "Gil, how long have you and Ruth and the boys been farming this place?"

"Oh, about fifteen years … this will be our fifteenth harvest,"

Papa, looking around at all the woods in the area, asks, "What was the land like when you got here?"

"We initially bought fifty acres, mostly woods, with about four acres cleared. A couple of creeks, two ponds, and gentle hills. Reminded us of home."

"You've done a great job with the place," Albert remarks.

"Well, the first few years were tough, no doubt about that. The first year, we planted what we could and then started felling trees and clearing brush. Couldn't take the time to remove the roots, so we just hoed between the stumps and planted there."

As we look at the fertile soil, our eyes take in just how good a land this is. Gil grows oats, hay, corn, and wheat. In addition, he has four draft horses, two mules, several saddle horses, several cows, five dairy cows, a bull, and many pigs and chickens. He also sells pigs, eggs, chickens, and an occasional cow. The dairy cows, of course, provide an ongoing supply of milk.

He explains that the grain is ground at the mill in town. It is then bagged and much of it sold and eventually taken to the river landing on the Mississippi River. From there, it is shipped north to St. Louis and then shipped both east and west to feed America. A great deal of it is also shipped downstream through Memphis to New Orleans and then through the Gulf of Mexico and across the Atlantic.

This is so different from what we were accustomed to in Bavaria. There, our number one priority was to farm to survive. The complexity of our grain going as far away as a busy port and into the international market is eye-opening. Gil explains it's just a completely different way of thinking.

As he shows us around, he is talking to his brother, Albert, and to Papa about their prospects for settling. He would like to have Albert and his family join them in farming and together buying and developing another 200 acres. He thinks that together they could make the operation much more profitable and be able to afford to buy some new equipment that is constantly being invented or improved.

Speaking to Papa, he says he knows of a farmer who is desperate for help. He had three sons, but one was killed in the Civil War. They also have one daughter. Neither of the two boys has his heart in farming. One wants to buy the General Store. The other wants to go to college and be a teacher and attend the soon to be opened teachers' college in Cape Girardeau.

Later that day, Gil wants to take Papa and me to meet this farmer friend he had mentioned. Albert, Papa, and I get in a wagon to go meet Theodore and Tillie Zilz. Mr. Zilz is glad to meet us and says, "Just call me Ted." He introduces us to his wife, his two sons, George and Joseph, and his daughter, Susanna. Tillie greets us warmly and seems genuinely interested in our journey and family.

She says, "Otto, tell me a little about yourself … about your wife and children."

Otto answers, "Well, we left Bavaria because we just didn't like what was happening as a result of Kaiser Wilhelm's and Bismarck's Unification. It just cost us too much. It even cost us our son … his name was Friedrich … who was killed at the Battle of Sedan."

Seeing Papa's eyes tear up when he mentions Friedrich, Tillie's eyes also well up. She wipes a tear as she excuses herself and leaves the room.

Seeing his wife tearing up and dismissing herself, Ted explains, "We understand. We lost a son as well in war … fighting for the Union … our oldest son, Leo … killed in the Civil War. He had been wounded south of here at Vicksburg. He later died in St. Louis, where he's now buried. But we've never seen his grave." Ted's voice and expression speak to his profound sadness. Almost as if he's talking to himself, Ted continues, "You never get over it. It's been ten years now, and you never get over it."

Papa, also expressing his grief, sullenly responds, “We don’t even know where Friedrich is buried … just somewhere in France … that’s all we know. I’m sorry for both of our losses. It’s not fair, is it?”

After an awkward pause that seems endless, Gil changes the subject … to farming. In no time at all, we’ve all joined in excitedly. Ted Zilz, I think, is trying to get at least some idea about the possibilities of working with us and inviting us to join with him in some sort of arrangement. I’m sure he must wonder if we’ll get along okay. He must know he’s taking a gamble. Plus, we come from Bavaria, which is very different from Prussia, where he is from. There are many cultural and political differences and even some language dialect differences between our Bavarian German and the German spoken in Prussia. That must play on his mind as well.

But, I think, more basically, he must wonder if we know how to farm. It’s a big risk for Ted and his family. Can we be trusted? Can we stick it out when things get tough? And just as importantly, are we willing to adjust our notions to fit this new challenge of learning to farm as they do it here in America?

Both of Ted’s sons, George and Joseph, are quite open about how their hearts are not into the grind of farming. Their interests and abilities lie elsewhere. It surprises me that they obviously feel at ease speaking their minds, and their father seems willing to accept them for their own desires. In fact, Ted even comments that he wants his children to be able to choose their own direction and pursue it. I can tell he means it.

I have some of the same questions about my direction and goals in life, but I don’t dare express them. I feel a duty to do what I can to make this work for Papa and Mama. After all, I am now their oldest child. That’s their expectation of me.

Bringing the visit to an end, Ted looks at us and states, “Well, Otto … Heinrich, Tillie and I and our family will think about it and talk it over. There’s a lot to consider. Don’t get me wrong, we do want a way to free up George and Joseph from the burden of the farm so they can pursue their interests and abilities. But still, it's a big decision."

Papa and I nod our heads in agreement. In unison, Papa and I say, "We certainly understand."

Ted concludes, "We also want to meet your wife and family. After all, this is a family affair for all concerned. And let me also advise you to think about this long and hard too. Even if we Zilzs' want it to work out, it's a two-way street, as they say."

Again, Papa and I nod in agreement. Ted wraps it up, "None of us would want you to jump into something too soon or out of a sense of sheer necessity or emergency. We're talking about an important personal arrangement that we all have to want."

Papa responds, "Ted, I understand, and I appreciate your forthrightness. You don't beat around the bush. I like that."

Ted reaches out and shakes our hands goodbye and says, "Why don't you and your family come back by in three days … on Friday about mid-afternoon. Then we can talk some more."

May 5, 1872

To my dearest Amelia.

At long last, I have a chance to write you. I miss you so much and think of you so often. I have faced many changes over the past five weeks, but one thing that hasn't changed is my love for you. When I close my eyes, my memory of our last night together is so vivid. I want to hold you in my arms again, but we are thousands of miles from one another.

I am still very angry about Papa's decision to emigrate. It's just not fair to the rest of us! But life is not fair, is it? If only

Friedrich had not been killed, if only Papa had been able to be strong ... if only ... if only... if only.

At this time, I will not describe the voyage over ... maybe at a later time. Suffice it to say that, though it was not easy, we arrived safely.

But instead of immigrating to Michigan, we are now living in Missouri! It's a long story how we got here, but it looks like this is where we will stay.

We are hopeful that a kind family named Zilz will invite us into their farm operation where we can work to get settled and have a roof over our head - even if it will only be in a barn for a while. Then, we can take our time to buy our land. The Zilzs', too, had a son die in a war. And then his two other sons have freely declared that they do not want to be farmers. Their father, Ted, seems to have accepted that decision without getting upset or feeling betrayed! That's why he's interested in sharing it with us. Things are definitely different here.

I hope that this works out for the Zilzs' and us. I think it will be good for all concerned.

I will tell you more at a later time.

And now, my final very important subject. Amelia, please know that my love for you has not dimmed in the least. But I also am realistic to know that we will most likely never see each other again. All I ask is that when you no longer feel the same about me, please tell me. And I promise to do the same myself.

Realistically, we are on two very different paths and in two very different worlds. I want to be happy. I want us both to be happy.

In the meantime, until I hear otherwise, I will continue to write when I have the opportunity.

All my love!

Heinrich

As I take the letter to the general store to mail it, I know that it will be many weeks before it arrives and then many more weeks before I hear back from Amelia.

Having finished and sent my letter, tonight I fall asleep with Amelia on my mind. I can picture her. She seems so very real. And during the night, she steals her way into my world, into my dream. I welcome her in. And what a beautiful dream it is.

It's a spring afternoon in Bavaria, and Amelia and I have ridden our horses up on a nearby hillside. Leaving the horses to graze, she and I are walking hand in hand, smelling the powerful fragrance of the wildflowers. Bees are buzzing from one to another and colorful butterflies are lighting onto these flowers.

We stop and laugh as we sit down in the grass and watch two squirrels chasing each other in nearby trees … running and jumping from limb to limb and tree to tree.

It's a perfect day ... just being with Amelia again ... in such a wonderful place ... back in my homeland ... back in Bavaria. The cool mountain air, the fragrance of nature, the devilish playful grin of Amelia, all come together in a harmony of sheer joy and peace.

And then, Damn! Suddenly I am awake. The dream is over; the beautiful dream has ended. I feel so empty inside. It was just a dream! A dream that will never become reality for Amelia and me. I ache. It will never be true without some kind of miracle. A miracle! I pray, "God, please let it be true someday. Please, God. Please." I hurt inside because I want this dream to become a reality for me ... for Amelia and me. But it's just a dream.

In the middle of May, the Zilz family invites us to come alongside them for at least this year's season. Mama and Tillie seem very compatible. Not far from their house is the original small cabin they built twenty years ago when they first immigrated. That's where our family will stay… at least for now. At least we won't be sleeping in a barn!

They graciously allow us to use their possessions such as tools, washtubs, etc. They say, "Why buy it when we've got it all right here? Save your money. You'll need it later." We have free access to their well and even their privy. They have gone so far as to open their food supply to help get us started.

The Zilz family is for Papa the tangible proof of what it can be for our family. They own over 100 acres of land ... some being farmed, acres needing to be cleared, and unfarmable woods left alone to be the place for hunting deer, fox, squirrels, rabbits, and turkey ... even raccoons … a major source of food. The river, stream, and ponds also provide fish.

As it was back in the homeland, we're up at dawn, eating a hearty breakfast and off into the fields. The crop is not yet completely planted.

The horses we bought in St. Louis a few weeks ago take to the plow under our direction extremely well. With double the manpower, much more work can be accomplished and more efficiently. Both George and Joseph Zilz seem very willing to answer any questions we have about farming here in America.

Susanna is older than Clara, and she is very much an extrovert. She's never met a stranger, and she has taken it upon herself to do all she can, so Clara is made to feel welcome and included.

But Clara, being quite shy and introverted, is still not quite ready to venture beyond her immediate family to relationships with others. Clara's at a very awkward stage of life and has had so much happen in the past two years. She needs time to come out of her shell in which she has taken refuge. Susanna seems very willing to let Clara have the time she needs.

The Zilzs' raise the usual livestock – a few cows, and some dairy cows, some goats, many chickens, and hogs. Of course, there are also their horses and a mule. They own two Percheron draft horses for the heavy work of farming, and several quarter horses for riding and pulling a wagon or a carriage. They also own a Percheron broodmare to provide a new colt every year or two.

Ted has decided that we can expand the land for farming by clearing some of the wooded acreage. And so, in our downtime, we begin felling trees and removing stumps. Much of this is new to us since our farmland at home had long ago been cleared. It is hard work – swinging the ax for the smaller trees and using a two-man crosscut saw for the larger ones, trimming off the branches of the felled tree, cutting the trunk in sections, and dragging the logs off to the side to later be sent to the sawmill and cut into lumber.

For most of these stumps, we're told that we will use a stump extractor that is powered by our horses. For the large deep-rooted stumps such as oak, Ted says he has a small supply of dynamite. We will use it sparingly and carefully. He reasons, "The manpower, horsepower and tree extractor don't cost money, while dynamite is quite expensive. Plus, it is dangerous."

During the day, Clara works for a man named August Gaebler, taking care of his four children. His wife had died in childbirth. The baby died as well. The surviving children are a handful. They are nine-year-old, Lydia, seven-year-old, Augie Jr., five-year-old, Hildegard, and four-year-old, Elisabeth.

Clara doesn't like to be around Mr. Gaebler. She says he

drinks too much beer, and she doesn't feel comfortable around him. I assume it's because she has never been around people who drink to excess. But it does pay some money, which we need.

Fritz, our dog, seems happy as can be. He follows Clara almost everywhere she goes. It gives Clara such pleasure. Not long after we arrived at the Zilzs', their female dog, Sadie, went into heat. Fritz obliged her and will soon be a father!

No one warned us about the heat, the humidity, and the biting insects. We're used to the higher altitude of Bavaria … cooler temperatures especially at night, low humidity, and none of those pesky biting insects and blood-sucking mosquitoes. The chiggers are horrible. But the worst is what they call a buffalo gnat. They go first for my nose, my ears, my mouth … and wherever they bite, it leaves a horrible painful welt that lasts for days. These gnats even suffocate chickens, attacking and blocking the nostrils in their beaks.

These bugs are driving us crazy. Ted says it will take some time, but our bodies will get used to them. I can't wait. He simply says the heat and humidity are just something we must accept being this close to the river and in this part of America.

This afternoon as Papa and I are walking home and talking about these nuisances, he says to me, "Maybe we should have tried Michigan after all." I look up at him, expecting an argument, and he's smiling. I know by this that he is okay with life in Missouri.

We're fashioning a new life … a life of freedom, opportunity, and great promise. All is going well. Some call it "Good Luck", others call it "God's blessing." Perhaps it's a lot of both. Life is looking up!

The Fourth of July is coming in a couple of days. We look forward to celebrating our first Independence Day in America.

It's July 4, 1872. The community is having a celebration both to honor America as well as our German roots. Everybody is being urged to share some of their traditions from Germany and join in recognizing both our German unity and our American spirit.

Even though our family has been here only a brief time and we're still adjusting, we want to participate and do our part. Being the only Bavarians in the community, we are encouraged to wear traditional Bavarian clothing. For women, it's the dirndl and for men, the lederhosen. Since we had originally planned on going to Michigan to join other Bavarians, we had packed these items of clothing.

And so, Papa and Mama and Clara and I don our traditional clothing. Papa is delighted as he dresses in his lederhosen. He is quite physically fit and looks very good in his outfit. Mama feels self-conscious because she had put on some weight over the years. But Papa assures her that all the other women of the community have also plumped up a bit … some quite a bit. Mama goes along with the request. I'm proud of my heritage and have been looking forward to wearing my lederhosen. I dress with pride and ask Papa to check me over to make sure I look worthy of my heritage.

Then there's Clara. She doesn't want to be conspicuous by wearing her dirndl and pleads with Mama and Papa not to make her put it on. But she loses that argument. Mama tells her that she looks cute in it and reminds her that Mr. Heins had looked forward to seeing her wearing it. She remembers and smiles, but still, she feels self-conscious. But she asks Mama to allow her to take a change of clothing so she can change later in the day if she wants to. Mama consents.

And so, we all get in our wagon and ride into town. As we approach, the smell of bratwurst sizzling on the griddle is thick in the air, and soon we hear the gaiety of the festivities. Mama has brought Schweinshaxe and Sauerkraut, a Bavarian favorite.

She has also brought a large batch of buttery bread pudding called, Semmelschmarrn, and takes it to the women who are handling the desserts. They receive it with enthusiasm.

The afternoon is convivial as we meet many people we hadn't known except in passing. I've seen many of them around town or at church but haven't yet had an opportunity to get to know them. Today changes that.

There's also a horseshoe tournament. It's a fun game, even though neither Papa nor I have played it often. Then, the highlight is the shooting contest … these have become an extremely popular pastime in Germany as well as here in America. Each participant pays his entry fee and then contends to win the prizes of meat and pies and other baked goods. However, it's the men who had fought in the Civil War and those who love to deer hunt that rule the day! But it was all fun!

Everyone greets us warmly, and, of course, offers us beer. Since most in the community have come from the region in and around Prussia, in Central Germany, they are quite taken with our traditional Bavarian attire. At any rate, both because we're new to the community and because of our unique dress, we're the center of much attention.

Papa is soaking it all in and having a great time. Mama, too, is pleased to be accepted by the other women of the community. She's especially happy to hear the compliments about her ham hock dish and, of course, her dessert. At their urging, she promises to bring the dessert to all the church dinners, filling her with pride.

Susanna Zilz makes sure that Clara is introduced to the other girls. They all warmly welcome Clara and comment enthusiastically about her dirndl. The little children can't get enough of staring at her and smiling. And of course, some of the older boys take notice as well. She looks cute as can be … quite pretty!

For the first time, I realize that Clara is beginning to develop into an eye-catching young lady and that I, as her big brother, will have to keep that in mind and watch out for her. Seeing Clara in her dirndl brings back thoughts of Amelia the last time I saw her, and I miss her even more. But I'm also happy about being so well received.

There's a lot of good-natured ribbing, especially of Ted Zilz. Papa and I are told repeatedly not to let him work us too hard. They tell Ted that he ought to work to build us a bigger and better house. It's all in good fun.

All in all, it's a great afternoon. We've received a heartfelt welcome and feel like we belong here. We're no longer strangers.

As we are gathering up our belongings to return home, out of the corner of my eye, I notice August Gaebler. He has had too much beer and is staring … gawking really … at my little sister in her dirndl. It is a look of lust, and it bothers me. I don't like it.

As we ride home, Mama and Papa and even Clara are talking animatedly about what a fun day it's been. But I sit silent, lost in thought. For one thing, I miss Amelia. Also, I keep replaying in my mind the sight of August Gaebler's ogling Clara. Am I just imagining it, or is there something just not right going on with him?

CHAPTER 5

Dear Heinrich,

It is a great sadness that I inform you that my sister, Amelia, developed consumption. We followed what we believed to be the best and newest medical advice and took her up onto the nearby hillside so she could breathe fresh air and eat a healthy diet and hopefully recover. However, she died.

The pastor had very comforting words and a hopeful message as he spoke of Jesus' promise of going to prepare a place for Amelia. And when Christ returns, what a great day that will be when there will no longer be pain, sickness, or sadness, and Amelia will be able to breathe easy again. We have buried her in our family cemetery here on our farm.

Your letter addressed to Amelia arrived two days after her funeral. We took it upon ourselves to open it. We hope you don't mind. We thank you for your love and respect for my sister, as expressed in your letter. Through our pain, we also recognize that this letter to you will bring you great sadness and pain.

Thank you for your love for Amelia. Thank you for giving her a taste of a wholesome caring kind of love.

Papa and Mama, of course, now ask themselves, "What if we had allowed her to go with Heinrich to America?" She would likely still be alive. But as you noted in your letter, life is full of "if only" and second-guessing. You are right in saying that life is unfair. Death takes the dearest and most beautiful and pure.

Heinrich, be assured that her love for you continued throughout your time of separation and her illness. She worried that you and your family had not survived the journey. Near the end, she thought that perhaps she would see you in heaven. Though thankfully you have made the journey and are very much alive, we believe the promise of our Lord that Amelia is happy and safe.

May God go with you through your grief. We know that Amelia would want you to remember her and grieve for her and then find another to be your life mate. We will remember you in our prayers as we hope you will also remember us in yours.

Again, I am so sorry to have to break this news to you.

Louis Dilger

"A place prepared for Amelia?" "Prayers?" God didn't answer mine! Where was He? What are prayers good for? Honestly, I'm beginning to wonder about the whole question of God.

Sometimes, I even wonder if there is a god. Our modern German theologians and philosophers say things that are different from the way I was raised to believe. Many of them say that God is not the traditional God we find in the Bible, calling that a very primitive idea.

Some even say there isn't a god at all, that the god-idea came from man's attempt to make sense out of this short life and death, to find solace when facing tragedy and death. In other words, God is a made-up idea. They say that life is all mere chance and happenstance. They even say that there is no real meaning in life; it just is.

I'm beginning to understand how and why they say such things. I am angry ... angry at Papa for taking me away from Amelia … angry at how my life is going … even maybe angry at Amelia for getting sick and dying. I know that sounds crazy, but it's real.

But most of all, I'm angry at God. Part of me hopes there is no God; that would make more sense. It would sure solve a lot of problems. There would be no question about whether life has meaning or purpose. If there was ever anybody who did not deserve to die … least of all from that horrible disease of consumption, it was my lovely Amelia. I also wonder why a decent God would do nothing as my brother Friedrich was killed. A God who is supposed to be all-powerful but has taken the two most important people in my life is not to be trusted, let alone thought to be gracious. The days of having simple faith are over for me.

How can I justify this god with the loving gracious God that I hear about in Church? Maybe the philosophers and theologians are right. Maybe there is no god … may be that mankind's only hope is in Man!

Let's face it, in this century, mankind is making astounding strides in understanding nature through modern science and making a better life all by ourselves. We don't seem to need God. There has been incredible progress. The industrial strength of Britain and Europe, including Germany, and, of course, America, is amazing. The knowledge and inventions that have come from science and technology are astonishing. I'm beginning to think that life may make more sense without God.

I intend to ponder this question as long as it takes to find the answers I'm looking for. I want to be realistic. What makes the most sense based on the evidence? Does the evidence point to Man as his own "god" in terms of his genius and ability to solve our problems, answer our questions and bring about a better and more just world? Or does the evidence point to the traditional Christian assumption of a good and gracious and all-powerful God? Or perhaps, does the evidence lead to a whole different idea about God? I need convincing and I'll not accept anything on blind faith … not any longer. Not merely based on the authority of the Church or of my parents. Those days are over.

But I'll continue to go to church. It's the expected thing to do, and it'll keep my parents off my back. And who knows? Maybe the minister will have an insight or thought that will be helpful. Hopefully, somehow, I will find answers.

Tillie and Mama have become good friends. It began in mid-July when Mama invited them over for a traditional Bavarian dinner. She and Clara prepared quite a meal! The Zilzs' had never tasted Nurnberg Rostbratwurst which is a small finger-size bratwurst pan-fried with sauerkraut and potatoes seasoned with spices and onions and served with horseradish and German mustard. Mama also made Spaetzle, a type of noodle, covered with warm cheese. And for the vegetable, she served Gurklen-salat, which is a cucumber salad. And, for dessert, Mama and Clara put together another batch of Semmelschmarrn that she had taken to the July 4 event. All accompanied by beer served before, during, and after the meal. It was an outstanding evening.

The highlight of the evening came, when Mama unbeknownst to any of us, publicly thanked the Zilzs' for welcoming us into their lives and giving us a sense of hope. She went on to say that, even if the future working arrangement would not work out beyond this season, this was sufficient. It had come at a critical time when we were second-guessing our decision to come here from Bavaria. Her words were heartfelt and sincere.

Since that day, Tillie and Mama have visited often.

One rainy day, Tillie came over carrying a small box. She told Mama that it was the anniversary of her son, Leo's, death, who had been wounded near Vicksburg in the Civil War. She felt the need to talk to someone who would understand and knew that Mama would since she had also lost her oldest son in war.

Tillie reflected on her son's life. "Leo was the natural-born farmer, even more so than Ted." She then told Mama a fascinating account of how they happened to come to America. "We emigrated in 1850 because we had to flee from Prussia. Ted had been a professor in Berlin who had been one of the many involved in the independence and national unity movement of 1848 that had swept all of Europe, overthrowing the kings and rulers of the various territories … at least for a while."

Mama said, "Yes, I remember that time; it also happened in Bavaria, and King Ludwig had also been deposed."

Tillie continues, "It was so strange. It seemed like it was going to succeed. We came so close to democracy. But then, the political reformers couldn't agree among themselves over some basic issues. Instead of acting, they just seemed to talk. And they dragged their feet too long without getting enough done.

Our Prussian King Friedrich Wilhelm IV promised to abide by the new constitution, but then he reneged. And before we knew it, the whole movement was squashed. And in a very bloody manner. The wealthy class was afraid. Kings and rulers, the old dynasties, were returned to power. The movement for unity and democracy was ruthlessly put down by the rulers with their armies."

Mama recalls, "Yes, I remember that time. Our Bavarian king, Ludwig, though, never ruled again. The people were incensed with him for his having a no-good mistress, some dancer named Lola. So, when the monarchy was re-established, his son, Maximillian, became king."

Tillie continues, "Yes, and so many of the leaders of the independence movement became wanted men and had to flee. Many endured harsh imprisonments. Others were exiled. That was when Ted and I and little Leo emigrated."

Tillie relives moments of the voyage. Mama doesn't interrupt, just lets her talk. "It was a horrible voyage … just unbearable … it lasted almost three months. We sailed out of Bremerhaven and then lost the wind … sat still in the water for days … and then a storm … damaged the ship … had to return to Bremerhaven for repairs … finally set sail again … people seasick … the smell was sickening … and then cholera … it was horrible. People were dying … old, young children, pregnant women … didn't matter what age … their dead bodies were then dressed in their favorite clothes and thrown overboard, buried at sea. My Ted got sick and lay for many days until finally, he began to regain his strength. Thank God I was well enough to care for him. And then came the smallpox. It was just horrible, more deaths and burials at sea.

"Finally, we landed in New Orleans and had to wait there until the ice stopped floating down the Mississippi from the north before we could take a steamboat upriver. Along the way north, we saw slavery for the first time. Black men and women … even children … property … and being worked at the pleasure of their owners … and I know that they were being used in other ways, too, at the pleasure of their owners!"

"Yes," interjects Mama, "we heard some about that on our way down from St. Louis. It must have been horrible."

"We were so disillusioned. We never thought we'd see anything like this in America, the new land of freedom. It made us sick. Parts of Missouri, even around here, also had some slavery, but it was nothing like what we saw down south. I'm not saying that it's right, but slaveowners around here usually worked alongside their slaves. But still, it's not right.

"Actually, we didn't plan to stay long in America anyway … just long enough for the independence movement in Prussia to reassert itself, and then we'd go back … when conditions got better in Prussia."

Mama consolingly says, "But that didn't happen, did it?"

"No, it didn't." She pauses as she reflects on those days. "By 1853, we realized that we were here to stay. But now, what? Ted was not a skilled craftsman; he was an educator. What could he do to earn a living? He had been raised farming, and so we bought this land at a good price and tried to farm. But he wasn't much of a farmer any longer. He was a professor and, let's face it, an idealist. Others from thirty years before who had fled Germany for political reasons were called "Latin farmers" because they were people of learning, not farming. Well, we were still sometimes good-naturedly called that as well.

"If it hadn't been for the folks here who were willing to take us under their wing and teach us and help while Ted relearned farming and adapted, I don't know what would have happened.

"And so, we settled down here with our children, Leo, George, and Joseph, and, finally, we had Susanna. She is such an answered prayer for me."

Mama now speaks, "Well, all I can say is, thank God that America opened her doors to you and others fleeing Germany."

"Well, some people did. But then others thought that too many immigrants were being allowed in, especially from Germany and Ireland. Those folks formed a new political party, the American Party. There was a lot of secrecy and, if asked what they believed, they were told to say, 'I know nothing.' And so, they were commonly known as the "Know-Nothing Party."

Mama asks, "Know-Nothing Party!" What were they all about?

"Stopping immigration, as I see it. They wanted an immigrant to have to wait twenty-one years before he could become a citizen. They wanted no Catholics, only Protestants … thought there were already too many Germans and Irish."

"Heavenly days!" blurts out Mama. "Surely, they didn't get far with their ideas!"

"It's surprising, but they did. There were several governors and even congressmen in Washington DC who were part of the 'Know-Nothings'. If there was one good thing that came out of that Civil War, it was that it pretty much put an end to the 'Know-Nothings.' The question of slavery was more important than the issue of immigration. By the time that war was through, so were they."

Mama turns her attention to the box Tillie had brought with her. Opening the box, Tillie explains, "I have here letters that Leo wrote home after he was wounded. Every year on this day, I read them. It's hard, yet it makes me feel close to him again. Ella, I'm not trying to force you, but I am wondering … asking … if you could read them with me this year?"

Mama is caught off guard, and she immediately sort of freezes … not sure. She knows what it will also mean for her. It will bring back memories of her Friedrich, who had also died in battle.

She looks at Tillie, at her loving and gentle face. Mama realizes that Tillie's grief is much like her own. And Mama realizes that she has never really taken a time such as what Tillie is asking … no, not asking, inviting her to be part of. That's what it is … an invitation, not a request … an invitation to drop her German emotional armor and feel … and grieve in a place of safety … with her new friend who also needs her at this time.

Tillie reads the letters in chronological order. They are written in English, but you can readily detect that English was not Leo's first language. In the first letter, written on August 29, 1862, Leo describes how excited he is when in Bloomfield, about forty miles away,

we found that wee were to rout a nest of Rebels about 300 strong and wee were about the same number. In the evening about 2 oclock the first pickits fired on us and about 4 oclock wee were in the Rebels camp but they run away and left there guns, coats, blankets, there meat in the fire, the bread in the skillet theire Horses hitch and way they went.

A few weeks later, on September 18, Leo wrote again, sending home ten dollars, promising that more will soon follow. He also writes the following touching words,

My Dear Mother, I have left you but there is one that will never leave as long as I live and that Love. O Mother doan't greave to much about me onley trust God and he sertney will not forgit us. O Mother Shoud I stay at Home and Sea our Govrment lost? No indeed not so long as I have a arm to Strike. O if it be my time to dye I will go to my Father in Heaven where Rebels will never meat us any more, wee will live in peas and part no more. Mother I gefs I will Sea you al Sune.

As Tillie continues to read Leo's letters, Mama closes her eyes and can imagine Friedrich writing similar letters to her and Papa. She envisions Friedrich's battle conditions even as she hears those of Leo … though it was an entirely different war.

A couple of letters later, Leo describes how things are reaching a boiling point.

Gen Frank F. Blare is ours Gen. he toald us yester day morning that we wald Sune bea in a battel and doant dout that, for the River is full of Gun Boats and Steam Boats heare ... Doant ket this dis cureg cause it is a just

and in Goad is oure trust. And this is our Motto Be the Rebels they must Yeale.

On January 14, 1863, Leo writes,

Dear Mother, I was wounde on the 29 Dc 1862 in the left thy but it is gittin wal fast, there was non of my bones hurt at all. I was wonded 5 miles from Vix burg in a bayonet charg but we was driven back with a hevy loss.

Leo is loyal to his new nation. He has no use for those who would dessert. On March 8, 1863, he writes,

If you Sea any of the Deserts tell them that ar to be Shot for duing So. I for my part think So. Thare is honor in that all Reblion must be put down and it will never be done by thease Cowerds. Shame on any man that Deserts. I still goo for the Union.

Later Leo can rejoin his regiment of Company F of the 29th Missouri Infantry. In an undated letter, he writes,

Next morning they came round me like Beas. The Boys told me that the Engenere Regt was campt closed by So I went to Sea them yester day. Here they came round me like a Swarm of Bees Shaken Hands. "How are you Leo you got back a gane." "Yess I want to try the Rebels agan." '"Buley for you and So on."

Subsequent letters describe conditions of battles and how friends of his from home who are part of his regiment have fallen in battle. He describes how at Vicksburg, the surgeons were amputating arms and legs and throwing them into the river. It is heart-wrenching.

On August 4, 1863, he writes, *Dear Mother I am Sorey to in form you that I am Sick and I am so week that I cans onley Set up a little at a time but I think that I will git better Sune.*

He can manage to write just two more sentences and then later he writes, *I can not writ any more this time. My hand is tiared. So my love to all and writ as Sune as you can.*

These were his last words to his mother. He died on August 22, 1863, at Jefferson Barracks, near St. Louis. He is buried in the cemetery. Tillie and Ted have never seen his grave.

Both Mama and Tillie cried great tears together that day, mourning the deaths of their firstborn. Through the words of Leo, Mama felt like she was also hearing the words of Friedrich.

That day, Tillie and Mama became fast friends.

THE CROPS ARE GROWING AND LOOKING GOOD; WE'VE HAD JUST the right rains. It looks like a bountiful harvest soon. More and more, we are growing accustomed to farming in America. The soil is extraordinarily fertile, and the future looks bright.

Today, I see Ted and Papa talking some distance away. I can't hear what they're saying, but Papa is very animated. At the end of the conversation, I see them shake hands and Papa comes back over, smiling from ear to ear.

Papa calls a family talk. As we gather around, Papa tells us that Ted is very pleased with how it is going. He tells us about a hundred-acre farm next to his that will soon be for sale. He's interested in our buying it, if we want, and then the two families working out a long-term arrangement of farming together.

With all the new modern horse-drawn and even steam-powered farming equipment, we can work together to expand our farms. That farm will be available after the harvest.

Papa, Mama, Clara, and I go immediately to meet the farmer, Mr. Schubert, whose wife has recently died. He's up in years and is moving to Cape Girardeau to be nearer his son and grandchildren. His son teaches at the teacher's college there. He is wanting to sell out to us "lock, stock, and barrel", as he puts it.

We agree then and there on a price. Papa will make a down payment, and we will take possession on November 15 after the harvest.

When we come back and tell Ted and Tillie, they are thrilled. And then, Ted, who has such a wonderful giving spirit, makes an incredible offer. He says that we can have the timber from the trees we've been clearing from his land so that we can add on to the small house that Mr. Schubert will be leaving to us. Ted assures us too that he and his sons and, most likely, many others of our neighbors will help us build that house addition during the winter months when things aren't so busy.

When we thank him for his generosity, he says, "Well, if we hadn't had lots of help from our neighbors when we first came here, we would have died of starvation and cold. This, I think, is the Christian thing to do … "love your neighbor as yourself."

What an incredible place!

Yet, as wonderful as it is and as these people are, I still ache inside for Amelia.

CHAPTER 6

It's late on a Friday afternoon. As Clara is about to leave Gaeblers' to return home, August has come home drunk. He opens his wallet and pays Clara for her work this week. Clara is momentarily distracted as she looks down to put the money into the pocket of her dress. Without warning, Gaebler suddenly grabs her and pulls her down to the floor, muttering, "Come here, you sweet little thing." Clara, smelling the strong stench of beer mixed with his rank body odor, fights back as he clutches her and tears the front of her dress. Even though she, having been used to hard farm labor, is strong, Gaebler's huge frame is more than she can handle. He has her down under his brute control. She is trapped … helpless. She fights back desperately, scratching at him, but this only makes him madder and seems to empower him even more.

At this moment, Gaebler's four-year-old daughter, Elisabeth, comes in from playing outside. As she enters the house, she screams in confusion at what's happening before her. Gaebler is momentarily distracted and in turning back to look at his daughter releases some of his hold on Clara, just a little but long enough for Clara to kick and wiggle away from him. Bolting through the open door, she runs home.

A few nights later, Gaebler is walking home from the bar, drunk as usual. Papa and I, wearing masks pulled down over our faces, are lying in wait for him at the top of a hill. When he huffs his way to the top, we jump him and beat the tar out of him. Papa especially is full of rage, and I have to stop him from going too far. I want to punish Gaebler, not kill him! We leave him half-naked in the creek at the bottom of the hill.

He surely knows who did this to him, but, with our wearing masks, could he be sure? Besides, who's he going to tell? How could he explain his innocence? The truth would come out. We got him in a no-win situation.

TODAY, NOVEMBER 15, 1872, WE COMPLETE THE PURCHASE FOR the Schubert farm. All that Mr. Schubert took with him to town were his clothes, bedding, his keepsakes, his Bible, two horses, and his carriage. He left everything else behind for us. What a fantastic purchase we have made!

This afternoon, Mama and Clara, along with Tillie and Susanna, start cleaning the small three-room house and determining where everyone will sleep until we build additional space. I'm not fussy; anything will feel good to me.

Mr. Schubert has left us all his farming equipment, some of which is quite old and now out of date, but still usable. He also left everything we need to run a household. And of course, we have the privy, the barn, a smokehouse, even a small shed for drying tobacco, and a spring house down at the creek to keep perishable food cool and fresh.

And he even left behind two draft horses, and his livestock, three dairy cows, numerous chickens, two goats, and many hogs. Thankfully, his barn is filled with hay from the harvest as well as a good supply of oats.

When we are up and running, we'll be basically self-sufficient. We'll can survive on what we can produce and do ourselves. That's how it was in Bavaria. But here, our lives will flourish even more and we can grow to be more prosperous. We'll have our crops to sell, plus our garden produce that we eat and sell as well. And of course, the animals, especially the pigs … not only a source of meat for us, but they bring in good money.

The woods are filled with wild game. I regularly take the shotgun to hunt squirrels, rabbits, and turkeys. There are plenty of deer. For these, I take out the Sharps rifle that we had bought in St. Louis. It only takes one well-aimed shot, and the deer is killed instantly. Every time I dress a deer and see the damage that the slug from this rifle caused, I shudder to think that this was a rifle commonly used in the Civil War … so much carnage!

THERE'S A LITTLE EXTRA EXCITEMENT THESE DAYS. NEWS HAS leaked out of scandalous activity discovered among one of our church members. Rumor has it that Laura Oberdeck has confessed to the elders that she has acted inappropriately with a man. Everyone knows what "inappropriately" means, even though they won't come out and say it … at least not publicly in church.

But now, everyone looks at Laura Oberdeck differently. The women "tsk-tsk" behind her back and the men and boys just wonder … some more the others. Of course, how could I not but wonder, too?

Today, Clara wants to talk to me privately. She is extremely agitated and angry. I've never seen her like this. We go to the back part of the barn. She wants to talk to me about what Laura Oberdeck has been through and the gossip and rumors. She's asking, "But what about the man? Does he just get off scot-free?

Why doesn't he have to confess, too? That's just not right, not fair!"

Clenching her fists and with tears in her eyes, Clara paces in circles. Between her tears and heavy sighs, she hesitantly shares with me how she still vividly remembers that horrible day when Gaebler attacked her and she ran home, trembling with fright from the ordeal. She says of that the now-mended dress that she wore that day, "I still have to wear it," pausing, "and every time I do, it brings back memories, the horrid memories of that day"

She says, "In my mind, I still smell his repulsive drunken breath, still feel his brutish arms pulling me down onto the floor and still hear his lecherous voice saying, 'Come here, you cute little thing'!" At this, she breaks down in tears and sobs, shaking uncontrollably and with a look of sheer terror on her face. It's as if she's reliving it … maybe she is.

Between sobs, she cries out, "I was just so helpless! I couldn't make him stop! I was trapped. I was afraid that he … that he … would," she can't say the words, "that he would … would hurt me!" She turns and throws herself on the pile of hay and curls up into a tight ball as if to protect herself, shaking as she moans.

I sit on the ground and reach out to touch her, but she pushes my hand away, saying, "No, don't touch me." And now she's quiet … except for sniffing and whispering how she was trapped and couldn't help herself.

Her beloved dog, Fritz, comes over and licks her face and her tears and plops down beside her laying his head across her curled-up body. Slowly, she begins to relax and soon is cuddling Fritz to find comfort.

She continues very deliberately, remembering the trauma of that day, "When I ran home, I was panicked and shaking. I was crying and afraid and threw myself into Mama's arms, crying, 'Help me, Mama, help me.' Mama held me and asked, 'What happened, sweetheart? Tell me what's wrong.' I told Mama what had happened. Mama was livid but couldn't figure out what she should do about it. She held me a long time. I think she was afraid our family would be seen as troublesome newcomers." Breaking into anger, Clara cries, "I think she cares more about that than about me!"

Clara relates that Mama had her take off her torn dress and mended it. "She said she would talk it over with Papa. But that's all I know. Nothing more has been said; nothing more has happened. Mama's never brought it up again. It's like it's a secret, now … a family secret." And shaking her clenched fists with her eyes shut tightly, she says very slowly, one word at a time, "And it's all my fault.

"Now, I have those horrifying memories that I can't get away from. So often, I wake up in the middle of the night, sweating and shaking. And every time I have to wear that dress again, I see and feel the stitching of the mended tear. It's like it glares at me. In my mind, I hear and feel it tearing like it did that day, and I feel his disgusting dirty hands on me, groping me, and his sick perverted voice saying, 'Come here, you cute little thing.' A thing … a cute little thing … not a human … not a person … but just a thing. It just brings it back. It's not fair! Nothing is going to happen to him. He's a vicious monster and he gets off scot-free, just like whoever that man was with Miss Oberdeck."

Pensively, she asks rhetorically, "What would have happened? Would he have stopped? Could I have somehow stopped him?" And bowing her head with her eyes closed, sobbing with the realization, she states her answer, "No, I couldn't have stopped him. I was trapped." As she buries her face in her skirt, wailing, "O God, help me. I couldn't have stopped him. Thank you, God, that Elisabeth came home, and I could break away. Thank you, God, for Elisabeth; I was … helpless … he would have …". She still can't say the word. Then she whispers it, "… that he would have raped me." As the realization sinks in, putting her face in her hands, she throws herself back into the hay, and again curls into a tight ball, crying tears of anguish. She whimpers, "Oh God, he would have raped me." Her arms, with clenched fists, tighten even more as she continues to weep.

I sit quietly and wait while Fritz once again comforts her. After a couple of minutes, Clara has relaxed enough so that we can talk. Clara shares her impression of how the silence from Mama causes her to conclude that no one outside our family should ever know about it … lest Clara should somehow be blamed. "It's a 'secret'! But why should I be blamed?"

A long silence ensues as I remain silent, and she shocks me when she says, "But Heinrich, deep down, I do wonder if maybe, somehow, it was my fault. I recall that on the Fourth of July when I wore my dirndl, Mama said to me, 'Clara, you are becoming so grown-up and attractive. The boys are going to start noticing.' That had embarrassed me … in a good way. It caused me to think of myself differently. But now I wonder if I had taken Mama's compliment too much to heart and somehow enticed, even tempted, that man. He has no wife. Maybe … maybe somehow it was my fault." She sits there in the hay, looking down, wondering, and trying to make sense out of it, as she continues to pet Fritz.

At long last, I break my silence, "Clara, you are growing up … and becoming a beautiful young lady. That's how nature planned it … I guess you could say, how God planned it. That's part of the magic between a man and a woman." She looks up and gives a little smile.

I go on, "I experienced that with Amelia as we grew from childhood friends and, as we grow older, became two more grown-up people who loved each other. That attraction was just there, and it was strong … really strong. Yes, a big part of me wanted to have Amelia as my own, yes, completely. I was ready to marry her, but we were still too young. Or that's what they all said. I had such longing, and I think she did too."

Clara looks at me, raising her eyes with sort of a quizzical expression. I ignore her look and go on, "But, Clara, my love for Amelia meant that I honored her and would never ever want to hurt her. And I would certainly never want to take advantage of her. And the thought of what that lecherous old man was trying to do to you … it's revolting! More than that, I want it so that he can never try that with anyone ever again."

And before I know it, I blurt out, "That's why I'm glad that…" and then I stop myself from saying what I want Clara to know, but it is not my place to tell her. I want to say, "That's why I'm glad that Papa and I went after Gaebler one night when he was drunk and gave him a taste of his own medicine!" But I don't say it; I stop in time.

But Clara noticed. She asks, "You're glad that … what?" I lie quickly, "Oh, I just lost my train of thought for a moment." And I rebound with, "That's why I'm so glad that Amelia and I didn't cross the line."

I can tell by her expression that Clara doesn't quite "buy" the explanation but lets it pass. She wants my opinion. "Heinrich, I am just so confused. Ever since that day, I don't know how to act with boys, especially the older boys. What happened haunts me in my dreams. I'm afraid that it has tarnished my soul. I think maybe I need to go confess my sin to Pastor. But what have I done wrong? What sin do I have to confess? Even though I no longer watch Gaebler's children, sometimes, like at church, I catch a glimpse of that man, and I begin to shake, at least inside, and I break out in a sweat and feel like I need to throw up. Heinrich, what do you think is wrong with me?"

I think for a moment and then respond, "I think it is still so fresh, and you have not been able to talk about this. Promise me that you'll keep telling me how you're doing and how you're feeling. I don't think anything is wrong with you. Let's see how you feel in a few months." She smiles and promises.

And I promise myself that she must be told that August

Gaebler did not escape unscathed. And if Papa and Mama won't tell her, I will. It is only fair; it is the right thing to do.

TODAY, I SPEAK WITH MAMA AND PAPA, RELATING TO THEM A little of what Clara was struggling with … enough that, at least, Mama recognizes the need to sit down with her. Papa objects, "But Heinrich and I gave him what he needed. Besides, I just don't want to start any problem here; we're just getting to know these people. Some will feel sorry for Gaebler, having lost his wife not too long ago."

That's the wrong thing for Papa to say. Mama retorts, "Otto, you listen to me, and you listen good! Don't you dare try to defend that bastard, for what he did! Clara is my daughter … and your daughter. She means more to me than a few people not wanting to hear about it if it gets out. Who's Gaebler going to tell anyway?"

Papa shuts his mouth and walks out the door toward the barn. About a minute later, I hear the sound of firewood being split by the ax. Ella has spoken! Clearly, Papa doesn't like it, but he has no choice but to accept it.

I look at Mama, smiling at her, and say, "A mama bear protects her cubs."

"You're darn right I do!" She comes over and hugs me and says, "Thank you, Heinrich, for all you do for our family. I'll make sure Clara knows what happened to Gabler afterward. She'll find out that he didn't get off scot-free."

THE ADDITION TO OUR HOUSE IS NOW FINISHED. WE ARE MOVED in and extremely contented. We have spent our free time during the winter repairing some of the equipment that Mr. Schubert had left and taking some of it down to the local blacksmith so he can make some new parts.

What's being called the "agricultural revolution" is in full swing. This 19th century has seen more labor-saving devices and equipment introduced than one can imagine. Part of the reason is "necessity". As they say, "Necessity is the mother of invention." With the ever-expanding markets for our farm products and with the loss of many young men killed in the Civil War, newer and better ways of doing things had to be found. Otherwise, we would never be able to meet the demand.

THE NEXT SPRING, THE FAMILIAR ROUTINE BEGINS. UP BEFORE dawn, eat a hearty breakfast, and then out in the fields. We know the schedule and the routine. Shoveling and spreading stinky animal manure over the fields for fertilizer … plowing for days on end … disking the soil to further break it up and smooth it … removing stones that had worked their way to the surface during the winter … sowing oats and planting wheat, corn, and barley. Then comes the cultivating to disrupt the growth of weeds without destroying the crop, harvesting hay at just the right time … and finally in the fall, the harvest.

We can use some of the equipment left by Mr. Schubert. Of course, since we are in partnership with the Zilz's, we team together using their equipment as well. With the expected growing profits, we hope to buy more equipment to further assist and make the job easier. Thus, we are also able to expand our land under cultivation.

Life is good. The crops are growing. Looks like a good year. There's only one problem: I don't like farming! But I do it … whatever it takes … for the good of my family. I'm doing my duty.

CHAPTER 7

Summer of 1874. Many folks living in town are coming down with diarrhea that they can't seem to control, and some are dying. It's cholera. A friend of mine died, and I had seen him the day before. Papa and I are talking about this.

Papa asks me, "What do you think about this?"

"Well, Papa," I respond, "From what I read from the German newspapers, European doctors today think it's caused by bad infested water … that harmful living things, called germs, get in it and cause this sickness."

"Why don't the doctors here think that?" queries Papa.

"America seems to be quite backward when it comes to keeping up with medical advancement. Real progress these days is happening in Britain and Europe, especially Germany," I respond and continue, "American doctors just don't believe the findings from overseas. They don't keep up with what's new. There are all kinds of new instruments to help … the microscope, a way of checking blood pressure, checking the heart. But doctors here just don't want them."

Papa continues, "But don't most patients get better here?"

I snidely reply, "Yes, most do … sometimes, in spite of the doctor's care, I'm afraid."

"That's a worry," says Papa.

"Yes, it is," I resume. "I read recently that in London about twenty years ago, cholera broke out in a certain part of the city where everyone got water from the same source. A scientist named John Snow thought that it was the bad water and had the pump handle removed from a certain pump to prevent that water from being used. Soon, the outbreak ended."

Papa wonders, "Well, could that not have just been a coincidence? I mean, maybe the cholera just ran its course."

"Well yes, but there was a local brewery that got its water from that same well. And the workmen who drank their daily allocation of beer from that brewery did not get sick. Papa, as we both know, when we make beer, we must boil the water for a good while before we add the hops. It's the boiling of the water that kills cholera."

Papa queries, "So you think if we just boil our water before we drink it, that will keep us from getting sick?"

"Yes sir, I do … at least it's worth a try."

"Well, I guess that's what we have to tell everyone to do."

"But don't bother to tell Doctor Gilmore. I tried already and he didn't want to hear it." The doctor said, 'I am a doctor and I have amputated arms and legs of our soldiers in the Civil War. What have you ever done?'"

I said, "Well, I just know what I've been reading from overseas."

Then he told me, "Then why don't you just take your German ideas and go back where you came from?"

Papa asks, "Do they know how this water gets bad?"

"They suspect human and animal dung that gets into the streams and cisterns."

Disgustedly Papa responds, "*Scheisse!* … that's horrible! Then I guess we have to tell folks not to drink from the streams either."

"At least not without first boiling it … and let's tell them to boil their cistern water too," I suggest.

WE'VE ALWAYS KNOWN THAT CLARA HAS A WONDERFUL WAY with animals. We saw this when she was very young still living back in Bavaria, and again when we first came to America when our dog, Fritz, started following her.

Fritz is our dog, but as far as Fritz is concerned, he belongs to Clara. Papa has also been fond of Fritz ever since that night on the road down from St. Louis. But still, Fritz's first loyalty is always to Clara. We all know it.

It is a shame that Fritz had not been with Clara that fateful day in August Gaebler's house. It probably would have been a different story.

Clara's gentle, loving way with dogs extends to other animals … especially to horses.

Farms depend on having healthy well-mannered and disciplined horses. Ted owns a Percheron broodmare that recently gave birth. Clara had watched for the signs that the birth was imminent. She stayed with her while the birth took place, soothing and calming her.

And then, when the foal was born, Clara became its primary human contact while incredible trust and mutual respect developed. She began breaking and training the colt when it is just a few days old.

That's how she is with all horses. She speaks with such a soothing calming voice and never gets irritable, subduing it with kindness rather than by force. She gets to know the individual personality of each horse. Horses are smart animals and have a great memory.

Clara's interest in horses has naturally meant contact with our local blacksmith, Rudi Schmidt, and his son, Gus. In addition to blacksmithing, Gus has become the local harness maker, working with the tanned hides to make and repair harnesses, collars, halters, bridles, and sometimes, even saddles.

Gus is twenty years old, and Clara is now eighteen. There are sparks in the air at the blacksmith shop that has nothing to do with a hammer beating on hot iron and steel, but these are sparks of romance. Clara takes every opportunity to take a horse into town for new horseshoes or "just to check" that a nail has not been bent and causing the horse to be a little lame. And when Clara "happens" by, Gus easily finds an excuse to take a break from his tedious leatherwork.

They are an attractive couple and are pretty much the latest talk of the community and church. Gus has to tolerate a lot of ribbing, while the women just sort of wink at Clara. She blushes so easily. It's obvious.

I am delighted for Clara. Gus is very gentle and caring, and I can tell that he would never hurt her.

Today, though, Clara has come back upset and wants to talk with me privately. One look at her eyes and I know she's been crying. Again, we go to the back part of the barn. When we're out of earshot of others, she can't hold it anymore and breaks down and sobs, "I just … I just messed up … badly … I just messed up badly with Gus."

I'm immediately thinking, "Oh boy, they went too far, and she is no longer a virgin." But when she starts to explain what had happened, I discover that isn't it and, condemning myself, I think, "What a jerk I am to assume that of her! I'm just a typical dumb male!" But at least I haven't said what I had at first thought.

She tells me that she and Gus were talking privately and sharing their feelings for each other. And Gus said to her, "Clara, you are such a sweet little thing." Of course, he has no idea of the Gaebler incident. How could he or should he have?

But when he called her a "sweet little thing," it touched a nerve deep inside of Clara, and she exploded at Gus. She tells me some of the nasty and dreadful things she called him, and that was when she ran from him and rode home as fast as she could.

After a pause, she continues, "Heinrich, I'm afraid that I've ruined my relationship with Gus. I didn't mean it for him. But I know I hurt him deeply. On the way home, I realized that Gus meant it as an expression of love, but he used that word. He called me a 'sweet little thing.' That word, 'thing'. That's what August Gaebler said … he saw me as a thing … to be used however he wanted … for his sick pleasure.

"And I took my hatred of Gaebler out on poor Gus." Looking at me with eyes of desperation, she continues, "Heinrich, I feel so vulnerable and helpless. There's nothing I can do. Gaebler … that horrible man … who hurt me, who has haunted me, who leers at me and undresses me with his eyes. He … he … he tried to take from me what I wanted someday to give."

Throwing herself onto the thick pile of hay, she is crying and beating her fists into the fresh hay as if she's beating Gaebler, calling him names … both in German and in English. "You bastard … you piece of *Scheisse* … I hate you, and I hope you burn in hell."

Before long, she is exhausted. She looks at me with a frown. She has her hand covering her mouth, with worried eyes. She says, "Dear God, I can't believe I said those words." She sits there now with hands folded in her lap, her eyes looking down. She won't look up at me. "Heinrich, my brother, help me. What have I done? What has Gaebler done to me?"

Bursting into tears, she buries her face in her hands, crying out in despair, "What can I do? I've ruined everything with Gus … dear gentle Gus … he doesn't deserve this … I don't deserve him!" She moans and whimpers like a hurt puppy.

After a long minute, I venture, "Clara, do you want to know what I think?"

Eyes cast down, she nods and softly says, "Yes, I think so."

"Clara," I begin, "strong relationships and love can handle a crisis. And yes, you and Gus have a crisis right now." She looks up at me, biting her lower lip, blinking back tears, and nods in agreement. "I suggest that you go back to town to see Gus after he closes his shop." She looks at me with anxious eyes. "Clara, I remind you … again, you did nothing wrong with Gaebler. Can you tell yourself that and believe it?"

She looks up at me with a more hopeful smile and eyes, and I say again, "You did nothing wrong with Gaebler. It's not right that you carry these wounds." She smiles at me and then looks down again, thinking as I continue, "And I also think that Gus deserves to know, needs to know this part of you, the wounds that you carry. He needs to know the whole Clara. I suggest that you tell Gus about that day and how it has affected you.

"And tell Gus that you never again want to be called a 'sweet little thing' even in the most romantic passion." That makes her smile. "If Gus loved you this morning, he will still love you tonight, no matter what inner hurt you carry." She looks at me with an anxious look. "And if he can't handle this ugly episode in your life that was <u>not</u> your fault, then he doesn't deserve you."

She looks down, biting her lower lip … as she thinks.

I leave her alone with her thoughts.

Two hours later, Clara, having eaten but little dinner and refreshed herself, gets on her horse and heads off. She returns just after dark. She comes in and walks over to where I'm sitting and sternly says, "Get up". Somewhat uncertainly, I do so, not knowing what she might do, and she throws her arms around me and hugs me, and says, "Thank you, big brother." I love you. You are so good to me and so wise."

Papa and Mama look at us quizzically but figure it's none of their business.

Three months later, Clara becomes Mrs. Gustav "Gus" Schmidt! The church is full, and the party is grand. She moves to town into a small house that the folks of the community had joined with the Schmidt family and us to build. Clara's advice is still sought about horses. They're making quite a name for themselves … a combination blacksmith shop, harness shop, and now wise advice about horses.

It's Saturday night and Papa and I are in town at Brun's Bar, and we're sitting in conversation with several others about life back in the Homeland. Somehow the subject turns to religion in Germany and the differences between Catholics and Lutherans. As they are discussing it, I sit there and quietly drink my beer.

On the way home Papa says, "Heinrich, you didn't have much to say tonight in that religious discussion."

Silently deliberating whether or not to open up, I eventually say, "Papa I don't want to hurt your and Mama's feelings and be disloyal to my church. But honestly, the differences between Catholics and Lutherans are not all that important to me, right now."

"What do you mean, they're not important? That's what Luther's Reformation was about."

"Well, Papa," I continue, "I just don't know where I am in my faith. My questions are a whole lot more basic than what you were all discussing. Sometimes, like when I recall the history of the Thirty Years War, I think religion has been the cause of war."

Incredulous Papa says, "Heinrich, is that what you think? Religion causes war?"

"Well, Papa, remember the history. That Thirty Years War, 200 years ago. It was horrible. So many millions of our people died in the war … the devastation of our land and cities, famine, starvation, sickness. ”

“But that wasn’t just religion. Politics got all wrapped in it too.”

“Yes, I know that, too. But Papa, Karl Marx said that religion is like an opiate, something that dulls people’s pain. It promises future rewards for their faithfulness and obedience today. That way, their rulers can keep them stuck in hopelessness and poverty, forced to endure the social constraints that the rulers want. And so, yes, I do think that religion is used to keep people in the social class the rulers want them to be in. And then, when they have had enough of it, the people rebel.”

Papa irritably responds, “Karl Marx! His ideas are dangerous. That's a bunch of *Scheisse* as far as I’m concerned, and I can't accept that.” Pausing for a moment, he continues, “As you know, I'm not a real religious person. I leave most of that to your mother. But I do know what I believe. I do believe that God exists and that he has brought us here for his purpose. If I didn't believe that, I would go stark raving mad! I have to believe that there's a reason why Friedrich was killed, and, I think, too, there's a reason why your Amelia died so young. There’s a reason for all the lousy things that happen. Maybe God is testing us. I don't know all the answers. I just have to trust.”

“I don't know either, Papa. I wish I did. I don’t want to upset you and Mama. I'm just struggling. Maybe someday, I'll get it worked out.”

Papa suggests, “Son, why don't you go talk to Pastor Bachmann? He’s an educated man … the most educated person we have here. Maybe he can help.”

I brush him off and say, “No, I don't think he would understand. He just keeps pounding away at having pure doctrine. And that's fine as far as it goes.”

Papa again interrupts, “Well, pure doctrine is important, you know.”

I continue, "And I really can't agree with him when he talks about the nature of man; he's so negative. Always talking about how bad we are. And I guess that doctrine's important but that's not important to me right now. I'm trying to figure out some bigger and more basic questions. I don't think he'd understand, and he certainly wouldn't appreciate my questions. I just want to see something more relevant to my life right now. I just have to figure this all out by myself."

Papa, "Well your mother and I just don't want you to leave the Church."

"Well Papa," I respond, "I don't know where this will take me. I wish I did. But I think that if there is a God, he wants me to find the truth about everything. After all, I think that all truth is God's truth … that is if there is a god."

Shaking his head and giving a big sigh, Papa brings the matter to a conclusion, "Well, best of luck to you, son. I hope you get your answers. You just got to watch who you're listening to." Shaking his head and looking down, Papa mutters under his breath, "Karl Marx!"

With that, Papa and I rode in silence the rest of the way home.

CHAPTER 8

Today, I'm in town and go by to say "hi" to Clara. I innocently ask her, "How's marriage?" and she looks at me with an impish grin and, lifting her eyebrows, says, "It's great! I'm pregnant! It's all great! Thank you, big brother!"

I am overjoyed for them, but I immediately feel that always-just-beneath-the-surface spasm of grief as I remember that Amelia is gone forever. I feel my eyes tearing up, and all at once, my mood turns melancholy.

Looking at me and with a serious tone in her voice, Clara ventures out boldly saying, "Heinrich." I look up at her. "I got something on my mind that I'd like to talk with you about."

"What is it?"

"Heinrich, you know I love you. And you have helped me through some hard and bad stuff over these last crazy and hectic years. All that's happened since Friedrich died. Wow! And now, I'm at peace with myself … and happy … so much of it, thanks to you."

I think, "Uh-oh, she's up to something."

"Heinrich," Clara begins, "remember how we both knew even before we left Bavaria that Papa was jumping too soon into leaving … all because of his grief in losing Friedrich? And how you thought Friedrich would be sad about how his death has so negatively affected our family?"

"Yes, of course … I think Friedrich would have said that he wanted us to remember him and grieve him but also to get over it and move on with life."

Boy, did I ever just walk right into Clara's trap. Clara responds pleadingly, "Yes, Heinrich, that's what Friedrich would have wanted." And then, hesitantly, but with inner strength, she ventures, "And don't you think … well … that's what Amelia would also have wanted … for you?"

I am stunned by Clara's question. I glare at her, but she continues in her caring tone, "I know you love her, and I know you feel that her death was unfair and without any meaning. And it was … is unfair. I agree." Getting to her point, she asks, "But Heinrich, do you think that she still wants you to carry this grief like a heavy cloud? Any more than Friedrich would have wanted that for us?"

Defensively, I lash back, "I don't do that. Nobody knows what I'm feeling. Nobody can see what's going on inside."

Shockingly, she shoots back, "The hell they can't! Many lovely women would love for you to look at them. But you won't pay them any mind."

I reply emphatically, "No one can replace Amelia."

Expecting an argument from Clara, she agrees, "Of course not! Nobody can replace Amelia. She was one of a kind. I know that. But there are others, Heinrich. And they're each one of a kind, too. There's someone out there who can give you happiness if only you would open your eyes and heart just a little." Looking straight at me, she lovingly, boldly, even pleadingly asks, "What are you afraid of?"

I am struck silent. I walk a few steps away and stop and look up to the sky and clamp my eyes closed and wonder. What am I afraid of? I suck in a big gulp of air and blow it back out. Looking down, I shake my head … confused. I'm angry at my sister for barging into my sacred space. Yet, I also know she loves me and doesn't want to hurt me. It's a tough question.

Am I afraid? And if so, of what? Is it fear that if I find another to love, that she too will die? That to fall in love again will be too painful? No, I don't think it's that. That I won't love her properly? Maybe, because I wonder if I'll constantly compare her to Amelia? Maybe, that's part of it. But I'm also wondering if my remembrance of Amelia is idealized, unreal, just a dream … like the one I have had repeatedly for so long. Maybe it never really was what I think it was. I don't know.

Nor do I know how long I ponder … but as I do, Clara sits quietly and waits. Eventually, I respond, "Clara, that's a good question. I don't know if it's true. Maybe I am afraid. I need to think about that.

"But frankly, Clara, what you said hurt me. You smashed in and meddled in my very private world. I got angry … at first. But I know you did it because you care about me and want to see me happy. But I just don't know if you're right or not. I need to think about that and sort through my thoughts and feelings. I need some time."

I reach out and give her a big brotherly hug, saying, "Congratulations again about the baby. Take care of yourself, and congratulate Gus for me, too." I quickly get on my horse and head toward home, reflecting on that question all the way. Thankfully my horse knows the way home.

When I get home, I immediately go to the special place where I keep the letter that Amelia's brother, Louis, had written. I read it with tears. And then, near the end, there's that line that reads, *May God go with you through your grief. We know that Amelia would want you to remember her and grieve for her and then find another to be your life mate.*

Maybe they're right. There will always be a grieving spot in my heart for Amelia, but maybe I do need to face the hard truth: Amelia is gone! But even in and through the pain of my grief and sadness, life can go on and there's a new day and new life. I know it in my head, but I'm not sure about knowing it in my heart. I say out loud since nobody is here to listen, "Thank you, Clara. Even if you are my little sister, you are wise and brave." And I whisper, "God … if you're there … help me to get through this."

WHAT CLARA CONFRONTED ME WITH THAT DAY IS A MIXED blessing. It hurts. My little sister has a mind of her own, too. She's no longer willing to sit back and keep quiet about what she thinks. So, she let it all out. I admire her for that. Like Mama, she has a backbone of iron when she needs it.

But I admit, I was peeved. Clara had no right to plow into my private life as she did. But I knew deep down that I needed to consider what she said. She had a good point. The last thing Amelia would want is for me to grieve for her for the rest of my life, to never get through it, but to stay stuck in 1872 … in a dream that can never be reality. Amelia is gone! I can say that now. "Amelia is gone."

A couple of weeks go by. This morning while in town, I intentionally stop over to see Clara. I want to tell her what has been going on in me since that day.

At first, Clara appears very reticent and anxious. I bring the subject up. "Even though I reacted with anger at first, I've thought about what you said. I knew you were not trying to hurt me, and that you love me." As I see that Clara's tension is relaxing, I continue, "And I began to realize that what you said is pretty much the way it was. I was afraid of facing her death, afraid of the hurt and the anger."

With a profound sense of relief, she says, "Thank you for telling me. I have second-guessed myself so many times since that day."

Taking hold of both her hands and looking into her eyes, "I'm sorry. I should have come by sooner, but I had a lot to think through. Probably no one else could have done what you did. Thank you for taking the risk and helping me to see."

Tears come to her eyes. Embracing one another, Clara says, "Heinrich, I want only the very best for you, to be happy … to find contentment … joy."

Continuing to hug her, I say, "Thank you."

Then, I pull away and point to her slightly distended belly and lightheartedly ask, "By the way what's that bump there?" She laughs and punches me hard in the arm. "Ouch!", I exclaim, feigning great pain. We laugh together as I leave for home.

My eyes have been opened. I know that I will never forget Amelia, yet it is possible for me to move beyond grief to a new beginning.

WHEN I GET HOME, MAMA ASKS ME TO GO TO THE ZILZ'S TO borrow a cooking pot. It's just right down the road so I walk. Susanna appears at the window and then comes to the door. As she opens the door, I see her smiling face and notice her lively sparkling eyes. I'm instantly struck by her, knowing already her exuberance about life and her loving spirit. Now, though for the first time, I notice, I mean really notice. I see her! Not just Ted and Tillie's daughter, but Susanna! I sense a big smile coming over my face.

Susanna comes out to meet me. "Well, you certainly look happy today! What's the occasion?"

"Mama sent me down to ask to borrow a pot. But…" I pause for a split second, "I'm not, I'm not in any big rush." Not knowing exactly what to say next, I clumsily stammer, "I just came from Clara's, and she says, 'Hi'." We talk a little about Clara's pregnancy and her new life.

For, at least the next two hours, we sit on her front porch and talk. Susanna tells me about her family and how her father and mother had fled from Berlin for political reasons. She explains how it happened that her father ended up farming out of necessity even though he had been a professor. I am so amazed that her parents have always challenged their children to learn and grow and dream of what they wanted to do with their lives. That's why her two brothers' desire not to farm was met with such acceptance by her father and mother.

Susanna explains that even though her parents' hopes for Germany back in 1848 had not materialized then, they feel that they had been a part of the movement. It finally did lead to the unification of Germany, even if it was over twenty years later. They feel that their earlier role was meaningful. Susanna is proud of her parents.

I also share with her some of our family's story. She asks me about my personal plans and dreams. "Well," I respond, "after Friedrich was killed, I've always felt the responsibility to take his place in the family … to step into his role. But I don't know if you call that a plan or a dream. It just sort of happened."

She asks, "Now that your parents are getting established here, do you still feel that way?"

"That's a hard question." I pause, feeling a little uneasy, "I don't know. I like farming well enough, I guess. It certainly does seem to offer me more than what I used to think." I pause and think how best to say it or even if I should articulate it, fearing perhaps that to do so would someone be disloyal, "But can I see myself still liking this ten years from now?" I pause and think. Susanna sits quietly. Frustrated and feeling stupid, I stammer, "Susanna, I've never had the luxury of being able, let alone encouraged, to consider exactly what I want … especially since Friedrich died. I feel that I have always had to be there for the family."

Susanna looks at me with those perceptive kind eyes and

smiles and in all sincerity, says, "Heinrich, that is so very selfless of you … generous … to give up your own dream for the good of your family."

Embarrassed, I respond, "Well, it just had to be done, and I guess it still does."

We both sit quietly for an awkward minute. Susanna doesn't pursue that any further. Instead, she delicately changes the subject to an even more difficult topic, "Heinrich, would you be willing to tell me about Amelia?"

Immediately uncomfortable, I look up at her, and again those kind eyes meet mine. I can tell that she really does want me to share this with her. She's not being nosy. Her pleasant gaze and tone of voice invite me … invite me to tell the story.

But how did she know? But then again, how could she not know at least something about Amelia! Our parents have become close over the past few months. Surely Mama had said something, or maybe Clara, or maybe even Papa.

So, I find myself telling her about Amelia, about how I had to leave her, and about the day I received the news of her death … how crushed and angry I was … and still am. Susanna is remarkably sympathetic. When I felt tears welling up in my eyes, Susanna softly smiled and gently encouraged me, "Heinrich, it's okay; go ahead … go ahead … it's okay."

But thankfully, I was able to blink hard and stop the tears. Again, we sit in silence.

"It takes a long time, doesn't it," she ventured. I sat quietly just looking down at the floor, and she continued, "But then again, why shouldn't it … if you care. It should take a long time." Pausing for a short time, she ventures, "Can I tell you something that I learned when my brother Leo was killed in the Civil War?"

"Yes, I'd like to know that."

Susanna begins, "I was only eight years old, but when I first heard that Leo had died of his wounds, it seemed like I saw him everywhere I looked. There were so many nights when he even came to me in my dreams; it was as if he was right there still. But then as time passed, he was no longer everywhere. Slowly, he seemed to be only in certain places, like in the empty dinner chair, or when I fed his favorite horse, or when I remembered how he taught me how to clean a fish so that even now, whenever I go fishing, I still think of Leo.

"And then, gradually, even those places began to lose their power to bring on such grief. But still, sometimes even yet, a little thing will just happen, and there it is again. They are not things you can plan or expect; they just come out of the blue. And I still remember him, and I miss him again, and I cry.

"But as I said, I was only eight years old. I can't begin to imagine what it must be like to lose someone you were so close with … as you were with Amelia."

As she related her own experience, I find myself realizing that it applies to me, "I know what you mean … at least I think I do … that happened some with me too … first with Friedrich and now it's also happening some with Amelia, too. At first, it seemed all the time, like you said, I saw her everywhere." Again, feeling a little guilty, I say defensively, "But I don't think it's right that I should forget her."

Susanna sympathetically asks, "Forget her? Do you think it's possible to forget her … to completely wash her out of your heart?"

"Well, no but…" I don't know what to say. I'm feeling awkward. Even though what Clara had said is true and what Amelia's brother had written to me is also true, I still have this nagging sense … that somehow I'm failing.

Susanna looked at me with her amazing smile and said, "Heinrich, I don't think you can ever forget her, even if you wanted to … nor should you. Amelia was a special person. Your memory of her will always be very special and precious. And it should be, I think."

I look at Susanna, smiling slightly, and nod, simply looking at her expressive eyes. I lower my gaze, take a deep breath, and say, "Thank you, Susanna." I look up at her again, see her empathetic smile and whisper again, "Thank you … for listening … for understanding."

I need to leave … to be alone and examine what's happening. So, I intentionally look at the angle of the sun, and say, "O man, it's getting late. I have to get home."

I get up and start off, and Susanna calls out, "Heinrich, thank you." I turn and ask, "For what?" And she simply says, "Thank you for talking." I look at her eyes and her smile and say, "You're more than welcome. Thank you!" I look at her smiling face and continue, "for listening." I turn and head home, forcing myself not to look back. When I'm about 100 yards away, though, I look back and Susanna is no longer standing on the porch.

And when I get home, Mama asks, "Where's the cooking pot I sent you to get?"

Feeling stupid, I respond, "Mama, I'm sorry, but I forgot?"

Frustrated, Mama asks, "Well, what were you…". She stops herself, pauses, smiles at me, and says, "Well sometimes it happens that our minds do get diverted to more important things."

I'm sure my face turned red, and I said, "I'll go back and get it." And she said, "No, I don't need it any longer. I made do with what I had."

Like it or not, the seeds of Susanna are now planted. And I don't feel like I'm cheating Amelia! That is a breakthrough. I remember again those final words written in that letter from her brother, Louis, *May God go with you through your grief. We know that Amelia would want you to remember her and grieve for her and then find another to be your life mate.*

☆

Susanna is so self-confident and so open. She's not afraid of delving into almost any subject or question. Her home life has been so very different from my own. Instead of having to keep her thoughts and desires and feelings to herself, she's always been encouraged to explore her interests and questions and to chart her own future.

However, this is not easy for a woman in this day and age. Women are simply expected to get married, have children, and be pretty much subservient and obedient … "submissive" is the way the Bible says it. And if they get a job anywhere, it is usually as a housekeeper for someone else.

A growing number of women are not satisfied with that role. There's even a political movement to give women the right to vote and gain other rights. Susanna is of that same mind. She just does not understand why women aren't able to vote and why more positions are not open to them. She refuses to think that men are innately smarter or more capable than women. I agree. It makes no sense that women cannot vote. But that's an uphill battle.

Susanna can tell that my heart is not in farming, even though I'm good at it. She's right, but what am I to do? She reminds me of all the new and laborsaving farm equipment appearing every year … that between our two fathers they can make a go of it together. And she points out how my younger brother, Karl, is a natural-born farmer and is the apple of Papa's eye – the true replacement son for Friedrich. All of that is true.

My biggest deterrent, though, is this sense of responsibility to Papa and of having to meet his expectations. But Susanna sensitively but continually encourages me to be who I want to be and do what I want to do.

We both know what's happening. We're falling in love. For me, it's easy to understand why. Looking into Susanna's eyes, I see her heart. She is the most fully engaged person I have ever known. Not just to me … to just about everyone … but it seems especially to me.

But I can't see what she sees in me. It's sheer grace, a gift.

Susanna seems to creep her way into almost every thought I have. I discover I begin making decisions with her in mind. I plan when I have the best chance of seeing her. We want to spend as much time together as we can.

One day, when I'm in town, I stop by to see Clara. As we're talking, Susanna's name keeps getting mentioned. It doesn't take long before Clara looks at me with that devilish know-it-all grin and says, "Heinrich, you got it bad!" She's right.

That evening I stop by to see Susanna. "Susanna, I know what I want to do and who I want to be!"

Smiling, she looks up at me and asks, "What is it?"

"Well," I say, "I want to marry you and I want to be your husband!"

She throws herself into my arms. That evening I ask Ted if I might have his daughter to be my wife. With a smile on his face, he consents and firmly and warmly shakes my hand. Tillie embraces me and welcomes me into their family.

We don't want a long engagement. The sooner, the better. Three weeks later, we are married! We move into that original cabin Ted and Tillie built so many years ago.

That night … our wedding night … incredible … what a gift!

Susanna and I have been married for one month now - one glorious month. Since both of our families have joined together in their farming operation, our days are taken up with the annual springtime farm chores, as we work together to prepare the fields and sow the oats, and then plant the other crops. Susanna also continues to play an integral role in the farming operation, having been raised helping her family do whatever it took to survive and thrive.

At night we both come home to our small house exhausted but not too tired to have time for one another. It is a glorious beginning; she is an incredible woman.

It is not too many months later, though, that family strains are developing. We laugh at how this is a strange operation - trying to blend two families with two different backgrounds but involved together in farming, and then, to add to the pot, a son and daughter of the families being married! And we're all living within walking distance of one another.

Susanna, in her own way, is struggling for independence from her parents, and I'm struggling for the same from mine. At the same time, I'm trying to deepen my relationship with Susanna's parents, and she is doing the same with mine. But it's not easy.

In addition, Papa and Ted Zilz are, "cut out of different cloth" – very different. I think they each define love and loyalty very differently. Unfortunately, Papa's is a grudging, conditional kind of love. And then, there's the question of loyalty.

The other day, Papa said, "Heinrich, Ted and I been thinking … thinking about whether we should buy a new piece of equipment, a binder, that will both cut the grain and bind it into bundles for drying. Ted says it would make our harvesting go faster and eliminate the need for manpower. But I don't see it that way. The way I figure it, we don't need to save on manpower. We have you and Susanna, and your little brother, Karl, who is a natural-born farmer. He's catching on and helping. But Ted says that we can't really count on you and Susanna to be with us forever. Wonder where he got that idea. Is that true? What do you think?"

Speaking of the binder, I am in a "bind"! Papa assumes that I'll follow in his footsteps and be a farmer all my life. But why shouldn't he think that? I've never said anything to him about my desire not to do that. He has never taken the time or has had the insight to think any other way.

In a non-committed response, I say to Papa, "Well, I don't know. I can see both sides. I need to think this one through."

"Well," says Papa, "Don't think too long. Ted's ready to order one and put down the earnest money right away."

That night after supper, Susanna and I have a talk.

"Susanna," I begin. She looks up at me, as always with those incredible inviting eyes. I continue, "Today Papa said something to me about your father wanting to buy a new binder."

Susanna puts down the book she'd been reading, and she looks down. I can tell she's uncomfortable. So, I continue, "Papa says that Ted said that they can't necessarily count on our being here with them and farming for the long term." Susanna continues to look down. I go on, "How do you suppose Ted got that idea?"

She audibly exhales, "Well, he asked me the other day if you and I thought we'd be taking over all the farming operations someday. And I asked him, 'What makes you ask that, Papa?' And he came back with something like, 'Well your brothers haven't wanted to, and, as you know, after coming to this country, I kind of got stuck in it myself - to survive.' And he said, 'Susanna I know you're wanting more of a city kind of life - continuing to learn and maybe even get involved in politics. Plus, Heinrich, I think, has done this farm work pretty much out of duty too … and his heart is not really in it either. I think he'd rather do something else. So, I'm just wondering'."

"So, what did you say?" I ask irritably.

"Well, I told him that pretty well describes the situation."

"Damn!" I interject, "I wish you hadn't said that."

She looks annoyed, "Well, what was I supposed to tell him when he flat out asks me? Do you think I should lie to my own father?"

"Well, you could have said that we didn't know … that there

are advantages and disadvantages. That would be sort of noncommittal."

Her eyes now spark with a tinge of anger, "Heinrich you know that's not the way my family works. If we're thinking of doing something, we just come right out and say it. We don't beat around the bush. We come right to the point."

"Crap! Now, Papa is wondering if we might be bailing out on him and the family."

With a tone of disgust, she puts me on the spot, "Would that be so bad? Maybe he needs to consider that! Besides, I don't think you should blame me for what you would rather do with your life."

And then I said the wrong thing, "Well," exasperated, "I wish you wouldn't take what we say and do in private and share it with other people!"

Now she is livid. Her eyes flash with anger. Enunciating each word slowly, she almost shouts, "What do you take me for? That is one of the most ridiculous things you've ever said. I didn't take anything to my Papa, but I'm not going to lie to him, especially something that's in his interest to know. And I resent that you would think that I am telling others what we do in our private lives."

Both of us get loud and argumentative. It goes on for quite a while. This is our first argument of substance since we've been married. Finally, we've hit an impasse. We just quit talking. She's stuck with her feelings, and I with mine. And both of our feelings are hurt.

What is this all about? Family. We're both so connected, overly connected, to our families, acting in the way that we were brought up.

So, Susanna and I drop the issue. We just quit talking about it, and soon life seems to return to normal. We both love one another deeply. Life seems good again.

After Papa saw how one of those binders works, he slowly

but reluctantly came around, agreeing that it would be a good idea to have one. Our productivity could expand and become even more profitable. He continues to assume that I will be with him for life. After all, his philosophy is, that's what families do, and I don’t tell him otherwise.

But that doesn't settle everything in this unique situation that we find ourselves in … I’m part of Susanna's family … Susanna’s part of my family … and these two very different families working together. We continue until one day in early August, Susanna tells me she's pregnant! Wow!

CHAPTER 9

It's fall, 1876, and time for the harvest. By now, Clara and Gus have a six-month-old baby boy named Robert. She and Gus are thriving in their business, and their love for one another is evident to all. They are the most joyful wonderful couple! Everyone I know loves them.

Our harvest is bountiful. The new binder works perfectly … well almost … a few problems. But all things considered, it is quite a machine. Even Papa says privately to me, "I guess we did the right thing."

Today we take the shocks of wheat that have been drying in the field after having been cut and bound by twine and thresh them, removing the kernels from all the shocks.

Harvest time is a communal affair. The farmers get together to help one another out. Today is our turn. A threshing machine was brought onto our property last night. It is operated by a steam engine. All the preparations have been made. A sufficient supply of wood is on hand to burn to heat the boiler. We have prepared a ready source of water to be used to replenish the boiler's water as steam is produced. Mama, Tillie, Susanna, and Clara have worked all week, getting the huge meals ready for the men.

The next morning at daybreak it all begins as the neighbors arrive in their wagons and get to work. It is an amazing operation to witness the kind of camaraderie that unfolds each year. This is what it's all about, the high point of the farmer's year, "Bringing in the sheaves."

All is going well; each person has his job … from young to old … and the coordination of the team is like clockwork. We break at noon to enjoy the huge spread that the women have been busy preparing all week long: three different types of meat, potatoes, greens, and of, course, plenty of delicious desserts.

In the afternoon, we're back at it. About mid-afternoon, there's a problem with the steam engine. It's either a stuck pressure valve or a defective boiler, but there is an explosion. Clara's husband, Gus, is standing too near and when the boiler explodes, Gus is killed instantly.

CLARA IS NOW A WIDOW WITH A SIX-MONTH-OLD BABY. SHE'S only 20 years old. Her world is shattered. Her loving husband is dead.

Today, the day after Gus died, we bury him on the farm in a place that we have dedicated as our family cemetery.

Susanna and I open our lives and our home to Clara and little Robert. But, as the days slowly pass, we feel discouraged and helpless, watching Clara's listlessness, hearing her cry at night, seeing this young, attractive widow dressed in black … mourning. She is lost … numb … in shock. It tears our hearts out to see little Robert looking around as if waiting for his daddy to come home. It's all so tragic.

She's not eating … losing weight … growing weak. Mama comes over to encourage her and cheer her up. Of course, she also comes to see her grandson Robert. But Clara is alone with her thoughts … and her grief.

And then there's Papa. He doesn't come over often, which is probably best. He doesn't know what to say and what he says is unhelpful. Just his usual advice, devoid of real sympathy.

To find comfort, Clara reads her Bible and prays. It seems to work … for her. One day, Clara comes to Susanna for guidance and solace. She'd been crying and her thin, weak body is wracked with trembling. Biting her lower lip, she says to Susanna, "I know that as Lutherans we're not supposed to pray for those who've died, but every day I pray for Gus. I can't help it. It feels like something I must do. I can't stop thinking about him; I can't stop my mind from seeing his lifeless and torn body lying there. I pray for him … that he didn't suffer … that he never felt the explosion … it brings me comfort. But I'm not supposed to pray for the dead, am I? But I can't help it. Susanna, please, I need your wisdom, do you think I'm wrong?"

Susanna, looking compassionately at Clara reassures, "Clara, I don't think God wants you to bear religious guilt on top of everything else in your life right now. If it helps … if it makes you feel better, comforts you, then do it. Do whatever you need right now to find peace. You can figure it all out later."

TODAY, MARCH 4, 1877, OUR BEAUTIFUL BABY DAUGHTER CAME into this world. We will baptize her Christina. Thankfully, Clara served as the midwife!

Clara is pretty much becoming established as the midwife for our area. It all started in January during a snowstorm when the Schroeder baby was born. Mrs. Schroeder went into labor several weeks too early. Because of the storm, there was no way to get to the doctor, and Clara was asked to see what she could do. Their baby boy was born prematurely. He was so small! He was too weak to nurse. Everyone assumed that the baby would soon die, and so Mr. Schroder baptized him since they could not get to the pastor.

Yes, everyone assumed that the baby would soon die … everyone but Clara. She suggested that they wrap the baby in a blanket and place him close to the woodstove to keep him warm. And then she told them to take about a cup of cow's milk and put a tablespoon of whiskey in it and to spoon-feed the baby every two hours, day and night. At first, people thought Clara was crazy, but since they had no other recourse, they tried it.

The next day, the mother was able to extract some colostrum from her breast and dab it from her finger onto the baby's lips and tongue, and soon the whiskey was being added to her breast milk.

Amazingly, the baby has survived and is doing well. He's now nursing from his mother and is growing stronger. Clara is receiving accolades, both for her ability to deliver the child as well for the suggestion for feeding him.

People ask her where she got that idea?" And she simply says, "That's what the old German mid-wives used to do."

People admire her spunk. Even though she is still a young widow and grieving, she can help bring new life into the world.

It was surely great to have her deliver our new baby girl.

Surprisingly, there has been little conflict between Ted and Papa. I know that Papa, thus far, has been so appreciative of Ted and his family that he has tried to take a subordinate position. Papa, by and large, seems content to let Ted be the boss. Of course! It's Ted and his family who took us in, gave us an opportunity, and have coached us through from the beginning of this transition. I've been wondering how long that will last. I have known that eventually, he will have a difference of opinion with Ted that Papa would blow all out of proportion.

It's happened recently over, of all things, wheat. Farmers have in recent years been immigrating from Russia into Kansas and have brought with them a different variety of wheat, called winter wheat. It's planted in the fall and grows just a bit before it lies dormant all winter long and then matures and is harvested in the spring.

To Papa, this is all backward. He has always planted wheat in the spring along with all the other crops. And to Papa's way of thinking, that's just how it's done.

Once again, I see the significant differences between Papa and Ted's personalities. Ted is always looking for new ideas that will make farming easier and more productive. To him, this is worth a try. He's been reading up on it and thinks it'll work here. Papa doesn't much care for unnecessary change. His attitude is, "Stay with what you know."

And this is the match that lit Papa's fuse. He vented his pent-up frustrations. And, as they say, "everything but the kitchen sink" was thrown in. From the smallest irritations to the significant acts where Papa has had to hold his tongue … it all got thrown in. Papa said some hurtful things as he released the pressure of the months' build-up. He was a human version of that steam engine boiler that blew up and killed Gus.

Ted also lost his temper a time or two in the heat of argument but was able to back off and regain control of himself. Papa, though, finally just turned and walked away in anger. That's typical.

A couple of days later, Ted once again approached Papa and patiently listened while Papa continued to have his say. When Papa had finished, there was still the unresolved matter of the wheat. Finally, Ted suggested a simple solution. Plant half our wheat fields this fall with winter wheat and wait until spring to plant the other half with summer wheat. Then see what happens. Somewhat reluctantly, Papa agreed to try that.

Today, Susanna and I are with Ted. As I sheepishly apologize for Papa's personality, Ted smiles and said, "Well, I'm not surprised. I am surprised, though, that it took this long for Otto to let the steam out." Laughingly he continues, "He's done an admirable job of holding it in as long as he has. I knew this day would come. I'm glad it did. I learned a lot about your father, and I think maybe Otto learned a few things too,"

That's Ted … always accepting of human foibles and differences … always willing and able to move on and through to better things.

And then, Ted, smiling, looks down, and shakes his head, "Actually, all I wanted at the start was to set aside a few acres for this new wheat." And then, looking up and still smiling, he continued, "I ended up with more than I had even wanted. I got half of next year's wheat crop to be winter wheat."

TODAY, PAPA DROPS IN UNEXPECTEDLY TO TALK WITH CLARA. Something's up. I can tell by his demeanor. They go out into the nearby woods where they can talk privately.

Though I cannot hear their conversation, I see their body language. It tells the whole story. It's obvious that Papa is in his advice-giving mode as he talks and wags his index finger in the air and then at her. I've seen that posture all my life when he feels the need to pontificate.

Clara, though, doesn't just stand there and take it. She is livid … red in the face … arguing back. She reminds me of Mama that day on the ship coming over when she told Papa exactly what she thought of him. Now, I see Clara emphatically point her finger over toward his house as she appears to be saying, "Get out of here and don't come back."

Finally, she buries her face in her hands and breaks down crying. Papa, looking at her as she hides her weeping eyes in her hands, apparently says one last thing to her. Having gotten in his parting shot, he turns and walks away. Clara tries to sit but more like collapses to the ground in tears.

I go out to check on her, and she snaps, "Just go away and leave me alone. I don't want to hear anything from my stupid useless uncaring family anymore. I just want to go away and disappear. I want to die."

I simply say, "Clara, I understand. You know that Susanna and I love you, and we want to be here for you." And then I smile at her and say, "Not everyone in your family is crazy."

Smiling through her sobs and tears, she simply says, "I'm sorry Heinrich. Thank you, but I just need to be alone." I smile put my hand on her shoulder for a brief moment and go back to the house.

Tonight, after the children are in bed, Clara is ready to talk. I can't believe what I hear, but I do believe it. It is so like my controlling father. Papa had suggested that since it's been a year ago now since Gus died that she remarry to Henry Steiner, whose wife had died of diphtheria about three months ago. Clara can repeat verbatim what Papa had told her, "Steiner has three children who don't have a mother, and you have little Robert who doesn't have a father, and you don't have a husband. Clara, you need a husband. Here's a way for everyone to get what they need."

As if this wasn't degrading enough, she says that Papa has even said, "Steiner is ten years older than you, and he would still like to have more children." She continues, "I asked him how he knew this and found out that he'd already discussed it with Steiner! In other words, I've now become the talk of the town, like a slave on an auction block, going to the highest bidder, the one who can take care of me and use me" … and breaking down, she sobs … "like a broodmare!"

To regain composure, she closes her eyes and softly says, "I am so sick and tired of this free advice that people want to give me." She sits for a long minute and her body calms from its trembling. Then, looking at us through her swollen eyes, she says, "Susanna and Heinrich, you're the only ones who care and just let me be." She leans back, closes her eyes again, and sighs heavily.

After a few more minutes, she is calm. She sits there, deep in her thoughts and feelings until she calmly utters, "Papa doesn't have a clue. All he has ever seen is how things can work out for himself and what he wants. He never connects how his ideas and decisions affect others. And now he wants me to marry Steiner. I don't know him. I don't even think Papa knows him either. He's just a bar buddy. This wouldn't be a marriage … but an arrangement … just an arrangement. I'm soiled goods that Steiner takes off Papa's hands. I become his housemaid, his babysitter, his broodmare" … breaking into tears, "and his 'sweet little thing'." She dissolves into tears, crying out, "Gus, why did you leave me? I just want to die. Please God, just let me die!"

Susanna gathers Clara into her arms and holds her close while she cries.

But, by now, my thoughts are scattered and conflicted. What does loyalty mean to this family of mine? How much of ourselves do we have to sacrifice? And will it ever be enough? Angry at myself, I wonder, "When can I say, 'Thank you very much, but I'm going my own way'?" How can I be free from all these insane chains that shackle me?

Today Papa and I are cleaning up equipment, and he keeps telling me how to do what I have done dozens of times before. "Oil this, grease that, scrape the dirt off this, and sharpen that." I am growing angrier by the second.

Finally, I blurt out, "Damn it, Papa, I know what I'm doing. I'm tired of you trying to always control me and always trying to control our family. Mama, Clara, me. We're sick and tired of it.

This has caused a strain even between Susanna and her parents as well as between Susanna and me."

I can't believe what I hear when Papa responds. What a lie! "After all I've done for you and the family, immigrating to this country, and ending up here buying this property, making a comfortable life for everyone, giving you a job, a future. And this is how you think of me?"

What is he saying? That he emigrated from Germany because of us? Bullshit! That he sacrificed for our behalf? Bullshit! That he thinks he's done all of us a favor? Bullshit! That's all bullshit!

"Papa that's all a pile of *Scheisse*, and you know it! Recall, will you, how it actually was. Mama and Clara and I were forced to emigrate because you couldn't deal with the death of Friedrich. Sure, it's worked out well, but that's just the luck of the draw or maybe you can say, 'it's God's will.' But don't give me this about all you've sacrificed for us! We have been the ones who have sacrificed our lives for <u>you</u> … for your impetuous decision. We had to go along. But if it hadn't been for us, just where would you be now?"

Papa doesn't even hear what I say, and continues, "Look at Karl. He's just seven years old now, and he's the real future farmer here. He follows in the footsteps of Friedrich. And he'll be farming circles around you in just a few years."

I've had it, "Well then, why wait a few years? Susanna and I want out now. We're tired of having to walk on eggshells to keep peace around here. We have kept our mouths shut rather than cause trouble. Do you have any idea how tough it is to navigate through this morass of confusion and family ties, all these different family expectations? We want out!"

"Well," Papa mockingly replies, "you don't have to wait to do what your little wife says you have to do. You can leave anytime you want."

Now I'm livid, "Don't put this on Susanna. She's the best

thing that ever happened to me. Unlike you, she sees what I want. So does Mama and so does Clara. You're the only one around here who can't see past the end of your nose!"

THAT DAY, THE RELATIONSHIP BETWEEN PAPA AND ME CHANGED forever. Unfortunately, the ripples ran through the family. Papa's reaction was drastic but predictable. His belligerence brought additional conflict and division.

At first, I just didn't care. "Let the chips fall where they may," was my way of thinking. But then that night, when my emotions had calmed down, I rethought it … replayed it in my mind … and sought to understand what had gone wrong. I got little sleep.

Sitting in the main room by the fire, I realized something ugly about myself. I was "a chip off the same old block", as they say. I was like Papa … lashing out … driven by raw emotion at times … just as willing as he to kiss the relationship goodbye without sober judgment.

The next day, I did one of the hardest things I've ever done. I walked over to Papa's house and found him in the barn. He saw me and turned away. I said, "Papa, I came over to apologize for my part in our argument yesterday."

Still turned away, he said, "You mean, you came over to grovel for your life back."

"No, Papa, someday soon I do want to talk to you about my hopes in life. But first, right now, I want to talk about yesterday and you and me."

Turning to me with fiery eyes, he curtly spits out, "There's nothing more to say. You said it all yesterday … all I need to hear. It came through loud and clear. You listen to your wife's ideas, and you turn away from me."

"Papa let's leave Susanna out of this. This is between you and me. I want to talk about that, you and me."

In a huff of disgust, he says, "You want … you want … you want", as he put an increasingly strong emphasis on the "you". "It's all about what you want! Well, I'll tell you what I want. I want never to have to see or work with you again. Now what does that have to say about what 'you' want?"

I got testy, "Now, how do you suppose it's possible to achieve what you think you want under our present circumstances?"

And then our argument once again derailed. Papa retorted, "Listen, dammit, this is my farm. I bought it, paid my money for it. Got that? It is mine! So why don't you just go back to your wife and pack your bags and get on down the road!"

At that point, he turned away. My last comment was, "Papa, I'm sorry about yesterday and my part in it. I hope you can forgive me. I love you." I turned and walked back to the house.

Clara felt responsible for having sparked the event that led to Papa's emotional tirade to cut me off and out of his life. Of course, she would. That's Clara … the bearer of the family's angst. I spent many hours trying to convince Clara that this had been simmering for years … this rebellion within me to Papa's demands and unwritten expectations, coupled with my knowledge that I could never measure up to Friedrich and now, Karl.

In the days that followed, subsequently seeing Papa's emotional door slammed in my face, it didn't take long before I no longer tried. It wasn't that I didn't care, but why keep trying to recapture what will never be? Some people are incapable of looking inward and realistically assessing themselves. Papa's and my relationship was done … over.

Clara now is struggling with yet another loss – the loss of her family. At a time when perhaps she needs it most, it is breaking apart. She is torn. She wants little Robert to know his "Grampa Otto". She wants and needs Mama but doesn't know how this will all play out. She wants her son, Robert, to know his Uncle Heinrich and Aunt Susanna, and Cousin Christina. And she yearns for the kind, sympathetic, understanding, and generous heart of Susanna. But how can she manage to juggle all of this? How can she hold all the disparate pieces together? It's a maze.

Susanna wonders if she pushed me too hard and, therefore, she might be responsible. I thought about that but finally concluded that she had done me a favor, as she had lovingly challenged me to assert myself and my desires. Any wrongs done had pretty much all been on my part.

I realize I did overreact because of the pent-up frustration over the years. I took my frustrations with me that day. A lot happened that day. The dam broke, and Papa's and my fragile relationship has sunk in the turbulence. But that's not Susanna's fault. She has only helped me to see and dream of something better.

It's getting colder as winter sets in. The agreed-upon acreage of the winter wheat has been planted, and the farm operation is at its slowest pace. It gives us a respite from the highly charged emotions of recent months. But what will it be like in a couple of months when the spring farm chores pick up again? How will Papa react if the winter wheat experiment proves very successful and he is proven wrong? The big question is about the future. What will this partnership between the Zilz's and us look like, and how will it function?

Susanna's parents, Ted and Tillie, have been laying low for the time being. We visit with them often, partly so that they can see their only grandchild. But they also want to be clear that while they understand, they cannot become part of this latest brouhaha. But they support and love Susanna, Christina and me. They too are tentatively and tenuously charting a difficult course.

One day, in the middle part of December, Susanna tells me that her mother wants to see me. When I arrive, Tillie hands me a letter that Mama had written and has asked Tillie to give it to me. As I walk back to the house my hands are shaking, anxious because I don't know what Mama's letter will say. Yet I am eager to open it and find out. But what will I do if she's angry at me as well? Of all the people whom I want to please, it's Mama. She and I have always had a special understanding and closeness. I sit outside on the cold front porch in the late afternoon twilight and cautiously open Mama's letter.

My Dear Heinrich,

When your father told me about his argument with you, my world came crashing down. Since I know your father, I knew immediately that he would not bend ... that he would dig in ... as he did back in Bavaria after Friedrich died. He said that it was over with you, and I knew it was.

And it still is. My tears, my pleas, my anger, my threats ... nothing has budged him, nor will it. My efforts have only served to harden him. But honestly and sadly, I also have become very hardened ... toward him. And he knows it. But that is not your fault in any way.

Heinrich, deep down ... as much as I hoped and prayed it wouldn't ... I knew this day would come. I knew Otto's regard for you was not what it had been toward Friedrich or like it is now for Karl. I also know that you are not cut out for farming. You have done so out of loyalty to our family even when it has meant a loss to yourself.

Our next steps in life look murky. The future is now again uncertain. Please know my love and my desire to maintain my connection with you and your family, especially little Christina. I thank God for this partnership with the Zilz's, if, for no other reason, then it has brought you and Susanna together.

By the way, when your father is out in the field or in town, I plan to see you, your family, and my only granddaughter!

Nothing Otto can do will prevent that. I am sad that he will probably never get to know his granddaughter. But that's his choice.

All my love,

Mama

I put the letter back in its envelope and am relieved. I should have known that Mama would understand.

We go to Christmas Day worship. The church is packed. It is a beautiful worship service. The pastor has one of his best sermons, but I think, you can't miss with the Christmas story. The service climaxes as we celebrate the sacrament of Holy Communion, the special mystery of receiving Christ's real presence in the bread and wine for our forgiveness.

As I await my turn to go forward, I notice that Papa does not take Holy Communion. Lutherans are big on being sure that we do not receive the sacrament with anger in our hearts. I quickly wonder, "Should I stay away, too?" But it's been so long since I've had the sacrament, and I need it, so I receive it. Maybe I should not have, but I pray, "God help me if I'm wrong." But I figure God has so much else to be upset about with me and all my questions. And, so, I take communion, doubts and all.

Susanna's brothers, Joseph and George, and their wives have also come home for Christmas. We all have dinner with the Zilz's. It is a wonderful family celebration.

Clara and baby Robert are having dinner with Papa and Mama. I wonder how that's going. It must be hard especially for Clara … having lost her husband last year and now this most recent family rift. I wonder, too, if Papa has any regrets.

After dinner, Joseph wants to talk about something important. He announces that he has reconsidered and that he no longer wants to be a teacher. He says that he would like to return to farming. He says he has missed the outdoors and the physical labor and having his hands in the warm soil. He can't see himself stuck indoors and having to put his energy into teaching. He asks if he might be able to return to the farm.

This opens up a huge discussion. Where would Joseph's family live? What would this do to the partnership with my parents' family? Is this what they really want, or are they only coming back because it's easy? All kinds of questions. As they discuss and think these things through, I am amazed that the questions can be handled without pronounced emotional passion. Even when there are different perspectives, they're all free to chime in with their opinions. The discussion concludes with an agreement to keep thinking about the possibilities. They keep the door open for one another.

CHAPTER 10

Today, the day after Christmas, Mama comes over to see us, and especially to spend time with nine-month-old baby Christina. She has brought a new baby quilt that she has lovingly made. We can even detect an occasional tiny stain of her blood where she accidentally pricked her finger with the sharp needle. She calls them her "love stains." She stays longer than she had intended.

When she arrives back home, Papa has already returned and is waiting impatiently. As Mama enters the house he irritably demands, "Where you been?" And when Mama tells him, he says, "I figured as much." And then he adds, "Well, I'm hungry, and why did you stay so long and why isn't dinner close to being ready?"

Mama fires back, "Dammit, Otto. I am not going to miss seeing my loved ones at Christmas time because you might be a little hungry. I am not going to let your stubbornness interfere with my relationship with my granddaughter and children. I couldn't see them yesterday on Christmas, and so I went to see them today. So quit being such a gripe!"

"Well, what's for dinner?"

Cantankerously Mama replies, "You'll see when I get it

ready. Some leftover ham from yesterday and some other left-overs. Thought I'd make some potato pancakes."

"Well, I'll be outside. Yell when it's ready." He leaves and, within a couple of minutes, she hears the steady splitting of wood. She knows he's angry. This is his standard procedure.

After about fifteen minutes, dinner is ready and, no longer hearing the ax hit and the ripping sound of wood splitting, she goes to call him in. As she looks out in the fading light, she sees him lying on the ground.

She runs to his side. He's breathing but is not responsive. She runs over to my house and calls out for me to come help. I run to his side, but he still cannot talk. He's breathing but has a blank distant stare in his eyes. With the help of Ted, we carry him inside and lay him on his bed to make him comfortable and cover him with blankets to get him warm.

Seeing what has happened, Clara immediately goes into town for the doctor. Papa has had a stroke. It's bad.

After all the confusion settles down, Mama insists on sitting with Papa, who continues to stare with that blank expression. She holds his hand and speaks to him and prays. Over the course of the next few hours, she lovingly reviews the story of their lives together from the earliest days of their relationship and their marriage up to the present.

Meanwhile, seven-year-old Karl, who has been crying and is confused, comes over and cautiously looks over into Papa's eye and says, "Papa, wake up." He keeps repeating, "Papa wake up. Please, Papa, wake up." Mama tells Karl that Papa is very very sick and probably will not wake up but that he will soon be going to heaven … to Jesus." Eventually, Karl settles down, and goes into his room, and falls asleep.

About midnight, I come over and insist that Mama get some rest. I promise I will awaken her if anything changes. I sit with Papa. I have so many mixed emotions going on inside. So many memories … both good and not so good. I share them with Papa in the hope that he can hear me. I don't know if he can or not. Maybe I'm saying all these things for my own sense of peace. I speak about how our relationship has deteriorated and how that saddens me. I see that his breathing is becoming labored.

Finally, I take hold of his limp hand and say, "Papa, thank you for your love for me. Even though you maybe didn't say it, I know that it's been there. Even though I know it's been hard at times … I want you to know, despite everything lately, I love you. I forgive you where I feel you have been wrong, and, if you can hear me, I ask that you forgive me too."

As I sit back and stare at him. I am sure I feel his hand tighten just a little for a split second. He heard me and squeezed my hand with love, I think. It's not long before his breathing becomes more labored.

I awaken Mama who comes to hold his hand while I run over to get Clara. We leave Robert with Susanna, and both run over to Papa's side. Clara takes his other hand and through tears assures him of her love. We awaken Karl, who still wants Papa to get up, but slowly seems to understand. And as a family, we sit together for a couple of hours, speaking to him in the hope that he can hear. And we comfort one another. Sometime in the middle of the night, Papa takes his last breath. We all break down and cry together … holding our hands … as a family … not always the model family, but still a family … where still there is love and compassion, and let's not forget, there's allegiance, family loyalty!

Two days later, Papa is buried in our family cemetery … not far from Gus.

CALL IT COINCIDENCE … CALL IT DIVINE INTERVENTION … I don't know how to figure it. I don't want to sound crass, but, ironically, Papa's death helps our families reach clarity and a new direction. In February 1878, we prepare and plant our joint fields as usual. Joseph and his wife, Hannah, come in early summer after school ends and dig right into farm work, staying with Ted and Tillie.

Mama and Karl are all alone and having a hard time. It made sense that Clara and Robert move in with her. Karl is almost eight years old and a handful. He misses Papa constantly. He seems angry and is very belligerent with Mama and even with Clara. I make sure I check in with them all at least once a day. I have my hands full surrounded by all this grief.

Then there's my grief. I live with a nagging sense that if only I hadn't had that confrontation with Papa this would not have happened. But Papa had such an explosive temper when things didn't go his way. He was like a stick of dynamite with a short fuse … ready to explode at a moment's notice. But even knowing this, it doesn't exactly calm my guilt and sadness. I do treasure those last few hours with Papa, especially remembering how he squeezed my hand. I believe that that was his way of expressing his love for me. But I fear that this will follow me all my life as a personal failure, bringing with it a lingering sense of guilt.

Yes, our entire Mendorf family is grieving. But God bless Susanna. She is incredibly generous with her love, her listening ear, and her comfort.

And then there's Tillie. What a saint she is with Mama! With the arrival of Joseph and Hannah, her life is full of a new sense of joy. And yet she has the energy and desire to be there for Mama. In Susanna, I have stumbled upon the most giving and understanding in-laws imaginable.

Together, we will get through this.

In June 1878, Joseph and Hannah share the great news that Hannah is pregnant. They think that she is due to give birth in early January. Ted and Tillie are beside themselves with joy at the prospect of becoming grandparents again.

Clara and Susanna comment to themselves that Hannah is a very small woman, and they are worried that there may be difficulty with her pregnancy.

It is during a snowstorm in mid-December that Hannah goes into labor. Clara is summoned and Susanna says to Clara, "You're the midwife. Just tell us what you need, and we'll do what we can."

I am told to take Joseph and the children, Robert and Christina, next door for the duration. Susanna will come to tell us when to return. We leave immediately. The atmosphere is tense. Joseph, too, is especially worried. As he paces, he keeps saying, "I hope everything's okay. I just hope she can deliver our baby."

Hannah, as they had feared, is having a very difficult delivery. When Clara looks down at Hannah during a contraction, she sees major trouble. "*Gott in Himmel!*" she cries. And then to the others, she whispers, "The baby is breach. Pray, we don't lose both Hannah and her baby."

It is hard labor. Finally, enough of the baby's foot and leg are presented that Clara doesn't hesitate to take hold and gently feel up around the foot and leg. Thankfully, she finds the second leg, and, with the next contraction, she gently but steadily pulls. The baby is born, but an enormous flow of blood follows. Clara commands Susanna to get Joseph immediately.

The baby is not breathing. Clara hands the baby to Tillie and tersely tells her to jostle the legs firmly pat the baby and do whatever she can to stimulate the child in the hope that it will begin gasping for breath. Having passed the infant to Tillie, Clara begins applying pressure through cloths in a desperate attempt to stop the flow of blood, but the hemorrhaging is too profuse. Hannah is dying, and no one can prevent it.

Tillie's effort pays off, and the child gasps and begins crying. At the same time, Mama ties off and cuts the umbilical cord. Amid all the confusion, it is only then that they discover that the baby is a boy.

Next door, Susanna orders Joseph to come quick. "Baby's born, but we're afraid we're losing Hannah." Joseph leaps to his feet, crying "Please God, no," In a flash, he's at Hannah's side, and, seeing the massive amount of blood, knows what it means. Immediately taking hold of his young wife's hand, through tears he tenderly expresses his love and tells her that she gave birth to a healthy boy. He kisses Hannah on her cheek and says, "Hannah, I love you." Hannah opens her eyes, smiles, and passes away. Joseph breaks down in devastating sobs.

Joseph's tears and sobs are heartrending. We are all stunned, speechless. Hannah was such a charming young woman. What a sense of humor … never a cross word to say about anyone … so happy to be pregnant and so in love. She can't be gone! I half expect that she'll walk in the door any moment.

All at once, with the baby's cry piercing our gloom, we suddenly realize that he must be fed. But Susanna, who has not yet weaned Christina, is quick to offer, "I can take care of this. Clara brought him into this world, but I can make sure he eats well." And taking the baby into her arms, she begins unbuttoning her dress. He immediately starts rooting. Slipping into the bedroom she coos to him, "You worked hard for your first real meal."

Two days later, Hannah's body is placed into the ground in the expanding family cemetery. Three untimely deaths in two and a half years.

With all the wintertime sickness, we ask the pastor to come to the house to baptize Joseph's and Hannah's infant son. He is named after both of his parents, Joseph Hans Zilz. Of course, everyone calls him "Joey".

In the marriage ceremony, there is the familiar passage from the Bible, "The two shall become one." But in our case, it seems that that applies as well to the Mendorf and Zilz extended families. We all laugh at all the interconnections. The joint farming … the marriage between Susanna and me … families drawn close through shared death of firstborn sons … and now Susanna before weaning our daughter, Christina, is being able to be a wet nurse to her brother's baby.

About a year later, one night as Susanna and I are lying together in bed, Susanna out of the blue starts laughing. I ask, "What's so funny?" She giggles and says, "For people trying to establish their independence from their families, you and I have certainly gotten intertwined. I smile and respond, "Yea, I wonder what will happen next."

The next Sunday at our joint family dinner we find out. Susanna's brother, Joseph, and Clara announce their intent to be married! Susanna looks at me and starts laughing again, I can read her lips as she whispers, "I guess that answers the question of what will happen next!"

But why shouldn't they get married? It makes perfect sense. A bond was forged between them that night when Clara tried desperately to save Hannah's life as she brought little Joseph into the world. Everyone who was there that night is convinced that Baby Joey also would have died if not for Clara. That bond between Clara and Joseph was strengthened in the later months as each faced his and her grief and loss. If ever two young people deserve to have a new start and a new hope and a new family, Clara and Joseph are at the top of the list.

Later that night, when we are alone in bed, Susanna breaks

down in tears. "Heinrich, I feel so terrible and guilty. I am so happy for Clara and Joseph, but I'm going to miss having little Joey at my breast. He is a dear child, and I don't want to let him go. He's like my own son, and I don't want to say goodbye. But I am being so selfish!" I cuddle her and let her cry.

The next day, Susanna begins to wean Joseph.

Three weeks later, Clara and Joseph are married. Little Robert and Joey have now become brothers. Mama and Tillie embrace each other and beam with tears of joy.

Like a mobile hanging in balance, the pieces of the Mendorf-Zilz conglomerate are shifted around during the next months, settling into a new configuration of equilibrium. Susanna's father, Ted, is now at the top. We humorously refer to him as, "Kaiser Ted." We could not ask for a more qualified man in charge of organizing and coordinating the operation. He seeks the well-being of everyone.

He informs everyone that he wants us all to attend a family meeting this Sunday after our weekly dinner. When all have settled, he begins, "The twists and turns that have brought us together to this place are incredibly remarkable. We've all realized, commented, and even laughed about all of that." Smiles of agreement are seen around the room. "Looking back over the past few years, I see it as the hand of God." Everyone nods in assent. Even I'm beginning to see his point, that maybe this isn't just all coincidence. Ted continues, "Not that I think God wanted these tragedies to happen, but these have certainly made us a strong and united family." We all agree, many of us with tears in our eyes or flowing down our cheeks.

He continues, "We are all in this together, and I want every single one of us to have the opportunity to realize his and her personal goals. I know that this is considered radical by some folks, but to me, this is what liberty means, 'the pursuit of happiness'."

And then looking at Susanna and me, he goes on, "There are two here who have labored hard and long for the good of our families to make this dream come true. And I think it's time that they have the opportunity to realize their dream as well." Everyone expresses a word or gesture of agreement … "absolutely" … "you bet" … or nods their heads in agreement. Everyone knows who he's talking about. Everyone's looking at Susanna and me and smiling, Mama and Tillie with tears running down their faces.

That day, the discussion was initiated that would lead to a mutual agreement that would enable Susanna, Christina, and I to move to Cape Girardeau where I could enroll in the teacher's college.

We would return to the farm, when possible, on weekends and at other times of year to help out as best we can. But our number one job, now, is to pursue our goal.

In the Fall, I enroll and begin my studies. Meanwhile, in 1880 Susanna and I have a baby boy, Henry. In 1882, I graduate from college with the certification to teach. Amazingly, I am asked to stay on at the college where I now teach German and European history.

In 1883, Susanna again gives birth to a second boy, whom we name William. William is not a healthy baby and dies when he is only six months old. It is so hard … to lay your own flesh and blood in the ground … his small lifeless body. We try our best to explain it to Henry, but still, he keeps looking all over the house for his little brother. There are days when the grief seems unbearable … most especially for Susanna.

CHAPTER 11

It's January 1, 1885. I'm slowly making my way through what we now call the Mendorf-Zilz Cemetery. Both families know that over time, it will probably be the final resting place for most of us. Death is a common and often sudden occurrence. Giving birth is risky for the mother, infant mortality happens far too often, diseases can kill in a day or two, and life-changing accidents are numerous.

We can recall the stories and count the years in our families' lives by walking through our cemetery.

I stand at the grave of William, who died just a couple of years ago, still a baby. I also see the grave of the stillborn daughter of Clara and Joseph. They had named her Sara. It's especially sad, I think, to see those small graves of infants and babies, who never had a chance at life.

And there's the grave of Gus, Clara's husband, who had died suddenly when the boiler exploded during that harvest. And just a few feet from his grave is that of Hannah, Joseph's wife, who had died in childbirth. Both died when they still had so much to live for. I'm sure, though, that they'd be glad if they knew that their spouses had married.

THE COUNTRY IS GROWING. IMMIGRANTS, MOSTLY FROM EUROPE, but especially from Germany arrive daily, seeking a better life, escaping political unrest, military conscription, and the putrid air and filth of European industrialization.

It's no wonder that they're coming from Germany. Bismarck is still the Chancellor. He continues to push Kaiser Wilhelm to keep strengthening the military. France and Russia keep upgrading their militaries to keep pace with Germany. It makes no sense to me. Why can't they sit down and talk and work out their differences and resolve some of this nonsense? After all, just about all the kings and rulers in Europe are related … all being descendants of Queen Victoria. If only they could divert the money that's being spent on the military build-up toward programs that would help the people! Karl Marx predicts that the people will eventually get fed up and rebel to rebuild a better and more equitable world.

Great Britain's Empire is worldwide, the Empire "on which the sun never sets" because it claims territories in Africa, Asia, Europe, America, and numerous islands. To connect this vast empire and to protect it, Britain has a powerful worldwide navy.

IN THE YEARS THAT I'VE BEEN LIVING IN AMERICA, THE advancements in farming have been astonishing. It seems that hardly one new piece of farming equipment comes out of the factory when it is surpassed with something better within just a few months. The former vital need for horses and mules is being reduced. The steam engine is transforming our way of life. This mechanization allows us to do formerly back-breaking work more easily, rapidly, and productively, and with less manpower.

These advancements have resulted in two major changes.

People are now freer to leave farm life and pursue other avenues of work, and secondly, smaller farms can now grow both in size and productivity. What had started as just a hundred acres when Papa purchased the Schubert farm in 1872 has now more than doubled in size.

With the continuing immigration and the population increasing and standard of living improving - especially in America and Europe - the markets for our grain and livestock continue to expand. All of this is creating more and more wealth here in our new land.

After Papa died, Ted and Joseph Zilz took the primary responsibility for the farm operation. As Karl grows older, it becomes evident that he will be capable of filling Papa's shoes. He's now fifteen years old, but he can handle as much hard work as any man, and he knows the ins and outs of farming. On the other hand, having inherited Papa's temper and still being a young man, he needs guidance and direction. Thankfully, Karl respects Ted who can provide this function for the benefit of all.

ON FEBRUARY 2, 1888, TED CATCHES DIPHTHERIA AND DIES within a day. We are all stunned with grief. Somehow, I guess, we all seemed to think that Ted would live forever; we'd never considered that he would not be here. He had become the patriarch, and we all have benefited from his wisdom and his desire that all achieve their dream. Everyone pretty much accepted his judgment and opinions because we all implicitly trusted him. He was truly a great man.

Karl is grieving and angry at the loss of Ted. He had grown to respect Ted's judgment and his guiding hand. But Karl can't handle his anger very well; in this, he is like Papa and is keeping it all inside. He can't bring himself to attend the funeral service. Instead, he goes to Brun's Bar. His drinking only serves to make him angrier. When he comes home later today, he reminds me of Papa. He goes out in the cold and chops wood!

KARL IS EIGHTEEN YEARS OLD AND IS NOW VERY MUCH HIS OWN person. Ted's death left a vacuum that needs to be filled. After weighing the options, I was chosen to try to fill Ted's role because Susanna and I have strong ties to both families which should provide a sense of balance and fairness if need be. Secondly, since I am not involved in the day-to-day operation, I can have a more impartial perspective about any matter that needs attention. A third reason, unspoken, at least from the Zilz-side of the operation is that, as Karl's older brother, I will best be able to deal with his turbulent personality and hopefully be able to rein him in when necessary.

Unfortunately, this also means that if Karl and Joseph are not in agreement about a matter, then it falls on me to negotiate and, perhaps, even make the decision. I don't want to be in that position. I am no Ted. No one can fill his shoes. This puts me in an uncomfortable, vulnerable, and thankless position.

It's not long before tensions begin to build. As usual, it starts with little things … some second-guessing priorities … misreading tone of voice … mishearing what the other person says and means. But in the middle part of April, the pot boils over when Karl wants to buy a new piece of equipment, and Joseph wants to wait and see how the operation is working for the first year after Ted has passed from the scene. Karl's temper gets the better of him, and Joseph tries to reason with him as Ted would have always done. But Joseph isn't Ted any more than I am. Karl respected Ted but has little respect for Joseph.

The subject of the disagreement makes little difference in this match between emotions. I'm expected to solve it, to make the final decision. This is a no-win situation. Trying not to take sides, I finally insist on a compromise. "Let's hold off until midsummer to see how the operation is going, and then revisit the question." They agree but neither is particularly happy.

We all now realize that this arrangement is not working as it should. We know we need to change it. But again, our interwoven families through the marriages of Susanna and myself and Clara and Joseph have created a challenging situation.

It takes some very diligent deliberation and negotiation until we finally come to a new agreement that will provide for the continued care for Tillie and Mama, as well as providing an equitable payment to Susanna and me and Joseph's brother, George, who owns the general store in town.

We come up with what we hope is a peaceful splitting of the farming operation. We work with a local attorney "to dot every 'i' and cross every 't'." I think both Karl and Joseph are relieved to be through with the other. They both admit to me that they were not comfortable with the original decision. And I am certainly happy to be out of that messy arrangement. It was a costly but valuable lesson to learn. Thankfully it didn't cause any major rifts.

TILLIE DIED YESTERDAY, AUGUST 23, 1889, JUST EIGHTEEN months after Ted. What a solid marriage she and Ted had. For the most part, they seemed to be of the same mind and way of thinking. And even when they differed, they could talk and resolve their differences without rancor. Together, they shared the joy of learning with their children. I see Tillie still in the wonders of my wife, Susanna. What a gift Tillie gave me!

Today, as I go to the cemetery to help dig her grave, I see Ted's grave, the ground still mounded up over him. It hasn't been that long since he died, and my memories and emotions are still fresh. With tears in my eyes, I recall what an incredible father-in-law he was!

He taught me a lot about true freedom and manhood! Even though his and Tillie's early hopes were dashed in the failed 1848 revolution in Germany, they never lost hope. And even though they had to settle for farming, Ted, as a former professor, continued to exercise and expand his mind with the challenge of learning. He and Tillie passed that challenge and love on to his children, wanting them to pursue their own dreams. Together they passed that attitude on to me as well. What a team they were! I miss Ted, and I know that I'll miss Tillie.

KARL GETS MARRIED IN 1890 TO A SWEET YOUNG LADY NAMED Emma. We all hope she has the fortitude to stand strong against Karl when necessary. Mama and she have many heart-to-heart talks as Mama seeks to help her understand Karl, based on her own experience with Papa. As a result, Emma has gotten very close to Mama. It seems to be working. Karl and Emma have three children in the first five years of marriage. Mama is thrilled to have more grandchildren to love.

Karl and Emma and their growing family are doing well. Karl makes sure that his farming operation stays current with all the latest machines and techniques. He continues to buy acreage, increasing the size of his farm, since he is convinced that his children will all follow in his footsteps someday. I can't help but wonder, though, if it isn't just a way of showing others what a "big man" he has become.

I keep my nose out of it. Whatever he does is fine with me, just so long as I continue to receive the designated portion of the profits each year.

Mama died two days ago, June 5, 1899. She was buried next to Papa today. That's fitting. She was always next to Papa … in life and now, in death. It must have been hard at times to love Papa, but she truly did. She stood stoically loyal even when she did not agree with him. There were times when she told him so, too. I still vividly remember the few times when she stood up to Papa, and Papa backed down. He learned when not to insist on his way and when to listen. What a strong bighearted woman Mama was!

It's funny how Papa had a special bond with Friedrich and then Karl, while Mama had a special bond with Clara and me. I miss her. I miss her love and understanding. So does Clara. She is having such a hard time saying goodbye. And her sons, Robert and Joey, struggle with their grief as well. We all agree that we didn't want Mama to suffer from cancer any longer, but still, we miss her.

We are on the cusp of a new century. Inventions and improvements continue to enhance everyday life for so many.

The power of the steam engine has transformed transportation throughout the world. Steamboats have been the primary means of river transportation. However, even with important improvements to make steam engines safer, there are still far too many boiler explosions. When that happens on one of these wooden riverboats, inevitably there is a tragic loss of life and crippling injuries. The boat typically burns and all its cargo sinks. Passengers and crew desperately swim for their lives.

Steam also powers our locomotives. The laying of rails is making it possible to transport goods into places where rivers do not run. The railroad will soon be laying track down toward us from St. Louis running parallel with the river. What an incredible way to move people quickly as well as having enormous potential for shipping heavy cargo, equipment, and livestock.

But the newest and most important development is the internal combustion engine. It promises to produce power more efficiently and will have even more numerous applications than steam. Running on gasoline, it will surpass the steam engine in its capability to transform life. Chiefly, it is being used in the automobile. I can only begin to imagine how the automobile will change our nation and our world.

Electricity is also making its way into our cities transforming the American way of life. It has not yet made its way into rural areas, but it will be there soon. The same is true for the telephone. To be able to talk to another person from a long distance is astounding. It, too, will transform our way of life.

OUR FAMILY IS GROWING UP. OUR CHILDREN, CHRISTINA AND Henry are grown. Christina is married to a mathematics professor in Cape Girardeau, and they have a boy and a girl. Susanna and I love being grandparents!

Our son, Henry, is in college now and wants to be a doctor, eventually going to medical school in St. Louis. Gone are the days when a man could become a doctor with as little as two years of study, simply by attending lectures and with no requirements for laboratory or hospital experience.

Instead, thankfully the European model of medical knowledge and treatment has been accepted, and our American medical schools have incorporated it completely in their training. At long last, the germ theory has been accepted in America, bringing with it the discipline of bacteriology and supervised laboratory experience.

The rigors of farming have taken their toll on Joseph. Several years ago, he was injured in a fall from a wagon and broke his leg. Since then, he walks with a limp and his back is often in excruciating pain. He and Clara have since quit farming but still live in their house on the farm. Clara, though, does continue to be a midwife and is often called upon for her services. Their sons, Robert and Joey, now run their family farm.

Robert and Joey are extremely close … so close that they even had both their weddings the same summer in 1898. Robert married a local young lady, Magdalena, and they now have a young son named Franz. Joey married a city girl, Louisa. He's having quite a fun time trying to make a farmer's wife out of her. Good thing she's easygoing and can put up with his pranks and foolishness. They also have a son, Eric. Each family has built their home on the family property, which is a delight to Joseph and Clara who are devoted grandparents.

CHAPTER 12

It's February 3, 1903. Joseph died suddenly today, most likely from a heart attack. Clara came home from delivering a baby and found him. He had been dead for several hours, but with no indication that he suffered, he must have died instantly. He will be buried in the family cemetery on Thursday.

Clara is devastated and, being Clara, second-guesses herself with her, "If onlys". "If only I had been here; If only I had been more aware of his health," etc.

Robert and Joey and their wives join Clara in her journey into this shadow of death. Her heart breaks when she hears her grandsons, Eric and Franz, asking for their Gramps. Thank God, she has her children and grandchildren close and can rely on them to give her comfort and joy.

September 15, 1904

SUSANNA AND I HAVE HAD AN UNBELIEVABLY EXCITING THREE days. Four days ago, we took the train to St. Louis. Rail service has just recently been established in this part of the state. What a way to travel! I remember the many days it took us to travel by wagon from St. Louis back in 1872 … more than a week as I recall. And now, to be able to cover that distance by train in less than six hours is unheard of … except it's true.

And that was just the beginning of the adventure. We spent three nights in a hotel on the site of the Louisiana Purchase Expedition. Most folks just call it the 1904 World's Fair. Talk about progress! What an incredible tribute to the genius of Man!

Huge buildings … modern architecture … modern construction technology. The Festival Hall has a dome larger than that of St. Peter's Basilica in Rome … incredible! And that's just the start.

The immense Palace of Transportation … over four miles of a railroad track on which are displayed the old and some of the newest locomotives and cars … plus more than 140 different models of automobiles.

The Palace of Mines and Metallurgy has displays of the immense equipment now being used to mine various metals and ore in the manufacture of iron and steel production.

The largest exhibition hall is the Palace of Agriculture. Here there are the latest and greatest farming machines and implements.

Words cannot describe it all. Statues, immense and spectacular fountains everywhere, a huge lake on which miniature ships reenact famous naval battles, a Ferris wheel that took me up almost three hundred feet in the air!

It just goes on and on.

But, for me, seeing the actual Liberty Bell that had been brought in from Philadelphia was such a highlight. It may not be all that big in size, but it is huge as a symbol of our new land.

All in all, as I now think about it, what a testimony to the greatness of the human spirit, the human genius! Mankind truly can accomplish anything he sets his mind to. Given enough time and cooperation, I think Man may be able to conquer just about any problem we have. It may take years, but he can do it all!

Reflecting on the past few days of exposure to such magnificent accomplishment, I cannot but think again about my questions about faith … faith in Man or faith in God? Honestly, there are times when I think that Man doesn't need a supernatural being, a god. Not any longer … we've grown beyond that.

I've been delving into study of the great thinkers in the past 100 years who have questioned and even denied the existence of God. I think of Ludwig Feuerbach who thought that Man has created God because he needs a god to be an answer for his deep struggles and fears. He said that the idea of a god is Man's dream, made-up. What he said, I think, makes a lot of sense. He makes a good case.

Karl Marx thought that Man's sorry economic and social condition was what created the desire for religion … to soothe our pain and give us a future hope. Religion, he said, keeps Man in bondage. Marx thought that the wealthy class and owners, the bourgeoisie, use God to control the workers, the proletariat. The God-idea, he said, keeps Man its place and, therefore, poor. Marx stated that if Man's economic status could be improved, there would no longer be a need for the illusion of a god. Therefore, according to Marx, class struggle and even revolution is the key to Man's freedom.

Then, there is Friedrich Nietzsche. What he calls "nihilism" posits that there is no order or predictability or meaning in the world. He considers faith in God as childish wishful thinking, and rejection of God is a step into freedom from the slavery to man-made rules and morals. To be realistic and to find true freedom, he said Man must realize that God is dead.

There have been others, too, who I have been reading. They all seem to be saying to me in various ways that belief in God is a crutch. The idea of God serves only to meet a deep psychological need for comfort and to give a false sense of hope. But it's all an illusion. There is only a "here"; there is no "hereafter".

These have brought me to ask, what if there is no God? It's hard for me to imagine such a world. It's mind-boggling. I wonder as I wander through this stupendous Exposition, "Is there any hope beyond Man's accomplishments? In the long run, would the world … would Man be better or worse off … freer or more in bondage without a god? That's the nub of my struggle. Would Man be better off without belief in God? Are we only fooling ourselves and need to face this realism so that Man can achieve his greatness? These are hard questions.

But these philosophers and thinkers are all brilliant men and certainly make important arguments. Furthermore, for the most part, they're all brilliant Germans! But are they right?

CHAPTER 13

1907... Brun's Bar – "Wars and Rumors of War"

Ludwig is talking about developments in Europe, "From what I've been hearing and reading, sounds like ole Kaiser Wilhelm II is envious of England, and his cousin, King George and the fleet of British Navy

Ernst picks up on it, "Yeah, England produces this huge new ship, the *Dreadnought*, and Kaiser's foaming at the mouth to get himself some of these ships."

Helmuth chimes in, "That has to be quite the ship with those huge guns, this new steam turbine power for speed, and that armor plating … ten inches thick!"

Arnie weighs in, "Well, I can see why Germany wants some of those, too."

I disagree, "Well, I can't see it one bit. The Kaiser thinks he can build a navy to match Britain's. But that's a pipedream!"

Ludwig concurs, "That ain't gonna happen … not in his lifetime … Britain has ruled the sea for a hundred years … ain't no way Germany's got a chance."

I add, "I can see why Britain wants them. Her empire stretches all over the globe! Their prosperity depends on protecting their trade routes. That's what the Royal Navy's for … it has to remain strong and modern. But Germany? Why does Germany need Dreadnaughts? What do they want them for?"

Ernst states, "But this only goes to show again that the Kaiser is just like his father, Wilhelm I. Every new weapon that comes along, he has to have an even better one!"

Ludwig questions, "But why? I agree with Heinrich. That's all Germany's been thinking about ever since Bismarck. Germany's strong enough now. Who's gonna mess with her?"

I jump in again, "Those Dreadnaughts … they're not designed to defend but to attack. They can fire a shell up to ten miles … think about that … that's like from here to town … holy crap!"

Arnie adds what he knows, "You could be sitting on a ship ten miles away and not even see it coming … just bam, and the whole side of your ship is gone in a flash!"

Ernst replied, "But, Arnie, you wouldn't know what hit you."

Ludwig responds, "Yep, you'd be gone. At least it'd be a quick death.

Ernst, "Maybe some of those clowns that advise the Kaiser think that Germany should go to war. After all, they loudly sing, *Deutschland, Deutschland uber Alles*.

Ludwig objects, "Don't give me that! You know that song came out of the unification movement back sixty, seventy years ago! It was the peoples' appeal to the princes and rulers to prioritize a national union and not focus on their own petty desires. It wasn't saying that we should rule everyone else in the world!"

Ernst defends his statement, "But try explaining that to our neighbors, the Cunninghams, down the road. They've come right out and said they wish we never came over here … they think we're trying to make a little Germany over here."

I redirect the conversation, "Well, getting back to those ships, I can understand Germany strengthening and adding to their merchant fleet. The German economy is booming … as is everyone's. Merchant ships, yes. Makes sense. But those Dreadnoughts are only going to create more tension."

Ludwig again, "Somehow the thinking everywhere seems to be, 'Well if we can do it, then we should do it.' What kind of crazy thinking is that?"

Arnie, "I guess they think that you have to do it before the other guy does."

I respond, "That's why I'm afraid. They're gonna mess around over there, and someone's gonna make a mistake, and then, all hell will break loose. They keep modernizing their militaries with more powerful weapons and pretty soon someone will want to try them out."

After a few more minutes, I decide that I've had enough of this barroom philosophy. I get up, excuse myself, plunk some money down on the table and leave. I'd rather be home with Susanna.

But on the way home, I do wonder what in the world Kaiser Wilhelm could possibly want with those new warships! Why is it that ever since Germany's many smaller nations and territories united … why has Germany consistently been so focused on building its military? I think it's that Prussian mentality, first instilled by Bismarck. It concerns me.

January 1911 Brun's Bar

I'M HAVING A FEW BEERS WITH MY GOOD FRIENDS, DAVID AND Peter. I comment, "By the way, I read today in the newspaper, the *Deutsche Volksfreund*, that tensions are building over in Europe."

Peter, joking about how all the major rulers in Europe and Britain are either grandchildren of or married grandchildren of Queen Victoria of Britain, "She's not called the Queen of Europe for nothing! Her grandchildren aren't playing so well together these days, are they?"

David chimes in, "Typical spoiled brats, if you ask me … out-doing each other, seeing who can build the biggest and meanest military. But they're playing with some mighty big stakes!"

I state my concern. "You'd think with all the capability of mankind, they'd be able to figure out a solution. All the progress and advancements in every area of life! But why in the world can't they make progress in controlling their ambitions?"

David shares his fear, "They're going to mess around, and something will happen, and it will blow up all-over Europe. And well, if that day comes, the United States better stay out of it. We can't solve Europe's problems; they'll have to figure it out by themselves … or fight it out, I'm afraid."

Peter gets serious, "It doesn't look good. Who knows what new kind of inventions they're working on to kill the other guy!"

David adds, "And what kind of plans no one knows about except the top brass and the rulers themselves!"

Peter concludes, "And what kind of under-the-table alliances have been going on with whoever."

I give my perspective, "We all know the French and the Germans have hated each other since even before Napoleon a hundred years ago. But ever since that French and German war forty years ago, the hatred has kept escalating."

Disgustedly, Peter goes on, "The poor souls in Alsace-Lorraine. That's where my wife and I used to live. First, Napoleon had it, and then Bismarck took it. Some of the folks speak French; some speak German. They live under the French King, then, the German Kaiser. Every time there's war, the winner takes all and it changes hands."

I interject, "But I'm still hopeful they can figure something out over there! Surely, Man is better than this!"

David adds, "Well, the new Kaiser got rid of Bismarck, and

say what you will, but at least Bismarck was able to see the big picture and use diplomacy when necessary to stay out of war."

I add, "But who does the Kaiser have now to advise him? Only his cronies! And they just feed into his desire to continually modernize the military. Sometimes, it looks like they want war."

Peter, again returning to his theme, "Which brings us back again to Queen Victoria's family feud. Those cousins just don't like each other!"

I conclude with my opinion, "The Kaiser's got everyone over there on pins and needles about what he might do. He has this huge army and, now to add to it, he's expanding the navy. It makes no sense."

Afterward, as I head toward home, I think about Kaiser Wilhelm. He's scary … he's the scariest of the bunch. So erratic. He plays cruel jokes on people for his pleasure. But he's been given so much power … especially over the military. Germany's Constitution designates him the Supreme War Commander. He makes wild and crazy statements that are sure to rile up the others. Who knows what he'll try … just because he can?" As I park my Model T and head toward the house, I mutter, "God help us!"

August 5, 1914, at Brun's Bar

KARL AND HIS CRONIES HAVE ALL ARRIVED AND ARE JUST getting seated. I join them.

As I sit down, Edward is saying, "Well, shit! It's started. Those *Dummkopfs*, those dumb asses, couldn't help themselves. Belgium's been attacked. Here we go."

Wilhelm shakes his head in dismay, "And it looks like it was Germany who started it."

Arnie, with his typically unthought-through ideas, expounds,

"Well, sure hope America jumps in on Germany's side. Looks to me like they've got Germany surrounded and have been trying to push her around for a long time. Germany's had enough of that, seems to me."

"Arnie!" exclaims Edward, "Why do you want America to go in at all? As I see it, it's their war."

"But what if Germany loses?" continues Arnie. "Are we just supposed to sit here and watch her go down in defeat? I still have relatives, cousins, over there."

"Hell, we all do, man," says Richard. "But I'm not ready to volunteer my son to go. Are you? Are you ready to sacrifice your son? That's the chance you'd be taking. I left that country to get away from that filth and dirty air … the industry that's building those huge guns and ships. My sister couldn't breathe it, and she ended up dying from it. I say they have to figure it out for themselves."

This is a touchy subject that generates strong feelings. Our arguing about it seems pretty useless. What difference can we make?

Fall Semester, 1914 … First Day of teaching my "European History" class

As I enter the classroom, I see that this is a very large class. Apparently, the war has caused great interest. Seeing so many students, I'm especially heartened, "Good morning, class. I am Professor Mendorf, and this class is, 'European History.'

"A lot has been happening over in Europe this summer. And as you can tell from my accent, I, myself, am an immigrant, having come here when I was about your age from Bavaria in 1872.

So, I'd like to take this first session of class to help us all understand this war that has broken out in Belgium and France. Plus, I really would like to hear your perspectives about what you or perhaps your parents think."

One hand goes up immediately from a young girl on the front row. "Mr. Mendorf, my name is Nancy, I don't understand what this war is about? I mean, I don't get it … how did it start? And why? I mean, who was that man who got killed over there in some little country I've never even heard of?"

I reply, "He was Archduke Franz Ferdinand. He was next-in-line to the throne of Austria-Hungary. Near the end of June … just a couple of months ago … he and his wife went to the city of Sarajevo, the capital of Bosnia. You likely have never heard of either of those places until a few weeks ago. Bosnia is one of the small Balkan countries that just doesn't fit in the Austria-Hungarian Empire."

I go to the large map on the wall and point them out. "See they're way over here. These are countries with different languages, religions, and cultures … but they're part of Austria. These little Balkan territories have been pretty much impossible to manage. They can't stand the Austrians because they want independence."

I continue, "The archduke and his wife had no business being in Sarajevo. But there they were, parading through the city in an open car when their driver made a wrong turn. As he stopped to turn around, "BAM", they both were shot and killed! The assassin was a radical from Serbia. It was a tragic and unfortunate incident."

Nancy continues, "Well, how would that … I mean, it's sad and all … but how would that cause what's happening now?

I respond, "Well, you see, there were treaties and alliances … agreements between nations pledging support in time of war. France, Russia, and England formed one of these alliances, which included protecting Belgium. They were very concerned about Germany and Austria-Hungary and pledged to support one another in case of German aggression. Germany and Austria-Hungary had a similar agreement.

"When Austria threatened to attack Serbia in retribution for the assassination, Russia wanted to defend Serbia, so it mobilized its army as well. To make a long story short, it wasn't long before it all broke loose. The agreements and alliances kicked in and war began.

"Ironically, forty-five years ago, Otto von Bismarck … who we will learn more about later in the course … he predicted that the next war would be ignited by, 'some damned foolish thing in the Balkans.' And so, it would be. In the Balkans … that's where it started."

I return to the map and point out the various countries. "Notice also how France, Belgium, and Russia surround Germany and Austria-Hungary. Bulgaria and Turkey are also in league with Germany. But it's Germany that they're all afraid of."

Someone calls out, "But why? Why is everyone afraid of Germany?"

I respond, "We'll get into more of the details of this later in the course. But briefly, ever since Germany became united back in 1871, when I was a boy living there … my older brother was killed in a war then and that's why my family immigrated … but for the past forty years, all the nations of Europe have been developing bigger and more powerful weapons and ships and now even airplanes and airships. They do this in order stay even, equally as powerful as the other guy.

"Germany has especially been building up its military. All of Europe has been trying to keep up with Germany and outdo one another. Plus, Germany's King, Kaiser Wilhelm II, is really," I pause, "well, he's not very wise. He does and says foolish things. He keeps irritating and threatening other countries. He got them all 'on pins and needles', as my mother used to say.

And so, when Germany and Austria do something, like move

some troops, it's like a chess game. Austria threatens Serbia and Russia counters. One thing leads to another. Or maybe think of it like dominoes standing on end and lined up. When the first one falls, they all follow. It started over there with Austria in the East, but within a few days, just last month, on August 5, Germany invaded Belgium."

Another student raises his hand, "My name is Peter Dawson. My ancestors came from England. My father says all those kings and queens over there are related somehow."

"That's right, Peter. They're all grandchildren of Queen Victoria, which means they're all cousins and second cousins or are married to her grandchildren."

Nancy asks again, "Well, then, that only makes it even more confusing. Why did it start? Why would an assassination of some unheard-of guy and his wife cause this? Couldn't the cousins have figured something out?"

"Good point. You would think so, wouldn't you? That's what makes this so sad, even tragic."

Another hand is raised, "My name is James Dalrymple. My grandparents came from Ireland, and we don't like the English. So, we're hoping that the English lose this war. And I certainly don't want the United States supporting their side in this. I'd like to know what you think, sir?"

I respond, "That's the question that is on many people's minds. America is a nation of immigrants, and sides will inevitably be taken in this. At least for now, I think America does need to try to stay out of this war. And so, I tend to agree with you, James. It's not our war, and I hope America stays out of it."

Another hand goes up, "Sir, my name is Herman. My parents came over from Germany about twenty-five years ago. From what they say, the Germans are winning thus war handily right now. So maybe it won't last long before Germany wins it."

I respond, "That's right. The German Army has swept through Belgium and is deep in France. It has gotten within thirty miles of Paris, the capital. I understand there's talk of the leading government officials even leaving Paris to find safety someplace else.

"All this within a month! The young men went off to war with the promise that they'd be home by the time the leaves fall. The speed that this thing is moving makes it seem possible.

"But now, I hear that Germany's advance has been slowed. And the French and British are fighting back and beginning to regain some territory, so who knows what will happen? But until now, Germany has definitely been winning. "

A new hand goes up, "My name is Sarah Cooper. Do you think this may cause problems between people and immigrant groups here in America?"

I respond, "That's a hard question, isn't it?" I pause to collect my thoughts. "Well, America is more and more a nation of immigrants, especially from these European countries. And immigrants tend to group together, at least at first … until they can feel part of America. So, loyalties to our homelands and our native language and culture are deep. Is that true for many of you and your families?"

Many nod in agreement. I go on, "It's certainly true in mine. My parents and our community spoke German … most still do. We're sort of in-between languages right now. But thanks to my wife, who was born here … her parents came over twenty years before my family did … I have had to learn to speak English, too. Both of us can speak English and German, but we insist that our children learn English, and in our home, we speak only English."

A student pipes up, "Sir, if I say a word of French in my house, it's like a dirty word. My parents wash my mouth with soap." We all laugh.

I resume, "Good for them!" Getting back to the question asked, I continue, "But I do hope that the U.S. can stay out of this conflict. I'm afraid it could hurt America's unity as it continues receiving European immigrants."

Mary speaks up again, "Sir, it's almost time for our class to end. But can you tell us what you're personally really thinking about all this?"

"Well, understand that this is my personal opinion and what I think as of today. I may think differently as time goes on. Others may disagree." I pause before saying, "I think that it's an unnecessary war. So tragic! It's all about the big powers, the big weapons, and the big egos. With just that one little spark in Sarajevo, Europe's now in flames.

"The United States is neutral. It's Europe's war, not ours. There are so many people here in the United States that don't want to go to war. People are divided as to their allegiances. President Woodrow Wilson vows that he'll keep the U.S. out of it.

"For most of us, the war seems so far away … so removed from our lives here. Here, we're all trying to just be good hard-working peace-loving Americans. Sure, there is some sympathy for our various fatherlands. My family as German-Americans wants to continue our German traditions, and many still want to speak our language. But that's not disloyalty. We are loyal Americans too. I'm sure that I am saying a lot of what many of your own families are saying as well, no matter where your ancestors came from."

Wrapping up the class, I say, "This will be an interesting year as we study Europe today and put it all in a historical context. Well, this seems like a good place to end. And with that, see you next time."

July 11, 1915 ... Brun's Bar

TENSIONS ARE HIGH.

Wilhelm, sitting down at the table with a stein of beer in his hand, begins, "Well damn, I don't know what to think! Some idiot German shot that big-time Wall Street banker, J.P. Morgan. Morgan is one of the wealthiest people in America!

Louis adds, "And then that *Dummkopf* goes and brags that the night before, he had set off that bomb in the United States Capitol."

Edward is skeptical, "How could he have done both of those? Setting off a bomb in the Capitol in Washington D.C. and then traveling overnight to New York and shooting one of the richest men in America." Shaking his head in disgust, he says, "That's quite a feat! All by himself! Or so he says."

Karl sarcastically adds, "If you think he's done this all by himself, then I have a couple lame horses I can sell you real cheap."

Gunter suggests, "Sounds like another one of those conspiracy theories to me."

Arnie challenges, "Do you think all this is true, or is it some kind of set-up, just more political fodder to get Wilson to go to war?"

I state what I think, "Well, for sure, J. P. Morgan was shot, and a bomb was set off in the Capitol. From what I hear, there's quite a lot of damage. But whether or not we're getting the whole truth … who knows?"

Arnie, hitting his fist on the table, says, "No doubt about it, a lot of people want President Wilson to declare war. They're trying to force his hand."

Louis disagrees, "Yeah, but a lot of people don't."

I interject, "Wilson still says that America is neutral."

Karl jumps in, "Heinrich, I hate to differ, big brother, but that's bullshit! If capturing over eighty German ships and sending weapons and arms and ammunition and food and horses to the British, French and Russians … if that's neutrality, then I'm Cinderella!"

Arnie sarcastically snaps, "You don't look like Cinderella! More like the ugly godmother."

Karl responds, "Stepmother."

Arnie asks, "What?"

Karl again, "Stepmother, not godmother."

Arnie, obviously irritated, lifting both middle fingers high in the air, interjects, "Well excuse me, Brothers Grimm!"

Getting back on the subject of the war, Edward suggests, "But really, it's J.P. Morgan and his buddies who keep floating ridiculous loans to the French and Brits ... to subsidize their part in the war."

Arnie dejectedly concludes, "And Germany gets nothing … zilch."

Edward continues, "And then Wilson comes back with that asinine excuse saying, 'Well, America is open for business to Germany, too. Germany can buy all it wants from American manufacturers'."

Arnie angrily states, "And how are they supposed to get it there? As Karl just reminded us, Wilson's already captured so many of our … I mean, so many of Germany's ships! Wilson's got them under lock and key, stuck in U.S. harbors. They can't move. And then there's the British naval blockade. There's not a snowball's chance in hell that Germany's ships could get through!"

A silence follows. Then, Gunter, directing us back to the original subject, inquires, "Wonder what will happen to the man who says he did all this."

I say, "I just heard while ago, the bomber died mysteriously in jail. They're not saying what happened … all I know is that he's dead."

Arnie, with a laugh of disgust, says, "Now, isn't that convenient!"

But then Arnie, with an accusatory edginess in his voice, says to me, "Well, Professor, some folks kinda think you're sounding more like you might be partial to the French and British in this."

I respond, "Well, not really, but I do know that this war has to end. Looks to me like they're stalemated in those trenches. Any soldier that sticks his head up just a little gets shot. And before that, the carnage on the battlefields … senseless slaughter. Already many thousands are dead, killed … soldiers and innocent civilians. And Wilson has at least offered to try to negotiate an end. I respect him for that, at least."

Arnie argues back, "Do you think he's sincere? I don't. If he were, then why isn't he more genuinely neutral?"

I agree, "Well, America's claim to neutrality does get a little hard to swallow. And yes, J.P. Morgan and his kind want the British to win … that's why they're floating those loans."

Arnie presses me, "Then why the hell doesn't Wilson stop them?"

Growing frustrated, I respond, "Well, I think there are two reasons. First, our government can't just stop them like that. This is a free country. There would be all kinds of laws broken if he tried that. A president is not a king!"

Arnie irately replies, "At least not yet, he's not."

I ignore him and continue, "A more probable reason, though, is that it's good for business. The American economy is booming. Why? Because of this war. This makes Wilson look good to the voters."

Gunter now jumps in, "Well, that's sick if you ask me. We're thriving while they're dying!"

I add, "I agree. It is. About our president, Wilson is an idealist. He thinks that Man's nature is basically good, as I tend to do, too. He has a high opinion of himself … thinks he's got the answers to all the problems. I wonder if his answers are just too simplistic. He's a decent leader in peacetime, I think, but not in times like this."

Arnie rejoins, "But, do you want France and Britain to win?"

Cautiously I reply, "I don't think there's much doubt, but that Germany and its allies are the more guilty aggressors. Germany and Austria-Hungary started it. Germany's invasion of neutral Belgium was and is unconscionable. I think that what they've done to Belgium and to its people is inexcusable."

Arnie, raising his voice, "So, you're saying that you would like to see Germany lose."

Even more cautiously I comment, "Arnie, I want to see this damn war end. That's what I want. Realistically though, unless Germany can pull a rabbit out of the hat, with America leaning the way it is now, I don't see how Germany and the *Central Powers* can ultimately win this thing. As you've mentioned, America already controls the fate of so many German ships that are interned at our ports."

Gunter again joins in, "Well, that's just downright unfair."

I respond, "Yes, it may be, but that's the way it is. Add the fact that America's huge industrial strength has not been dented and it has all the natural resources imaginable. And what chance do the *Central Powers* have against that?"

Gunter asks for my final assessment, "So, you think, there's no chance for Germany. Is that right?"

I try to conclude, "If somehow, Germany could get America on its side, maybe then, it'd be a different story. But right now, Germany is on shaky ground with the United States. We all know that. Two months ago, a German U-boat torpedoed the *Lusitania* without warning, in violation of international law. Over a thousand souls were killed … civilians … men, women, and children, even babies. More than one hundred were American citizens. That enraged the American public, really putting all kinds of pressure on Wilson. And now this, setting off a bomb in the United States Capitol and wounding one of our wealthiest citizens. This kind of *Scheisse* is only going to further alienate the American people against Germany."

Gunter objects, "There's more to the *Lusitania* story. It had to be carrying war matériel, explosives of all kinds or one torpedo could not have sunk it. She exploded and sank in what … 20 minutes! They're not telling us the truth on that."

Getting perturbed, I reply, "Maybe they are or maybe they're not. Keep in mind, too, that Germany broke the international law of naval engagement. They were supposed to give warning and have all passengers in safety before sinking the ship."

Gunter argues, "Well, how were they supposed to do that from a U-boat. They bring the submarine to the surface, and they'd be blown out of the water.

I reply, "I'm not going to argue that. All I'm saying is that the American people are getting fed up with this kind of crap … coming from Germany."

Arnie asserts, "Well, there are about eight million of us Germans living here now. That says a lot."

Now I'm angry, "Yes, but, Arnie, that's not enough. Besides, now you're talking about an insurrection or another civil war."

Arnie interrupts, "Wilson's actions are pissing off enough people that there may well be one. Add in the Irish who hate the British and you have a major force to deal with."

I pause to calm down and ask myself if I want to proceed. I decide I will. Carefully choosing my words. "Let's all think about it, do we really want to see Germany win this thing?" A long silence follows. I continue, "Really … stop and consider … isn't this, the Germany that we see today … aggressive, militaristic … isn't it the ugly side of Germany our parents couldn't wait to get away from?"

Arnie against asserts, "But I'm just pissed that America isn't being even-handed in this. I'm afraid for my relatives back there, too.

I sympathetically say, "I know, that's true, and what will this do to our German heritage here? But if America were any different and supplied both sides, that would only prolong the killing and destruction and hatred."

Gunter emphatically states, "Yes, but if only America wouldn't help either side … if it really were neutral!"

I respond, "I agree, but that ship has already sailed. It's too late for that, I'm afraid."

Soon, we all leave and head to our homes. We've solved nothing … just inflamed some passions. We all go home at least a little drunk, some more than others. We all go home more depressed than when we came. We all love America … maybe some more than others … but we also love our heritage. We are torn.

July 31, 1916 ... Brun's Bar

ARNIE, WITH A SLIGHT CHUCKLE THAT SHOWS HIS POLITICAL leanings, reports, "I just read in the newspaper that yesterday the Black Tom munitions facility in Jersey City was destroyed by fire and explosions.

Karl remarks, "Yes, until yesterday, it was the largest shipping center of munitions, and guess who to, France and England!"

Gunter adds, "I understand they estimate more than two million pounds of ammunition, including one hundred thousand pounds of TNT exploded. Two million pounds … I can't fathom…".

I add, "Everyone knows that this was an intentional act of sabotage."

Arnie quips, "Yep, that's American neutrality for you. Before the war, France and England relied on Germany as the source of raw material for ammunition. We'd wondered what would happen if there was war, where they'd get supplies. We found out, didn't we?"

Gunter completes the thought, "American neutrality is a myth."

Arnie agrees, "You can say that again."

Wilhelm joins in, "Something else has been happening. It's not much in the news, but several ships carrying supplies over to France have been mysteriously catching fire out in the middle of the Atlantic and are sinking, with all kinds of supplies being lost."

Edward adds, "I hear, too, that ships out there are having their rudders damaged and even blown off by some kind of bomb. They can no longer steer and lose control … some of them are sinking, too."

Gunter asks, "Could they be submarines?"

Edwards replies, "Nope, not possible. That's like finding a needle in a haystack out there in the middle of the ocean. No, I think the Germans or maybe the Irish, or maybe both … here in America … are rigging up explosives and, somehow, getting them on board and setting them off."

Arnie proposes his answer, "German ships are sitting in our ports under guard by Americans … luxury liners, merchant ships, and cruisers. Wilson says they're interned, but I say they're captured. Meanwhile, their German sailors and dock workers have nothing to do but sit around and get more and more pissed off. They have lots of time on their hands and who knows what their German ingenuity is coming up with?"

Strangely, I find myself agreeing with Arnie's explanation, though not with his confused sympathies.

Hermann adds yet another report, "You know, we're sending horses and mules by the hundreds over there, too. Whole herds that have been gathered from different places are catching glanders or anthrax and have died."

Karl, shaking his head, says, "Yes, I know. Some that we bred and sold to the government all died in one of those shipments. They were already dying by the time they got to St. Louis, I guess. But we still got paid, at least. Still a shame to see them go like that."

I break my silence, "Yes, from what I'm hearing up at the college, that's pretty much all true. Intentional explosions and they suspect deadly germs injected into these animals. They think that at least one herd came from our area, shipped from Cape Girardeau. It probably happened before being loaded on the train cars to St. Louis."

Arnie interjects, "Well, someone around here seems to have strong feelings for the Germans."

Edward, looking at Arnie with a congenial laugh, says, "You mean someone else around here?"

Arnie raises both his middle fingers to Edward.

Sensing that tensions are beginning to build again, we pay our bills and head for home.

November 4, 1916 ... Brun's Bar

SEVEN OF US ARE SITTING TOGETHER: KARL, FIVE OF HIS friends, and me. Karl asked me to come along with him, and I did, even though, I have little in common with these younger men.

Karl, already with several beers in him, is having a hard time keeping his voice low, "Well, next Tuesday is the election. Who you gonna to vote for? Two lousy choices ... Wilson or Charles Evans Hughes? Can't say I like either one."

Arnie, also speaking with intoxicated bravado, "Wilson keeps campaigning on the slogan, 'He kept us out of war,' but just you wait. If he gets his second term next Tuesday, he'll get us knee-deep in Europe's war. And it won't be on the side of the Germans!"

Karl interrupts, "Yes, but Hughes thinks that we should rebuild our military to be strong … just in case. Just in case of what? At least Wilson says he wants to keep us out of war."

Helmuth adds, "It's hard to see where Hughes stands on some other things. Like on prohibition. Now that's a subject that scares me."

Karl observes, "Seems like more states are leaning toward it all the time … along with women voting."

Arnie complains, "Do you realize that about twelve states are going to allow women to vote? I wonder how that'll affect the vote? I'm afraid those women will go for Wilson."

Karl says, "No, I think they'll just go along with what their husbands think."

Edward adds, "That seems strange … some states allow women voting and others don't. Doesn't quite seem right."

Wilhelm adds, "Well, Hughes is for women voting."

Arnie asserts, as we already know, "But for me, the big issue is the war. I just don't trust Wilson. He's got it in for the Germans … keeps helping out only England and France."

Karl joins in, "Yes, but hasn't this war been great for us farmers? The price for everything we produce is up, and we're breeding horses and getting incredible money for them. Doesn't seem right, but we might as well take advantage of it while we can."

Wilhelm looks at me and asks, "What do you think of all this, Herr Professor? Do you think Wilson will win and take us to war?"

I reply, "He'll need a bigger reason than what he has now to take us to war. He'd have a tough sell to convince Congress to declare war right now. America isn't ready for war. That's why I lean toward Hughes for president. I think we do need to get ready … just in case. Plus, I'm for women voting." But I can tell that no one cares what I think, so I quit talking.

Helmuth changes the subject, "I just know the newspapers aren't giving us all the real facts. Remember, when the war began, the first thing Britain did was cut the five underwater cables from Germany to America. England made sure we'd hear only news coming from England. And that's what American newspapers publish."

Arnie disdainfully replies, "That's "freedom of the press" … when the voice of the other side can't get a word in edgewise!"

Gunter adds, "There's still the wireless telegraph, but I hear the British control a lot of that too."

Wilhelm reminds us, "Apparently, they can't stop it all. Thank God for our German newspapers."

Arnie again complains, "Well, we'll see how long they last! If this thing gets going like I suspect, you just watch. They're going to clamp down on them too."

I decide I'd rather be home with Susanna than waste any more time in this bar. What good does it do? I excuse myself, toss down some money for my share of the bill and leave.

CHAPTER 14

On February 1, 1917, Germany, seeking to end the supply of war matériel and food to England, declared unrestricted submarine warfare. This means that even neutral nations are now targets for Germany's torpedoes. This declaration was issued against the advice of several significant German political leaders who are worried that it will bring the United States into the war. But, as usual in today's Germany, the military won the argument.

On March 1, British Intelligence released a deciphered telegram from German Foreign Secretary, Arthur Zimmermann, to Mexico, pledging Germany's financial and military support to Mexico if it would declare war on the United States. Germany clearly hopes that this will divert U.S. resources from Europe to a home front war on its southern border. Germany has promised to help Mexico regain Texas, Arizona, and New Mexico.

These two developments have shocked America and swung more of the public against Germany.

For President Wilson, this is the final straw.

On April 3, 1917, Susanna and I hear on the radio that yesterday, April 2, President Wilson asked Congress to declare war on Germany. Congress is expected to do so within a few days.

We know that the *Selective Service Act* will soon follow, requiring all men between the ages of 21 and 30 to register for the draft. This includes the young men in our extended family. Deferments might be given for such reasons as marital status, caring for a dependent, physical ailment, and providing an essential service. The pastor will likely be performing many weddings in the days ahead so that young men can claim "marital status" as an exemption.

It is not clear whether farming qualifies as an exemption by providing an essential service. It will be left up to the local County Exemption Boards to decide case by case.

April 9, 1917, at the home of Karl and Emma Mendorf

SEVEN-YEAR-OLD HANS RUNS THROUGH THE FIELDS TOWARD home, biting his lip to hold back the tears. He'd been in a fight. His shirt is torn, his face dirty and his arms are scratched. He throws open the door and bursts into tears.

"Hans, what's happened to you?" his mother cries.

"Mama, some bigger boys from that other school caught me when I was walking home. They called me bad names. They called me Hans, the Hun!" As he tells the story with tears running down his face, Emma enfolds him in her arms. "They say that I am their enemy, and they hate the Germans. They called me a 'Dirty German'. Then they called Papa, 'Kaiser Karl!' And they're saying bad words about you, too, Mama. I don't know what they mean, but I know they're bad. So, I had to fight. They made me."

Hugging him close, Mama comforts, "O Hans, I am so sorry." She holds him as he cries in her arms. When he has calmed down, but still sniffing and tense, his Mama continues, "Hans, we are Americans. Those were hurtful things that they said. Yes, your Papa and I were born in Germany. We both came from Germany, but we are Americans. Sometimes people are cruel, and they don't understand." Emma continues to hold Hans until she can feel him relaxing.

After a long pause, biting her lip as she deliberates, Emma hesitantly continues, "Hans, Papa and I didn't know if we should tell you, but a few days ago, our country, the United States, decided to go to war against Germany."

"Why, Mama?"

"Well, Hans, it's really hard to understand, but Germany has done some very bad things lately. They're even trying to hurt Americans."

Looking at his mother with a confused expression, and still reeling from the incident after school, Hans cries and asks, "But why me, Mama? We're not Germans. What did I do to them? They say I'm the enemy; they say I am a dirty German!"

His mother tries to explain, "Hans, as I was saying, both Papa and I were born in Germany, but your grandparents brought us to America when we were babies. All your Papa and I know is America. We've never been back to Germany and don't want to go there. Yes, we still speak German, but we also speak English … and people sometimes laugh at the way we say English words, but we're Americans."

But Hans cannot comprehend and cries, "But why, Mama, why did they make fun of me and say those mean dirty things about Papa and you and then hurt me? Why?"

"Hans, you didn't do anything to them. It wasn't your fault. You just have to be strong. We all, especially now, just have to be strong."

Seeking to reinforce her point, she continues, "Didn't Pastor Brauer teach us this last Sunday … that we are to love even those people who persecute you, people who want to hurt you?"

"No Mama, I can't love bullies who beat me up when I

haven't done anything wrong! I can't do it. I hate them, and I hope the Germans beat them.

Firmly taking hold of his shoulders, she looks him squarely in the face and insists, "Hans, you cannot talk that way. We will not have that kind of talk in this house. We're Americans, Hans, and don't ever forget that."

Puckering up and crying, Hans blurts out, "But Mama, that's not fair!"

Sympathetically, she gathers him into another hug, saying, "I know." And wistfully she whispers under her breath to herself, "Life is not fair. This is not right … hurting a little boy who has done nothing wrong." Inside she is seething.

April 14, 1917 ... Brun's Bar

BRUN'S HAS BEEN DOING A BIG BUSINESS LATELY. Uncharacteristically, farmers are quitting their fields early, putting other things off as well, and heading to Brun's to find out and talk about events in Washington D.C. and Germany.

I happen to find a chair among Karl and some of his buddies. Karl, my outspoken strong-willed younger brother, states intensely, "For a man who promised not to go the war, Wilson's certainly going all in. They're doing all they can to make us Germans look like barbarians."

Wilhelm chimes in, "He's trying to stir the shit against us Americans who have German ancestry. He thinks we're the enemy and need to be watched. He's as much as said so."

Edward continues the thought, "Yea, he says that anyone who has a hyphen in their name is not a true patriot, as in German-American."

Hermann, who has already had several beers, defiantly declares, "I have no intention of taking out that hyphen. That's my right! I'm American, but I am also proud of my German descent. I am a proud 'German-American'." As he raises his hand to draw an imaginary hyphen in the air, "See, there's that hyphen, and I'm not going to remove it. And nobody, not even the President, can make me change that."

"I'll drink to that," shouts Arnie, as he stands and holds up his mug.

Edward says, "Arnie, you'll drink to anything."

We all laugh and tell Arnie to sit down.

Arnie, refusing to sit, continues, "Mr. 'He-kept-us-out-of-war' Wilson plans to bring back his desire for the Espionage Act, so they can spy on anyone they damn well please, and that will certainly put us Germans right in the bullseye."

I'm thinking, "Good Lord, I hope not, but I wouldn't be surprised."

Wilhelm looks at me and says, "Well, what do you think now, Herr Professor? Isn't this a damn shame? Now, we're all gonna be watched and have to prove our loyalty."

I agree, "It is a shame … not good at all." I pause, not wanting to go on, but I venture, "But let's be honest. The Kaiser didn't help himself when he started torpedoing U.S. ships. And then came that letter from German Foreign Secretary Zimmermann to Mexico.

Edward objects, "Do you believe that Zimmermann telegram story? That whole thing sounds fishy if you ask me. Something about it just doesn't hold water."

Martin says, "Well, even Zimmermann himself has admitted it was true."

Edward continues, "I don't know if I can believe that report either. It all comes from the British, you know."

Arnie jumps in, "And besides, do you honestly think that the U.S. worries about anything Mexico could do?"

Eugene, who had just been listening until now, suggests, "Well, I don't think this has been thought about much, but I think that Wilson has to make sure Britain and France win the war so that they can repay the huge debt that they've built up with the likes of J.P. Morgan and others."

Hermann, thinking this through, says, "Hmm, I hadn't thought of that. That's a good point. It all does come down to money, doesn't it?"

Martin suggests, "But remember France can't wait to settle the score ever since their humiliation by Germany back in '71. For almost fifty years, France has been waiting."

I'm thinking that Martin's right about that. I'm also remembering back to that day when we heard that Friedrich had been killed in that conflict.

Karl jumps in, "Yeah, Heinrich and I had a brother killed in the battle at Sedan. I never knew him; I was a baby. But Heinrich did, didn't you?" as he looks at me.

"Yes, I remember that terrible day. We emigrated soon after that."

Wilhelm throws up his hands and says, "That's my point exactly. I don't know about you, but my parents came over here to stay away from war. I say we shouldn't have gotten into this mess. But it's too late now."

Eugene adds his opinion, "Our army isn't strong. What have we got … 100 to 110 thousand men? And now Wilson has started this draft, this 'Selective Service' nonsense. How does anyone think we'll do anything other than lose our sons?"

Arnie pipes up, "I hear he's gonna draft four million. I hear tell that anyone who has a wisp of a chance of being exempted is going to apply for a deferment. My boys are going to apply for sure … claiming that farmers need to stay here to do their part working on the farm. But I sure as hell can't see them fighting against their own people."

Martin sadly states, "It would be a damn shame to send some of our good German boys back to get killed."

I'm thinking to myself, "Yes, we will lose some and it will be a shame … I think of my grandsons and my great-nephews. It's a sick feeling … losing our young men with lives ahead of them here … in some idiotic war, that we had nothing to do with … well, little to do with!"

The discussion goes on. I get up to leave and, as I do so, on the other side of the room in a smokey corner, two eyes are watching, two ears are listening. They are the eyes and ears of Augie Gaebler, the oldest son of the late August Gaebler. It's just a look, but something strikes me as odd.

April 25, 1917

TODAY, I AM INFORMED THAT MY TEACHING POSITION IS TO BE terminated. The German language that, until recently, had been the most common foreign language taught in American schools, is now considered *verboten*, forbidden.

I'm angry. It seems to me that anyone who speaks English with a German accent is suspect, anyone who speaks German is hated, and anyone who teaches the German language is subject to interrogation as a possible German spy. That pretty well sums up the tone of Woodrow Wilson, a sentiment that has now been made front and center for the American people. I will, though, be allowed to finish this semester of German, probably because they can't find anyone else who can teach it.

In addition, some on the faculty have expressed concern that what I teach in my European History course may now be tainted with a pro-German slant. And so, I am immediately removed from the classroom and replaced by another but less knowledgeable professor to complete the semester.

And so, I am out of a job, but I will be paid until the end of the semester. At dinner, Susanna and I decide that we will probably move back out to the farm then. Not much prospect for a

German professor in this political climate! It comes down to that same old question of loyalty.

A few days later, as I open the day's mail, to my surprise, I receive a letter from The United States Department of War. There is a desperate need for loyal American citizens who are also fluent in the German language. They are needed in France to interpret the interrogation of German prisoners of war fresh off the battlefield. It's ironic; I can't be trusted to teach German in a classroom, but I can be trusted to accurately interpret it in the vital war effort!

Susanna and I are confused. Why me? Do they know my age, how old I am? Do they expect me to go through basic training? What exactly will be my status? Will I be in the Army? Will I be a civilian under a contract of some kind?

A few days later, Susanna accompanies me on the drive to St. Louis to meet with the government officials. We get most of our questions answered. They know how old I am. They assure me that I'll be out of harm's way. I won't have to go through basic training. But the answer to my question of status remains hazy. I will be "of" the Army but not "in" the Army, whatever that means. I'm not sure they're even clear in their own minds. But they need translators, and this is an opportunity for me to help my adopted country to which I am loyal, and hopefully, to help bring this carnage to an end sooner.

By the end of the day, I am signed up … pending my passing a physical exam and my clearing a loyalty background check. I'm even now on the government payroll.

We spend the night in a swank hotel at government expense and have a very special night in St. Louis. The next day, I pass my physical examination, and we drive home.

Two weeks later, I receive word that I have also passed my loyalty background check. For the first time in more than forty-five years, I'm headed back to Europe. I don't know when I'm to leave, but I wait my turn.

November 15, 1917 ... Brun's Bar

ARNIE ANGRILY STATES, "IT WASN'T ENOUGH THAT A FEW months back Congress passed the *Espionage Act*. Then we got this *American Protective League*. Now they passed the *Trading-with-the Enemy Act*. This used to be a free country, but those days are gone."

Gunter, shaking his head, adds, "These laws are to ensure that no one can speak against or write against America's war effort. Now, the hundreds of German newspapers published in America are required to furnish English translations."

Edward, registering his disgust, "But first, there was the *Committee on Public Information* that ole Wilson established the first week of America's declaration of war. Trying to spur true patriotism…"

Arnie cutting in, "but bringing suspicion onto any of us who, in their view, don't show the proper enthusiasm for the effort."

Karl joins in, "How much did you guys have to come up with for the last Liberty Bonds Drive? Between my wife and me, they took us for $100 … or our names would be published in the newspaper! First time, we got by for just $50, but not this time."

Gunter joins in, "My son works up at the store in town. They even got him for five dollars a week for ten weeks."

Arnie responds, "Yeah, they came back on me, too … wanted $100, but I told them, 'No more than fifty.' And when he said he'd write me up, I told him that that'd be the last thing he'd do. Got to put the fear of the Lord in em, I say."

Gunter replies, "*Scheisse*, Arnie! You're going to fool around and get yourself in deep water."

Arnie comes right back, "Let them try. This arm-twisting crap is going to go all the way to the Supreme Court. This is un-American."

Gunter again replies, “But they’re saying you’re un-American.”

“Let ‘em say it,” declares Arnie, “I don’t care.”

Karl says, “Well, my family took that stupid Hoover Food Pledge … cut back on red meat so they can send it overseas to the French and English, and I guess, the Russians too. Makes no sense. Ridiculous! How can the roast that I don’t eat help win the war in France? I told Emma not to pay any attention. How are they going to enforce it, I wonder?”

I join in, “Susanna’s working on her second sweater to send overseas for the winter.”

Arnie launches into a new subject, “What in the hell is Augie Gaebler doing with the *American Protective League*? He thinks he’s some kind of a detective seeking to sniff out the supposedly 250,000 ‘highly trained’ German spies and traitors.”

Karl laughingly says, “Yeah, he even wears his badge, engraved with *APL* … now he has a permit, I guess, to spy on his neighbors and report them if they look suspicious.”

I remark, “What concerns me is that it can become a handy weapon to use to get even with an old enemy or settle a score. All he has to do is make a report, whether it is true or not.”

Gunter asks, “I hear that even the Attorney General of the United States has singled us out saying that German-Americans need to, ‘Obey the law and keep your mouth shut’ if we want to be seen as loyal Americans. Sounds like he doesn’t trust us … guilty until proven innocent.”

Karl states, “Seems to me like, around here, we’ve overdone our allegiance pledge. Look at all the oversized American flags hanging from our houses. And even Brun’s, here, took down the German flag from behind the bar, and replaced it with that even bigger American flag.”

The front door of the bar opens and in walks Augie, Jr. He orders a beer and goes to sit in the corner alone, drinking his first beer of the day.

After Augie enters, within a few minutes our gathering breaks up and we all head home.

As I head to my car and drive home, I can't help thinking about that incident so long ago when Papa and I got even with August, Sr. after he tried to rape Clara. She and I must be the only ones alive who know the full story.

I recall that night. Papa was like a raging bull when we tangled with August. It was all Papa. I never even laid even a finger on August. If I hadn't stopped Papa, I'm afraid he might have killed him. But before I could get him to let go, Papa had wrenched August's shoulder. I had hoped it would heal but it never did completely. I can only imagine that every time his shoulder hurts, it only reignited his hatred for Papa … and for all of us Mendorfs.

August told it around town and to his family that he had slipped and fallen down a hill and into a creek. He couldn't very well tell anyone what really happened.

From that day on, Augie's father hated my family. To my knowledge, Augie doesn't know why his father bore such animosity, but the old man's bile was passed on to his children. Augie hates my family, but I don't think he has any idea why. He just does.

The Gaeblers' dislike of us is general knowledge. When anyone asks me why that is, I just say, "It's a long story" and leave it at that. Nobody asks anymore.

I now suspect that, with Augie's involvement in the *APL*, he probably hopes that he can catch one of Otto Mendorf's descendants and accuse him of a lack of patriotism. That would be seen as his patriotic duty. But more so, that would be for Augie his ultimate act of family loyalty to his deceased father and a way for him to avenge a long-standing grudge.

January 14, 1918

TODAY, BOTH OF CLARA'S GRANDSONS RECEIVED THEIR NOTICES that they've been drafted! The County Exemption Board denied their requests for exemption as essential workers even though so many other farmers have been granted that exemption.

Clara is crushed. Her grandsons are the apple of her eye, and we were all sure that they would be exempted. She has had a lot of heartbreak in her life, from the sexual assault when she was fourteen, widowed when she was only twenty, her baby daughter dying at birth, then widowed again when she was forty-six. She is such a gentle compassionate person, and I hope this war won't cost her her precious grandsons.

She comes over to talk about it, "Heinrich, it's just not fair. I just don't understand it. Why this decision? Other young men all around us have had their exemption requests accepted. But why not Eric and Franz?

"Robert and Joey are angry and at their wits' end about their boys being drafted. They are pursuing an appeal. None of us can understand why Franz and Eric are not exempt, while other farmers are. It's like they've been singled out, targeted somehow."

"Have you seen Eric or Franz", I ask. "What do they think and how do they see this?"

"They're young and excited. They're proud that they can serve their country. But Heinrich, they don't know what we know about war. I still remember that day when we got the news that our brother Friedrich was killed."

"Yes, I know; that was a horrible day!" Pausing for a moment, "I remember it … only too well."

"Heinrich, you have always been there for me. You've always been the strong one on whom I can rely. You, and of course, God. I don't know what I'd do if either one of you weren't there for me. I just have to trust God to keep my grandsons safe." She closes her eyes, quietly praying. Then she continues, "I feel that He will."

"Clara, you've been there for me, too. I've always known you'd be there. Remember how you challenged me and my self-pity over losing Amelia? You took a risk and said what was on your heart that day. You know how it changed my life. Susanna is the best thing that's ever happened to me. If you hadn't told me to pull myself together and move on, there's no telling what might have happened … or not happened."

Clara looks at me and with a gentle smile reflects, "Thank you, Heinrich, for always understanding me … you and me … our relationship … it's very special." Looking at me with all sincerity she concludes, "I thank God for you, Heinrich."

With that last comment, I look away and down.

Clara gently says, "I know, Heinrich, that you're still struggling with questions about God. That's okay. We're so much alike, yet so different. I don't know what I'd do without God. I hope and pray that you'll find answers to your questions. I hope you'll find peace."

I look at her with a wry smile, "Yes, I do too. And Susanna does too. She's more like you; you know that. Just has that implicit faith and trust." Uncomfortable with the direction of this, I return to the matter at hand, "Do Franz and Eric know that their fathers are pursuing a re-evaluation of this decision?"

"Not yet, I don't think. Those two boys are willing and raring to go. At least right now they are."

"How much time do they have before they have to go?"

"They have to be at a place called Fort Dix in New Jersey by February 11 where they'll go through basic training. That's just four weeks away."

We talk a few more minutes. And when she gets up to leave, we hug each other for comfort and support. Clara, with tears in her eyes, looks up to me, smiles, and says, "Thank you, Big Brother."

As I watch her leave, I wonder, "Where does she get her faith? She may waver but she never breaks." I envy her.

A few days later, I receive word that I'm to report to New York on February 26 to sail for France.

February 16, 1918

I'M WALKING DOWN MAIN STREET IN CAPE GIRARDEAU AND bump into an old friend, a former colleague from the university, named William. We talk for quite a while, catching up on our lives and reflecting on the war.

When I tell him that we've moved back to the farm, William happens to mention that he sits on a panel with a man named August Gaebler who lives in my part of the county.

He says, "That Augie is one hell of a patriot and super-diligent in his role on the panel."

I ask, "What panel is that?"

"The County Exemption Board," he says.

I am stunned and feel sick to my stomach. Trying not to show my shock to William, I quickly excuse myself and head on down the street.

It's not enough that Augie's snooping around as a member of the APL. He's even managed to weasel his way onto the Exemption Board. Now that's a committee that has power! And Augie, of all people, is on it.

Now it all makes sense … why Clara's grandsons' requests for exemption were refused, and they've been drafted. But it's too late to do anything. They reported for basic training at Fort Dix five days ago.

I cannot tell Clara. It would hurt her too much, to know that Gaebler can still hurt her. And I certainly can't tell Robert and

Joey. No telling what they'd do. They might kill Augie and end up in prison for the rest of their lives, or worse.

But soon I'll be leaving for the war and may not come back. And so that night, I tell Susanna the whole sordid story knowing that she will use her wisdom and discretion concerning this family secret.

Six days later, I board the train and head to New York and, from there, board a troopship bound for France.

CHAPTER 15

Three days ago, on April 28, 1918, I stepped foot in Europe for the first time in over forty-five years. A year ago, when we declared war, our American Army had barely 120,000 men. We expect that by the end of this year, we will have brought over two million, and, it is anticipated that eventually, as many as four million American soldiers will fight in Europe.

The French and British had expected that our American forces would be amalgamated under their command to fill in their depleted ranks. But our General Pershing is having none of it. He is training our troops to fight as an American military unit. Pershing does not think highly of the French and British war leadership and strategy and does not want to put our men under the command of what he considers inept military leaders. This has ignited ill will and the mood is tense. Our Allies are hysterically complaining that "Pershing's stubbornness will lose the war."

As expected, I'm an interpreter. My main job is to translate the interrogation of prisoners taken by the Allies. Needless to say, it feels very awkward to be getting information from men who speak my native language, but who are now my enemies.

But I am personally convinced that this is a war that we must win. The massive killing and destruction must end. The longer it goes on, the more killing, maiming, and destruction there is.

I am convinced of this more and more as I listen to what POWs have to say. I hear gruesome and gut-wrenching stories of how dead men who had been buried in No Man's Land are then being disinterred by a subsequent artillery barrage exploding the ground, blowing their decomposing corpses back out of the ground. I hear stories of rats eating the dead, and then the rats themselves are captured by soldiers and consumed by the starving men fighting in the trenches.

From French civilians, I hear troubling tales of abuse by the desperate, hungry, and murderous soldiers – theft, rape, pillaging and senseless murder.

Russia has been in a state of rebellion for over a year since Tsar Nicholas II abdicated last March. With the collapsing Russian military no longer a major threat, Germany has been redeploying many of its troops and much equipment from the Eastern Front to fight on the Western Front. Russia has now signed a treaty surrendering to Germany.

This is bad news for the Allies, with the enemy's estimated 200,000 war-hardened troops and all the war matériel from the east being brought back to reinforce Germany's fight here in the west. The captured German prisoners are giving us vital information about aspects of the redeployment, and we can pretty much discern the expected scope of the operation. Having this information will make a huge difference!

IT'S CLEAR FROM RECONNAISSANCE AND OUR SOURCES OF Intelligence that German General Erich Ludendorff is building up for a major spring offensive. We figure they know that it's a race against time. It will take time for the American Expeditionary Force (AEF) to build an army, train its soldiers, and arrive in force. The British cynically state that it will be at least August before the AEF can take the field. We all suspect that the Germans are trying to land the knock-out punch before then.

It's a sick feeling to know that it's very possible. Maybe it is too late. The war may be over before we're even in it. I can't begin to imagine what the world will look like if Germany defeats the French, the British, and the Belgians. The French and the British are running out of men to throw into this quagmire, reducing the number of divisions fit for combat. It seems possible that with one last push, the Germans might be able to force France and Britain to the bargaining table to get a decent settlement. But, from Germany's perspective, it must be done before the Americans join the fight!

Information is critical to the Allied cause. Airships and airplanes are regularly in the air observing the enemy's buildup and deployment. Seeking critical information, I am now interpreting the interrogation of German POWs for the British.

On March 18, two German soldiers desert near St. Quentin at the River Somme. They vividly describe the horrendous conditions of illness, shortages of food and supplies, and how morale has been sapped within the ranks of the German army. When asked about the Spring Offensive, they tell us that it will begin on the morning of March 21.

Good to their word, the heavy bombardment begins in the foggy early morning of March 21. Germany strikes at the weakest section of the British line along a fifty-mile front. It begins with five hours of continuous heavy artillery fire, intermixed with poisonous gas attacks, and then followed by its fast-moving infantry. Five hours! As this horrible war has dragged on for almost four years, we have discovered that no one can stand more than three hours of shelling without becoming sleepy and numb … rendered pretty much unable to fight or retaliate. During the war, we have come up with a new title to describe this condition, men from both sides who have faced this never-ending trauma. We call it, "shell shock".

Thankfully, there is some resistance, especially from some of the machine-gun posts. Nevertheless, this first day of fighting is devastating for the British. Confusion reigns behind the lines. Thousands of British soldiers are killed, and many more thousands are taken, prisoner. Entire battalions just surrender. Over 500 British artillery pieces are captured, along with still intact rail bridges. It is a rout by the Germans. A nineteen-mile-wide gap at the front has been opened.

The next several days see more of the same. The German offensive is threatening to punch a hole between the French and British armies, separating them. It seems that the Germans have in mind to defeat one nation at a time, first the British and then the French.

But at this point, the German advance begins to slow. I breathe a sigh of relief.

In April, the German Army attacks in the north toward the English Channel. We know that the Channel is more important to the British than is Paris. We also hear reports that British defenses have been strengthened. In addition, we hear of a tank battle between the British and the few poorly designed German tanks. The Germans are no match for the British tanks. Add an effective and highly motivated combination of British and Belgian forces, and, as a result, the German offense is again halted … but at great sacrifice.

In late April, we detect German operations developing again in our area. Germany reveals a new surprise … totally surprising as well to our Intelligence. They call it the "Paris Gun". Now, Paris is under attack, being shelled, from seventy miles away.

It doesn't take long before our interrogations reveal important information about this new weapon. The barrel alone on these monstrosities is 115 feet long and can fire fifteen-inch projectiles up to seventy-five miles. We're not sure how many of these there are, but we know that there are at least seven. Some Parisians have been killed and injured.

What's most frightening is not its accuracy but its range, as Parisians are becoming more demoralized with each shell that lands. Reports are that the Parisians think they're being bombed from the air because they can't hear the cannons being fired. This only adds to their fear; they never know when the next one will hit.

French Intelligence concludes that there will be another attack at the end of May to drive deeper into France. Our Intelligence, however, concludes that the German Army will turn south and attack at a different location. Our conclusions are summarily rejected by the French because we are supposedly new at this and therefore regarded as incompetent.

On May 26, our interrogation of two captured prisoners makes it clear that the beginning of the offensive is imminent. It begins a few hours later, just after midnight … a huge offensive with a three-and-a-half-hour barrage of heavy artillery, including poisonous gas.

But it didn't begin where French Intelligence had been so sure that it would and where they were most prepared. It's the same story for the French as it had been for the British. The Germans draw their enemy in one direction and attack in another. I marvel at how quickly the Germans can change the direction of their attack.

Our Intelligence is not surprised. The Allies meet them with already exhausted French forces, and, at best, slow their progress. The German Army is now headed for the Marne River. They arrive at the north side of the Marne and take control of the northern half of the French village Chateau-Thierry. This village straddles the Marne, connected by a bridge. German troops are now less than sixty miles from Paris.

And when they cross the river, the Paris-Metz highway will lead them right in.

The French government is preparing to abandon Paris. French officers are beside themselves with fear, frantically explaining to the Americans that if Paris falls, the war is over.

On May 31, I am being moved forward not far from Chateau-Thierry. While the German army holds the village on the north side of the river, the south side of the village is still under our control. Two American divisions are moving past the defeated, exhausted French forces to prevent the German Army from crossing the Marne.

Our American troops have been ordered to the front. The goal is to form a defensive line on the river's south side.

I have been ordered to be ready for long hours of translation and interrogation. Accurate information must be obtained quickly. Minutes count in the fog of battle.

But getting to my assigned location has been incredibly chaotic. As I head forward, hundreds of refugees are streaming to the rear away from the Germans. It's heartbreaking to see the poor souls … men, women, children, worn out, terror-stricken, a woman pushing a baby carriage, carrying whatever little they have left. Many frail, old, and sick people are just sitting off the side of the road in the fields. I'm sure some have just given up. Others are leading one or two goats or a cow or a small flock of sheep. It is a pathetic sight.

Exhausted troops of the French Sixth Army are trudging in retreat as well … even their officers. They are an exhausted demoralized army. Many no longer carry a weapon. Some are even looking at us and shaking their heads, pointing to us to turn around. As far as they are concerned, all is lost! It is frightening.

I wonder, too, what our soldiers will face, soldiers who have not yet seen battle.

As all these people make their escape, however, they are blocking the roads, slowing down the important movement of our troops.

When I arrive at my destination, there is more chaos. Orders have been changed and changed again … and changed yet again. The only ones who seem to know where they're going are those who are retreating, the French army and the refugees. It seems that only the Americans are trying to find the battle line.

In the last few days of the latest offensive, the Germans have taken many thousands of prisoners, captured untold numbers of rifles and more than a thousand machine guns.

In the confusion and chaos, neither our artillery nor machine guns have yet arrived, and our fighting men have very little ammunition. They are hungry, but there is no food … at least not enough to sustain them for battle.

Several German POWs have been brought in for interrogation. We find out that this latest offensive is not going all that well for the Germans either. Having failed to capture important objectives along the way, their supply line has been strangled. And the Germans have not yet crossed Marne River. They also report that the deadly flu is taking a major toll. After four years of war, their men are worn out and demoralized. They claim to be sick, but many stay drunk all the time.

Today, June 1, German troops have taken control of an area that includes a high point called Hill 142 and a kidney-shaped dense forest of about one square mile … a place called Belleau Woods. There, they are dug in and ready to engage the French and Americans. Machine gun nests have been strategically placed looking out over an open field of waist-high winter wheat.

We learn from interrogating a prisoner that the Germans are diverting two fresh regiments to make a push to cross the Marne.

I pass along this vital information, and our troops are shuffled to meet them. On June 3, we are able to drive them back into the forest. I feel proud that my contribution to this has helped bring about this small but important victory.

June 6, though, is a day I will never forget. French Intelligence is telling us that Belleau Wood is lightly defended – that the Germans have pretty much abandoned it. However, one of our dare-devil Marines, a Lieutenant Eddy, and two friends, infiltrated enemy lines during the night and returned to report that the Germans have dug a defensive line through the woods, strung a barrier of barbed wire, and armed the woods with numerous machine gun nests and were gathering additional artillery. We passed the information on.

Our information is ignored, and no plans are changed. Our attack begins in the middle of the night, the first objective being the taking of Hill 142. Later in the day, we are to take Belleau Wood.

There is no real artillery battlefield preparation other than randomly scattered shelling for thirty minutes before the offensive begins. The fighting is brutal for divisions of the French Army and our American Army and Marines. They face withering machine guns and deadly sniper fire coming from the woods. There is the savagery of hand grenades, bayonets, and hand-to-hand combat.

From the relative safety of my position, I hear the sounds of war … the ear-splitting boom of our artillery, then soon after, the distant rat-a-tat-tat of machine-gun fire. I'm surrounded by confusion as wounded and dying men are brought in by the medics. Their cries of pain and anguish are excruciating.

This initial action lasts for more than a day. But it meets with success. Hill 142 has been captured. We at least have a foothold in Belleau Wood, and we reportedly have several men in the German-occupied town of Bouresches. Nevertheless, it is a devastating day for our troops.

The next day, I find out that the Germans can't figure out what has happened to their enemy. They are used to the British and French retreating, but not so the American troops, especially the Marines. Each of their attacks is repelled by our artillery barrages, our machine-gun fire, and our deadly accurate rifle fire. Plus, I hear that they object to our unconventional style of waging battle, not following "tactical principles" and firing "while walking with their rifles under their arms" The Germans have a new title for the Marines - *Teufelhunden*, "Devil Dogs."

Over the next two weeks, we hear of numerous engagements - brutal murderous fire, hand grenades, hand-to-hand fighting, poisonous gas – bringing heavy losses on both sides. But finally, on June 26, Belleau Wood is cleared of all enemy.

Strategically, the German advance toward Paris is halted! But at what great cost!

I have seen up-close so much that is disturbing, of Man's inhumanity to Man!

THIS SUMMER, I HEAR REPORTS CONSTANTLY OF HOW THE British and French tanks have now taken the field and are driving back the German forces. Germany's worn-out infantry and horse-drawn artillery cannot hope to keep up with this new "armor" capability of the Allies.

On September 12, Pershing launches the first all-American offensive. German prisoners and deserters stream in and are interrogated.

From them, it has become clear that Germany is struggling. For one thing, the ages of the captured men are revealing. Some are so very young, and others so old, getting close to my age. Obviously, Germany is depleting its available pool of soldiers. Also, clearly, they are poorly trained, poorly equipped, and poorly fed.

In this ghastly war, millions have been killed, riddled by machine-gun fire, blown to bits by artillery, shredded by shrapnel, choked by deadly poisonous gas, burned to death by the flamethrower. I have seen the remains of cities and towns pulverized by artillery throughout France and fields pocked with deep holes by the artillery shells. I have seen and heard the cries of injured and dying soldiers.

And when I translate what the German prisoners are saying, I repeatedly hear, "I just want to go home." They speak of friends who had deserted and then were found and shot by their own army. They speak of chaos in their command. Their eyes betray their trauma. They are in shock, "shell shock".

As I interpret, day after day, I see the same sad condition. I typically begin by asking, "How are you doing, soldier?" And he looks at me with fearful eyes, trembling uncontrollably, and he says nothing. I see their emaciated bodies, wracked by hunger and malnutrition.

Today, a prisoner is brought in. I ask where he is from, and he stammers out, "Nurnberg." I'd thought beforehand that I eventually would meet someone from near my home, but today, when it happens, I am caught completely off guard. If I had not emigrated, this young, desperate, frightened, tremor-ridden man could well be my son or even grandson. When I tell him that I am from Schwabach, he looks at me through blank eyes and in a lifeless monotone said, "Oh yes, I think I remember Schwabach. I just want to go home. Will you please take me there when you go home?"

But not a single battle has been fought on German soil. It's all been in France and Belgium where the battles have raged in and along the 500 miles of trenches running from the Belgian coast to Switzerland. But not in Germany! Its cities are still standing, its industry still producing, the railroads still running, the civilian population still safe, although hungry and destitute, but still safe from many of the horrors and atrocities of the war.

I learn from countless prisoners that, inside Germany, the government news keeps assuring the people that Germany is winning the war and that it is just a matter of time. But, in the cities and villages, the citizens are seeing the maimed and the despondent on the streets. They often greet old friends who had marched proudly off to war but who now, having returned, just stare at them blankly. From other veterans who have returned and have shared first-hand accounts of what's happening, German citizens have lost faith in what their government is saying to them. Distrust of the government is growing; it's all just a lie.

While Germany is running out of bodies to throw into the meat grinder, more than a million fresh eager healthy American troops have arrived and are ready to fight and another million are on their way. Plus, there are an additional two million lining up and being trained in the U.S. to come behind them.

As the summer fades, we discover that Germany's desperate need for manpower has now even begun to empty hospitals to send wounded men back into the fight!

But it's not just the war that is killing soldiers. The Spanish Flu is weakening and killing hundreds before they even reach the battlefield. The way we deploy our soldiers and the crowded conditions on board the ships that transport them contribute to the rapid spread of this insidious illness. The germs pass so quickly. It is an invisible enemy.

While the Spanish Flu is causing major problems for the Allies, from what we're learning from POWs, it is crippling the German ability to sustain an offensive. With food shortages and even starvation, the disease resistance is very low. This flu is thought to be a major reason why this Spring German Offensive has been slowed.

On September 26, a huge counterattack is launched by French, British, Belgian, and American divisions. It's being called the Meuse-Argonne Offensive. This territory was captured four years before by the Germans and has been heavily fortified. The fighting is intense.

October 10, 1918

My Dearest Heinrich,

As I write this letter, Clara and her family have received word that both of their boys, Eric and Robert, Clara's grandsons, are now on a ship, named the "Leviathan", on their way to France. Because of their background and familiarity with horses, they have been assigned to the Vet Corps, which hopefully should make it a little safer. It's astounding to think that 1,000 horses a day are needed ... horses we are sending that will likely be broken down and shot or killed by gunfire. Robert and Franz's job will be to take care of the horses and mules and keep them in the fight.

By the time you receive his letter, your grandnephews will probably be there and possibly already engaged in this brutal conflict. I am praying for them both as I continue also to pray for you....

I CANNOT READ ANY FURTHER. THIS NEWS IS A PUNCH IN THE gut. When the troopship they are on, the *Leviathan*, landed in the French port of Brest on October 7, we got word that the Spanish Flu had spread wildly on board during the journey. This is the German luxury liner, *Vaterland*, that had been interned and then confiscated by the U.S. It was renamed and turned into an unacceptably overloaded troop carrier with 10,000 men and about 250 women nurses on board.

From what I hear, hundreds had been sick and more than

eighty died and were buried at sea on the way over. After it arrived, several hundred more had fallen ill and were dying. Then, they disembarked and continued to spread it to other soldiers in the camp, which ran out of room to care for them. It's continuing to spread.

Where are Eric and Robert? Are they safe? How can I find out? That's just it; I can't.

I return to the letter but see it's mostly just news from home. I set it aside lay down and take a deep breath as tears come to my eyes. "O God, I hope it's not true!"

October 20, 1918

O God, Heinrich, it's happened! We got word that Eric died of that terrible flu on his way over. He is buried in France! That's all we know. Maybe you can find out more. Robert and Joey and their wives and poor Clara are just numb ... dazed. We all are, but I'm mainly worried about Clara. She has endured so much from war! First, your brother and now her grandson ... buried somewhere in France! What the hell were they doing in France? Sent there by their governments! That's what! Sometimes I wonder what we've created with all this nationalistic loyalty and this quest for glory and power that ends up in war and death and tragedy.

I think that historian Lord Acton from Britain some years ago stated the truth when he feared how smaller countries and states of Europe were uniting into nations. He said, "Power tends to corrupt and absolute power corrupts absolutely." I think he was right. Germany for all of its greatness is now reaping the harvest of what Bismarck brought about fifty years ago "by blood and iron." What we see happening today is not the Germany that we knew and loved!

Please, Heinrich, pray for Clara and her family as they mourn, and especially pray for Franz, that he will be kept safe and come home. Clara is just devastated. We all are. And when you read this, I know you will be as well.

Heinrich, come home safe. I can't lose you ... we can't lose you!

I love you, miss you, and am praying for you!

Susanna

I WAD HER LETTER UP AND THROW IT IN THE TRASH. I DON'T want to read again; I don't have to. I am … so filled with grief and rage. I blame that ignorant no-account loser, that asshole, Augie Gaebler! He is responsible for Eric being on that ship! He has gotten his revenge against our family. He has hurt my sister worse than his father did.

Poor Clara. So much loss she to bear. I hope she hangs on to her faith in God. He's all that's keeping her going now.

AS THIS MEUSE-ARGONNE OFFENSIVE CONTINUES, MORE THAN one million American boys are being sent into his fight. Slowly, ever so slowly, progress is made. At long last, in early November, Germany is being decisively driven back and its army annihilated. But at what great cost to our American men. At what cost to my own family!

One of the main objectives of this offensive is to destroy Germany's massive rail operation that has been supplying and reinforcing its army. That operation is centered in the city of

Sedan! Sedan! That's where my brother Friedrich died fighting the French almost fifty years ago at the time of the German Unification!

Now, with this Allied success, Germany is gasping for air. Our forces can see light at the end of a four-year-old dark tunnel.

CHAPTER 16

Back on January 8, 1918, President Wilson had presented his *Fourteen Points* to the United States Congress. In these, he had laid out his plan that he believed would provide an honorable peace for all combatant nations as well as establish a League of Nations to foster future world peace. He spoke of *peace without victory*, which would be a way for all to lay down their arms and maintain dignity. Being an idealist, he has dreams of a better world. Some are calling these *Fourteen Points* the "moral background for the settlement."

Therefore, based on Wilson's now-celebrated *Fourteen Points*, the German government has approached Wilson, rather than France and Britain. Germany is ready to bring the fighting to an end in the hope of receiving a settlement based on Wilson's stated intent. Germany is putting her trust in President Wilson. They hope he will not let them down.

Every day, I hear more and more of the sad state of Germany. Conditions are simply awful. The people are past being hungry and now are at the point of starvation. There is no denying that Germany is at the point of collapse. Its people have had enough … enough lies being told them by the government, enough hunger, enough of the loss of this precious generation.

Germany is in a state of political chaos. The Bolshevik revolution has now spread from Russia into Germany. Numerous political factions of various stripes have emerged and are fighting one another. The public support that was enthusiastic four years ago when the war began, slowly turned to frustration, then to anger, and now is turned into hatred of Kaiser Wilhelm II.

Prospects are becoming even grimmer for Germany. I hear the rumors and then hear the official word that Germany's allies are surrendering. The Austrian-Hungarian Empire has not only surrendered, but it is also breaking apart as smaller countries are declaring independence. The Ottoman Turks have collapsed. How long can Kaiser Wilhelm II survive? Politicians are taking cover, resigning, being replaced, and blaming others. The military leaders still think they can win. They are delusional!

The German soldiers in the field know it's a lost cause. Why risk your life any longer? Untold numbers are now deserting, completely worn out, hungry and sick. While the military leaders want to fight on, the soldiers have had enough. They're laying down their arms and walking back to Germany.

To satisfy the requirements laid out by President Wilson, Germany has had to abandon all submarine warfare. The submarines are ordered to return to port. In defiance, many of them are intentionally being scuttled, sunk.

In the North Sea, the highly praised German *High Seas Fleet* has been boxed in by Britain's *Grand Fleet* for most of the war. The only significant action that these huge Dreadnaughts saw was the Battle of Jutland in 1916. And even that was quite inconsequential. Meanwhile, both powerful navies just keep each other stymied, tied down, and unable to contribute to their respective causes.

The German ships have been just sitting and rusting along piers in their ports, The German Naval command seethes with anger and resentment because it has not had a chance to engage in battle and prove itself. For the officers, it's a matter of personal honor.

Meanwhile, the Bolshevik Revolution in Russia has stirred rebellion within the desperate and angry German sailors on board the ships. Faced with the never-ending severe discipline of their frustrated officers, they are ready to rebel.

From somewhere in the chain of command, a decision is made to have the German Navy engage the British in a last desperate massive battle. All the German ships, its huge Dreadnaughts, and battlecruisers, along with its smaller vessels and submarines have rendezvoused.

The sailors aboard the ships know that all is lost, so why fight and die? When on October 29, orders are given to the German sailors to get underway, there is mutiny. Orders are not obeyed. On several battleships, the stokers refuse to shovel coal into the huge furnaces to power the ships. The mechanisms to hoist the anchors are intentionally damaged and put out of commission.

It's impossible to get the battle underway. The order is rescinded. The German port of Kiel is the focus of the rebellion. Thousands of sailors and dock workers gather in revolt. The mutineers hoist the red flag of the Bolshevik Revolution. German soldiers sent against the mutineers lay down their arms and join in the revolt. By November 4, the red flag flies on all German ships.

The mutiny is spreading throughout Germany. Soldiers at home are creating Bolshevik organizations based on the Russian model. Munition workers are threatening to go on strike. Fighting forces in the trenches have been reduced to the barest of numbers. Who is even running the country?

On November 8, Kaiser Wilhelm II abdicates; he surrenders the throne and flees to the Netherlands. Later this day, Germany is handed its conditions for the fighting to end. Within two days, the twenty-five other dynasties of Germany have also abdicated.

Our Allied army has been relentlessly fighting its way toward the railyards of Sedan. German resistance is crumbling. The honor of liberating the city is given to the French. Even though Pershing is not happy about it, the French Army will lead the victory march into Sedan. I think France deserves this honor in retribution for its humiliating defeat suffered there in 1870. France, in recognition of the American role in this drive and as a cooperative gesture, has also invited General MacArthur to lead a detachment of Americans along with the French Army to liberate Sedan. Sedan … the final decisive battle in 1870 and now again in 1918!

ON NOVEMBER 11, 1918, AT 11:00 AM, REPRESENTATIVES from both sides sign an Armistice. This takes place in a railroad car in the Forest of Compiegne. This Armistice is meant to bring all fighting to a halt. This bloodiest conflict in human history is finally thankfully coming to an end.

In addition to its Army, Germany is forced to surrender its entire Navy … everything … including all its battleships and U-boats. In addition, Germany surrenders its airplanes and zeppelins, most of its locomotives and rail cars, all occupied territory, and all overseas territories. The humiliation of Germany begins.

Today, the world celebrates. The fighting has stopped … no more killing and maiming … no more destruction.

Warnings about spreading the Spanish Flu are ignored. Neither men nor women know whom they are kissing and partying and carousing with. But I fear that this flu is anything but over. As is often being said, "The Spanish Lady doesn't take sides."

We have won the war, but what about the future? We have won the war, but can we win the peace? This remains to be seen.

November 19, 1918

Dear Susanna,

I am so angry. I cannot come home for quite a while. I have been ordered to remain for the peace talks that will result in dealing with Germany and its allies and redrawing the boundaries of the nations of Europe, not to mention all over the world.

Why do they need me here? To interpret and make sure the Germans understand the terms. When I asked if the Germans won't have their own interpreters, I was simply told that I'm staying and that's that. I have no choice! I guess that this answers our initial question about what my status would be, civilian or military. I guess this is what they mean by being "of" the army, but it sure feels like I'm "in" the army. At any rate, I am not allowed to leave!

I am beyond frustrated! I know that when you receive this, you will be as well. You are certainly carrying a greater burden than me. And I cannot be there to help. I am so very sorry.
I am sick of this war, and I need to be home. I feel lied to by my government.

Plus, already, we're seeing signs of the flu spreading all over Paris, probably from the lack of caution and irresponsible reveling on the 11th. The same thing's happening in other countries, too. I'm sure America is probably getting hit hard with the flu, as well.

I can only imagine what's being carried onboard those transport ships taking our boys back home. How many will die not from battle but from this insidious germ ... or from some other disease they pick up over here? It seems the prostitution business was the most thriving part of the French economy during the war, and now, with all these diplomats in "Gay Paree" and away from home, there's a whole new clientele ... extravagantly spending their governments' money!

Susanna, if there's any way at all that I can be relieved, I will take it. Trust me!

I love you.

Heinrich

November 24, 1818

Heinrich,

We just received word that Franz was killed near the end of the war. Clara has lost both her grandsons! Franz also is buried somewhere in France.

Our family is again devastated, grieving another tragic casualty of this terrible war! We anxiously wait for you to return home. When will that be? We need you, Heinrich!

Susanna

O God, now this, and this heart-breaking request from my wife! What am I supposed to do? I'm needed at home. I'm needed here, I'm told. My hands are tied, Susanna. You should know that ... I have no choice. I am here, and I have to stay here. Can't you understand that?

I want to tell her all of that, but I can't … won't.

I also realize that my last letter crossed in the mail with this one from her. Susanna must be furious at my being trapped here while she's holding things together at home. I hope my brother Karl is stepping up and not just sitting at home counting his money. He can be such a … such a jackass! So much like Papa! But why wouldn't he be? He was Papa's little man.

My sister, Clara, and her family are shattered at losing another son/grandson to this war.

I close my eyes and envision in my mind Augie Gaebler smiling smugly behind an expression of concern. He's gotten his pound of flesh … again … for his father. I wish I hadn't stopped Papa that night from beating the crap out of August Gaebler. I shake my head, and tell myself, "Get a grip, man. Get control of yourself." But I am seething inside.

My family needs me. I need to be home. I need to settle the score with Augie. I need to comfort my sister, Clara, and her family. I just want to be home … in the arms of Susanna. She and I need to be together, especially now! But where am I? Stuck for God knows how long in this hell-hole country with this God-forsaken job of being the one to tell the Germans all the bad news.

I put on my coat and walk up the street to a cabaret. Paris has come back to life and has opened her arms to the hundreds of diplomats here for the peace talks. But why shouldn't they be shown a good time in the meantime?

I don't remember when I got back to my room or even how I got there.

Since the Armistice on November 11, American troops are now headed for home. It will take months to get them all back to the States. It's probably better for my health that I am not on these early transports home. These ships are like floating Petri dishes of disease.

It will be a while before they can get the peace talks organized. This means that I have a lot of free time now. So here I sit … with nothing but time on my hands when I'd rather be home.

I am using the time, though, to find out what happened to both Eric and Franz and where they're buried. Our American dead have been buried in hundreds of small and make-shift cemeteries throughout France. It will not be an easy task.

Franz, I discover, died on November 9 in the final push of our army in the Meuse-Argonne Offensive. This final action had as its objective the integral railroad installation at the city of Sedan! Did he die there as had my brother, Friedrich, almost fifty years ago? Franz certainly died in that final offensive. The very idea sounds so creepy, almost supernatural!

Eric had died of the flu soon after setting foot in France. He is buried in a small cemetery not far from Brest.

Already in 1917, soon after we entered the war, many of our dead soldiers were being buried in a dedicated plot of ground in the town of Suresnes, not far from Paris. This is the first of many cemeteries that will be dedicated to our fallen soldiers. I am using every avenue I can to also locate Franz's grave and to urge that these two cousins be buried next to one another in this cemetery. I have been able to speak personally with some higher-ups of the American Grave Registration Service and am confident that this will happen.

What more can be done for Robert's and Joey's families and Clara except to hopefully have their sons and grandsons' final resting places next to one another! I am writing Susanna today to tell her of this and, of course, to tell Clara and Robert and Joey and their wives. Hopefully, it will bring some peace to our family.

Plus, my being able to accomplish this lessens the total frustration of my having to stay in this lousy country for the next several months. I intend to see this thing through and get it done!

It's now early December, and I am told that it will still be several weeks before everything is for the peace talks to begin. With some time on my hands, I ask for and receive permission for a seven-day leave. I purposely don't reveal my plans, as that would mean my request would be denied.

I have been able to get counterfeit credentials identifying myself as a reporter for the *New York Times*. Dressed in civilian clothes, I board a train and cross into the danger and anarchy of revolutionary Germany. If asked why I'm there, I will show my reporter's credentials. Bavaria especially is in a state of political upheaval and violence. But that's where I'm headed. Avoiding at all costs the chaos of Munich, I head for Nurnberg. When I arrive at Nurnberg, I hire a ride in a horse-drawn wagon to Schwabach, my hometown. The icy wind rips through my clothing and stings my face. From there, I walk to my original homeplace.

I had not expected it to be the same, but I am not ready for what I see. Even though the infrastructure of Germany is in pretty good shape after the war, the people and their lives are in pitiful condition. So much of the population has been ground into the gears of the war machine. Years of neglect show in the barren fields, the broken fences, and the broken-down house I grew up in or what's left of it.

I meet one remaining relative, a second cousin, Adele. She's my cousin's daughter. My aunt Margarete and Uncle Charles, of course, are long dead. Adele tells me that her husband, one son, and one brother have been killed in the war. Another brother has survived but now has brain damage and suffers from "shell shock". Her other son, Martin, is not yet accounted for. She fears the worst.

I ask Adele about the Dilger family, the relatives of my girl-friend, Amelia. She tells me that Louis, Amelia's brother, is still alive, but two of his three sons are still missing. I walk the still familiar road to the Dilger home. When I introduce myself to Louis, tears come to his eyes as he hugs me and won't let me go … weeping because I have come back.

After we visit for a few minutes, he says, "I'm sure you did not come all this way just to see me, right? Let me show you where Amelia is buried." I nod. On the way out to her resting place, Louis surprises me, saying, "Heinrich, I'd hoped that someday somehow you would be able to come back, someday to see … to see where we placed Amelia."

And there, in a well-kept little plot of land, among the other graves of the Dilger family, is her grave. It is marked by a wooden cross, now old and weathered. Painted on the crosspiece, I can still make out her name, "Amelia", her date of birth "August 2, 1853", and her date of death, "June 2, 1872".

Louis leaves me alone and goes back into the house. Nearby is a large log on which I sit for a long time, staring at her grave, and memories, long forgotten, return. I look up and off in the distance and see the hill where we had last seen each other, where we had kissed and cried and said *Auf Wiedersehen.*

Why have I come here? What do I hope to accomplish? What has drawn me back here? Looking at her grave, tears come to my eyes. She was my best and closest childhood friend and then my first love. We had a special relationship, abruptly cut short by Papa's impetuous decision and by her death. "I am so sorry, Amelia, that I had to leave. And then, when I found out that you had died, I was angry … filled with regret that I hadn't insisted that you come with me. But that was unrealistic and childish, I know. I have come back, I guess, just to be here again … to say thank you for your love and for what you gave me in our relationship. And I'm glad that you did not have to face the horrors of the past four years … the tragedy of losing children in this war and what this war has done to your land."

As if she could hear, I tell her about my life, summarizing the big things since that day when I had left. I tell her about Susanna and my children. "Yes, Amelia, as I know you would want, I've found a wonderful life and a wonderful wife who I love very much, and we are very happy together. I know that would make you happy."

I sit and remember those simple days. Then I consider what has happened … the death of a generation, the scars on the soul of Germany, the vengeance that will now be exacted in the negotiations in Paris.

After a long time, I have to say goodbye. I walk over to her grave, kneel on the soft grass, lean forward, and place my palms firmly on the ground. I close my eyes and hold that position for a long moment, thinking that this is as close as I will ever be to her again. I run my fingers along the fading paint of her name on the wooden cross and do the same over her date of birth.

I stand and, looking for the last time at her grave, say, "Goodbye, Amelia," and then two words out of nowhere pop into my mouth, "*Auf Wiedersehen*," and I wonder if maybe it will be true that someday somehow, we will see each other again.

Before I turn away, I take a last look at the cross, and I realize that that is a symbol for Amelia of her life and her hope after death … her hope in Jesus. And I say out loud to myself, "I wonder if I can ever have such hope again?"

I walk back to say goodbye to Louis. He has hitched his horse and wagon and wants to take me back to Nurnberg. I get in. After a while, it turns to small talk. He asks repeatedly about life in America. I speak in generalities; I don't want to tell him much … it would only depress him. We say our final goodbyes. I find lodging for the night and catch the first train back toward Paris the next morning.

My trip to Schwabach at long last completes an old but important chapter in my life.

CHAPTER 17

On December 4, 1918, President Woodrow Wilson sails out of New York on the *George Washington,* headed for France. He leaves with great fanfare as America sends him off to be the arbiter of peace that he sees himself to be. This bloody, brutal, nonsensical war has taken the lives of millions of soldiers and ordinary citizens … we don't know for sure how many million.

With the fighting having stopped last month, we have come to this critical time, an opportunity for making a better future for our war-torn and broken world.

Each nation is sending six commissioners along with their support staff. Wilson, himself, insists on leading our delegation. He chose five men to be his fellow commissioners. Ignoring the advice of his counsel, Wilson chose no Senators and no Republicans except for one who hadn't been active in politics for ten years. This has infuriated the Republicans; it was an intentional snub. I fear he'll live to regret that decision.

He arrives at the French port of Brest on "Friday, the 13th" of December 1918. Wilson has always considered the Number 13 to be his lucky number. Would it be lucky this time?

He is welcomed as a hero. Across Europe, there are cheering

crowds chanting and shouting his praises. Wall posters cry out, "We want a Wilson peace." Even streets, parks, and city squares have been renamed in his honor. I hear that this adoration for Wilson extends even beyond Eastern Europe to the Mid-East and even to the Far East. Wilson is looked to as the "American savior." High hopes! But how will it all turn out?

WHY IN THE NAME OF HEAVEN DID THEY PICK PARIS FOR THE Peace Conference? How can there be a just and lasting peace settled here, in a city that wants nothing more than to "make Germany pay"? Walking down the street, I see men missing arms or legs, damaged buildings, malnourished children, faces of fear, trauma, and hatred. There are shortages of daily necessities, like milk, coal, and bread. How can the Germans and what's left of the *Central Powers* possibly get a just deal?

I had managed to get out of Germany unscathed when I went to visit Amelia's grave, but that was a scary trip. On several occasions, especially in Bavaria, my fake *New York Times* identification papers got me out of situations that could have been bad, even deadly.

Germany is in internal chaos … rioting, revolution, complete breakdown of authority and civility. Its citizens have been misled and lied to by its own government. They had been told repeatedly that they were winning. They wanted to believe it; after all, German soil hadn't been invaded.

And then all the other *Central Powers*, their allies, gave up the fight. Germany's *High Seas Fleet* then mutinies, soldiers lay down their arms and won't fight, and the whole thing is over, just like that.

The age of the German monarchy is over. The Kaiser fled to the Netherlands. But, what now? Who knows? Socialism in various forms, even Russian Bolshevism, is running rampant.

Others seek democracy and want the Reichstag, the Parliament, to step forward with more assertive governing than it had during the Kaisers. Fear has now taken hold. Killings, beatings, and violent demonstrations are commonplace. The military refuses to take responsibility for defeat; instead, it blames the politicians for quitting too soon.

Our American military command thought the war would last for at least another year, during which time we would invade Germany. That's what Pershing wanted and planned to do. Win an unconditional surrender, lest there be any doubt of Germany's defeat.

But our Allies are tired. After four years, they are drained dry of money, men, and matériel. Their people are hungry, their economies are in dire straits. This surprisingly early end of the fighting is celebrated.

So, with the expectation being that we'd still be at war, no one was ready for the peace process. It's ironic: we were ready for war but caught completely off guard for making peace! Total confusion. Idiocy!

About thirty different nations have come to Paris, seeking retribution and reparations from the defeated powers … actually, just from Germany. Thirty different nations, like vultures circling the corpse of a horse, preparing to swoop down and devour it in chunks until they have picked its bones clean!

France is already butting in line, planning on being first, hoping to get most of the meat. France will use this as an opportunity to get even.

All the other delegations seem to have the same goal: to get what they can out of this and make Germany pay up! That's the bottom line. Screw Germany!

There's a big question about the role of Russia. Because of the Bolshevik Revolution that had dethroned the Tsar in the middle of the war, Russia gave up and made a separate peace with Germany over a year ago. Russia surrendered, removing itself from the war. It's now in the throes of a horrible civil war. Who is even in charge? How could they have any part in this Peace process? Why should they?

So, as these talks begin tomorrow, I am not optimistic.

I fear that the cycle of war and hate will continue, that from now on, with more powerful weapons for wreaking death and destruction, mankind will eventually bomb itself back to the stone age. Isn't Man capable of more than this?

While President Wilson, back in 1916, had not been my choice for president, I am hopeful that the Allies which make up *The Entente* will listen to some of the good things Wilson has in mind. At least he has a plan - his *Fourteen Points* plan for peace. He has in mind a League of Nations that will provide an ongoing way of settling international matters to prevent any more of these wars. If only Europe could have had that back in 1914!

Wilson, not having been a politician but formerly a teacher, college president, and governor is considered by the professional politicians to be "a lightweight", "a push-over". This is my main worry. I hope Wilson can stand strong on his principles. I hope he will not let Germany down. Germany laid down her arms based on Wilson's proposal.

We need to think differently now. I'm sick of both the politicians and the military. They got the world into this mess. We now need to do something different, to do whatever it takes to prevent another one of these God-awful wars!

This ordeal will not be over quickly or soon. The longer this process drags on, the more chaos will result in what's left of the *Central Powers*, especially in Germany.

And now … I can't believe this latest development … but it's true. Germany's delegation will not even be invited to be present during the process! The treaty will be worked out by the victors and presented to Germany as an ultimatum. The diplomats, being "diplomatic," don't quite state it like that, but that's what it amounts to.

So why am I here? Because my government insists! My family at home needs me, and I'm stuck here! So unfair and maddening!

At least I'll be able to follow what's going on as it unfolds … for what it's worth. But I'd rather be home where I belong.

I HAVE GOTTEN TO KNOW ANOTHER GERMAN-AMERICAN, DIETER Walters, who, along with me, is also here to translate at the Paris Peace Conference. As a child, he had emigrated from Germany to Wisconsin. Back in the U.S. Dieter teaches Classical Greek and Latin at Columbia University in New York. It is good to have another similarly minded person with whom I can commiserate.

In the days leading up to the beginning of the peace talks, we are both disturbed by the preliminary political chess moves that are taking place.

Tonight, we're having a few beers in our room. In utter disgust, Dieter states, "This is not going to go well for Germany. All the blame for everything will be placed on them. Why can't they at least acknowledge that Germany didn't start it? It was Austria-Hungary who started it … that stupid assassination."

I continue with a tone of ridicule, "But then stupid old Kaiser Wilhelm tells Austria to do whatever it wanted and promises that Germany would support them all the way."

"And then, the damn fool went on vacation, for God's sake!"

"Well, the way I see it, Germany is being singled out because it's 'the last man standing.' It's the only one with any money and resources to pay. None of the other *Central Powers* even exists now. Austria-Hungary is imploding, all the Balkans have revolted and declared independence …"

"… including even Serbia and Bosnia, where the whole damn thing started! And the old Ottoman Empire won't survive."

"So, Germany is the only one left, and, what really pisses me off, Germany won't even be able to be present at the negotiations! It has to accept whatever the others dish out …"

"… or else. Or else, the Allies will go to war against Germany again. Or Germany won't get the food to feed its people, and then there will be a total revolution!"

"Damn right … there's already rioting. Is that what these idiots here want?"

As we talk and drink, our emotions heat up, our speech becomes slurred and gets louder.

"I've never had much use for Wilson, but he seems to be the fairest and is seeking a long-term solution. American doesn't want any reparations."

"Then, there's France! Mark my words, if sneaky ole Clemenceau has his way, he'll figure out a way of getting 99% of everything. He's crafty … as slippery as they come!"

"And I guess you and I will be the ones who will have to try to explain it all to the German delegation. I guess that's why we're still here."

"I don't know why we're here either. But we're stuck."

"Don't get me wrong, I have no real loyalty to Germany, except that it's my heritage, and I have extended family living here … I guess they're still alive. And I agree that Germany will have to pay a price for this. But just how big, and at what future consequences?"

We talk late into the night as we drink more beer, both of us having a sense of dread. We wonder what will happen.

The next day, we both have headaches.

January 12, 1919

Woodrow Wilson, British Prime Minister David Lloyd George, French Prime Minister, Georges Clemenceau, and the Italian Prime Minister, Vittorio Orlando, meet for the first time. Japan has also been granted a couple of delegates. These are the major players. They know the pressures they face. The clock is ticking. The fighting has been stopped for over two months, and there's been no final settlement. These delegates have a huge job and time is of the essence. The eyes of the world are on Paris!

Meanwhile, much of Europe is falling apart at the seams. Hunger, typhoid, cholera, revolutionary insurrections, and even armed fighting are breaking out. Influenza, the Spanish Flu, this invisible enemy that burst on the scene last year is bringing massive loss of life.

The mobilized military forces are now shrinking in power and number. With 300,000 American troops being shipped home every month, they will all be home by August. What if military force is needed again to maintain order and force compliance? After American soldiers get home, they won't be coming back. So, there is intense time pressure to settle this labyrinth of boisterous voices and desires.

Governments on all the home fronts are struggling with major domestic issues … food shortages, restarting industry for peacetime, restoring farm production, and resurrecting a normal life after this war. Plus, in France and Belgium, entire cities and villages must be rebuilt.

Untold numbers of journalists and reporters have descended on Paris and have already begun to complain about the closed-door nature of the procedures.

What is going on at the Paris Peace Conference? The first week is spent quibbling about procedures, about who can have how many delegates, etc. Name it, they're arguing about it. Smaller nations who think they also have a legitimate stake are crying for attention, too. But the major players are not paying them any mind. That much is clear.

Oddly, the first item of business does not focus on questions about Germany but the Bolshevik Revolution. It has spread from Russia and has found a firm foothold in Germany. How can its spread be contained? How can Germany be kept strong enough but not too strong? Strong enough to stop communism but not so strong as to be able to make war again.

The former German and Austria-Hungary Empires are being stripped of land, population, resources, and overseas colonies. This is also happening to the former Ottoman Empire. They are redrawing the map of a huge portion of the world. In effect, they are creating new nations and rearranging others, sometimes arbitrarily. With the spread of Bolshevism on the delegates' minds, these new boundary lines and rearranged nations of the old Austrian-Hungarian and German Empires are intended at least in part to serve as buffers to the spread of this Russian menace.

The process has become quite ugly. It's not long before Japan and Italy are no longer being included. So now it's the "Big Three", the leaders of France, Britain, and the United States. And clearly, none of them like each other. The other day, a reporter asked French Prime Minister, Georges Clemenceau why he gave in so often to British Prime Minister, David Lloyd George. Clemenceau responded, "What do you expect when I'm between two men, one who thinks he's Napoleon and the other thinks he's Jesus Christ?" That well summarizes their regard for one another. Neither David Lloyd George nor Georges Clemenceau respects Wilson. They think him a starry-eyed idealist. One British diplomat says that Wilson reminds him of an eager debutante attending her first ball.

Wilson's *Fourteen Points* along with his proposed League of Nations have been picked apart and pretty much eviscerated. Clemenceau has described them as, "the 14 commandments of the most empty theory." They are said to be vague, idealistic, and unworkable. Frankly, I agree. They sound good in theory but cannot be implemented, especially not in this post-war political climate.

Their differences are most clearly seen in the matter of German reparations, the future financial obligations for what Germany has done. A few months ago, Wilson made a major speech in which he stated that there would be "no annexations, no contributions, no punitive damages." But both Lloyd George and Clemenceau have promised their countries that Germany would be made to pay. David Lloyd George had even promised that he would get out of Germany "all you can get out of a lemon - squeeze her until you hear the pips squeak." Clemenceau was even more adamant, wanting to completely weaken Germany so that she could never make war again.

It's February, and we're taking a mid-winter break. The important committees will stay and work. The "Big Three" leaders have returned home for a while to deal with various domestic issues and problems.

During the break, Clemenceau is shot and wounded by an anarchist. Thankfully the bullet lodged between two ribs and didn't hit any vital organs. However, it's considered to be impossible to be safely removed. Lloyd George has gone back to Britain to deal with labor problems. And President Wilson has gone home to America to deal with a rebellious Congress. He is having problems with both Republicans as well as his fellow Democrats.

TODAY, DIETER AND I ARE TAKING TIME TO GO OUT TO A battlefield about a two-hour drive from Paris. It's hard to describe … splintered trees, remains of horses with their stench of rotting flesh, shrapnel everywhere we step, little crosses placed in the ground to mark graves, burned-out tanks, unburied bones, craters blown out by exploding artillery shells now filled with water, in what's left of a fox hole the remains of a German helmet, fragments of clothing, and spent shell casings everywhere. It is chilling … horrible, a visual display of man's inhumanity to man!

We visit what's left of what was once a pleasant village … now nothing but a pile of rubble. In the rubble, I see the broken remains of a little girl's porcelain doll. And under my breath, I mutter, "This could have been Schwabach!"

All of what I am experiencing first-hand is bringing back my decades-old question about God. If God is, if he exists, then why didn't he prevent this? Does he care? Is he really as powerful as we have always said He is … as I was taught by the Church?

I'm reminded of that strange vision of Ezekiel in the Bible … the valley of the dry bones … the valley of the dead. I feel like I'm living it. The question from the Almighty is, "Can these bones live again?" Good question! Ezekiel's answer, "Only you know, Lord?" Maybe so, but he isn't saying! The dead dry bones, the splintered trees, the burned-out tanks, the empty helmets speak only of death and chaos. Is that the answer? But what in the hell kind of answer is that? That's no answer … that's meaningless.

On the other hand, what does all this senseless killing and destruction say to me about my hope for mankind's ability to make progress? I remember back to the 1904 World's Fair and how impressed I was with Man's great achievements. Science and technology have so much potential to change the world. Since then, even more incredible inventions and breakthroughs have come along.

But that's not the whole story. On our way back to our lodging, I can't stop thinking about that field of carnage we saw where thousands of young men in the prime of life died! I can't make the images go away. I can't simply ignore the question. It challenges all my assumptions about the goodness of Man. Can I say that mankind has progressed beyond the caves? We possess the brains and know-how to achieve greatness but the emotional wherewithal of a rattlesnake!

So maybe there is no God and maybe mankind is destined to annihilate itself! Is it that simple? This is not a conclusion that I can live with. Then life has no meaning. That's nihilism. So why bother? Why care? Does this then mean that there is no such thing as beauty or love either? Is what we call love nothing more than disguised lust and the drive to pass on life to another generation?

So, if it's all for self, then where does the notion of self-sacrifice come from? Then why did these thousands die here? And the millions throughout Europe? What did they die for? And my willingness to die for Susanna … for my two children … for my family, for Clara? And what about patriotism … and loyalty?

I am no closer now to an answer. I'm probably further away than ever. The more I see, the more I question.

IT'S NOW BEEN FOUR MONTHS SINCE THE WAR ENDED. "THE BIG Three", Wilson, Lloyd George, and Clemenceau have returned from break. At long last, the business of what to do with Germany is being addressed.

On April 3, President Wilson comes down with the flu. The official line is that he has a severe cold but will recover. But confidentially, his doctor has called it the flu, the dreaded Spanish Flu, with all its symptoms of high fever, severe coughing, and need for total bed rest.

We shouldn't be surprised. After the Conference break, he returned to Europe on the ship, *George Washington*. This transport ship had been the scene of the deaths of more than eighty soldiers returning home to the U.S. on its previous voyage. They had all died of the Spanish Flu. A few days later, this was the ship President Wilson sailed for his return to Europe.

Now we're waiting. The all-important work behind the scenes goes on, but with Wilson ill and not engaged, nothing of substance can be negotiated and agreed upon.

Five days later, Wilson feels able to resume, but something about him has changed. His mental processes are not what they had been. He acts very strange, even paranoid, and refuses to yield over the pettiest issues. In addition, at times he can't remember what the previous meeting was even about. This goes on for several days.

But then he abruptly changes again, for no discernable reason. Now, he seems to have thrown away his earlier goals and ideals, and he yields to whatever the French Prime Minister wants. Except for his League of Nations, Wilson has abandoned his *Fourteen Points*. These had been the basis on which Germany had agreed to the Armistice back in November! They felt that this approach had been promised them. Wilson has now reneged on his earlier promises to Germany. He has no backbone. He has sold out!

Dieter and I shake our heads over our evening beer. What will be the result of all this? How much of our time and effort will have been wasted? Time when I could have been at home where I belong! And what will be the dire consequences for Germany now that Wilson is no longer in her corner?

After Wilson caves in, it does not take long for the treaty to come together with France getting just about everything it wants. But it's not only France that receives concessions when Wilson abandons his principles. He concedes to Italy much of its demands. He also agrees with Japan's insistence to take over Germany's colonial possessions in China. In exchange, Japan offered a verbal promise of future good behavior.

But for so many other nations … nothing! They get nothing!

CHAPTER 18

On April 28, 180 German experts, diplomats, secretaries, and journalists set out from Berlin for Paris. I watch as they arrive to discover the final terms of the treaty that had been cobbled together.

Some of them are cautiously optimistic that the final treaty will have Wilson's *Fourteen Points* as its basis, which they thought was fair and just. They know that Germany will be heavily penalized, but at least she will survive and be able to rebuild and thrive with a completely new government. They are putting their faith in America … in Wilson!

Others are quite pessimistic, knowing that the French, especially, would be demanding "blood" and that Germany would lose much of its land, natural resources, and overseas colonial possessions.

But even the most pessimistic are not prepared for the terms that are imposed. Germany will lose not only Alsace-Lorraine, but both sides of the Rhine River will be occupied for up to fifteen years by Allied troops. This is the most prosperous region of Germany. Furthermore, Germany will be left with a very small and weak military.

What about the money that Germany will be required to pay

for reparations? It will be a vast sum. That's all they're told. Yes, it will be a vast sum, but the amount has not yet been agreed upon. This portion of the treaty would be like a blank check to be filled in later! The "Big Three" can't agree on a sum, and so it is left to a future decision by a Reparations Commission.

To add insult to injury, Germany is initially not to be allowed to belong to the League of Nations! She will have no voice as a legitimate nation of the world until she "proves herself", whatever the hell that means.!

Most galling of all is that Germany seems to be singled out as the sole cause for "all" the war. Germany's guilt is stated three times in the treaty. But Germany didn't start it, and neither Austria-Hungary nor Bosnia and Serbia are even mentioned. The unfortunate wording bothers me.

German banker Max Warburg, says of the treaty document, "This fat volume was quite unnecessary. They could have expressed the whole thing simply in one clause, 'Germany surrenders all claims to its existence'."

Noted British economist John Maynard Keynes quits the Conference and leaves for home, calling Wilson, "The greatest fraud on earth."

A group of promising young American aides and diplomats meet to discuss also resigning in protest. One who does resign, in his letter of resignation to Wilson writes, "I am sorry that you did not fight our fight to the finish and that you had so little faith in the millions of men, like myself, in every nation who had faith in you. Our government has consented now to deliver the suffering peoples of the world to new oppressions, subjections, and dismemberments – a new century of war."

This is also my sentiment and expresses my profound disillusionment.

After the Treaty terms are presented, Germany is invited to respond. On May 29, 1919, German delegates present detailed and well-thought-out objections and counterproposals. The general thrust was that this treaty was not the just and fair one that had been promised based on Wilson's *Fourteen Points*.

But the French are outraged and reject Germany's concerns out of hand.

The British, even Lloyd George, realize that the treaty is far too harsh. He knows that it is not in Britain's best interests to have a weakened Germany to contend with the Bolsheviks and other revolutionaries. British Secretary of the Navy, Winston Churchill, reflecting on the content of the treaty declares, "The hatred of France for Germany was something beyond human."

Lloyd George tells Wilson and Clemenceau that he would not be authorized to sign the treaty in its present form.

Two additional weeks of acrimonious wrangling take place with Lloyd George being pounded by both Wilson and Clemenceau. Wilson is no longer the Wilson of the *Fourteen Points*. He cares about two things: keeping some form of the League of Nations in the Treaty and going home. His demeanor reflects what I interpret to be sheer hatred for Germany.

There are a few small changes, just enough to satisfy Lloyd George … so he can tell the British people that he tried.

But I keep thinking of the dramatic change that came over Wilson when just last month he caved in and quit fighting. I am convinced that his doctor is right; this has been brought on by the flu. What has the Spanish Flu done to the world's future? Will the broken world ever be healed?

On June 16, the government of Germany is informed that it has three days to sign, or a food blockade will be renewed, and invasion would begin. Within Germany, there is a breakdown of all law and order. The streets are filled with revolutionaries with uncontrolled rioting, including rampant murder.

The military brass, none of whom would sign the Armistice last year, insist that Germany has been "stabbed in the back" by its own inept government. They still think Germany could have won the war! Whatever struggling government structure that still exists is deadlocked and ineffective.

The Allies are informed by their agents inside Germany that Germany might not sign. Forty-two French divisions are mobilized for a massive drive into central Germany. The British Navy prepares to renew the blockade.

WITH THE ARMISTICE IN NOVEMBER OF LAST YEAR, ALL German ships were stripped of all munitions and the men of their weapons … stripping all sense of honor from the German Navy. Then, seventy-two of her finest ships were escorted to a large British Naval base called Scapa Flow and held captive under British surveillance. The German crews have been reduced to 5,000 total men. And there they remain while, in Paris, the victors will argue over which nation can claim which of these ships as her possession.

The men remain confined on their ships with poor food, poor mail service, no recreation, and having lived through another North Sea winter with its frigid temperatures, howling storms, and only four hours of daylight. They are miserable and angry.

A great many of the 5,000 sailors left on board have turned to the radical political views of the Bolshevik revolution. They have stirred unrest, and fighting has often resulted.

Today, June 21, 1919, the cease-fire agreed to on November 11, 1918, expires. Strangely, during the night, the British *Grand Fleet* sailed away from Scapa Flow, leaving only a hospital ship and two destroyers. What does this mean? Has the war started again? Has the devastating naval blockade that had starved the German people, been reinstated? The Germans simply do not know.

Not knowing what's happening, the anxiety is high. If the war is back on, they are totally defenseless. They have been stripped of all munitions, and they haven't sufficient crew to man their posts. In addition, there is insufficient fuel. Their submarines had been surrendered back in November. What does it all mean?

But there is one option: suicide. At noon, German Admiral von Reuter sends out a command to all vessels to hoist their German flag to full staff and for all seacock valves mounted through the hull of the vessels to be opened and pipe connections be broken to allow the sea to pour in. It isn't long before ships begin listing as they are beginning to sink. The German *High Seas Fleet* is being scuttled. The men onboard lower lifeboats and row to safety.

An urgent message is sent to the British fleet to return, but it's too late. Fifteen of Germany's huge battleships, five cruisers, and thirty-two destroyers are scuttled, intentionally sunk. In all, 54 of the 72 vessels have sunk, and most of the others have been beached.

When I hear the news, I have to smile. No one will be able to lay claim to these spoils of war … especially not the French. I'm sure this gives those German sailors some pride and dignity rather than the humiliation of turning their ships over to the enemy. Plus, they can end their forced exile in a foreign country and give their once-powerful ships honorable deaths. The ships have gone down with their German flags flying at full staff!

This is a major embarrassment for the British, and the French are beside themselves with anger. But what can they do about it?

The deadline for Germany to sign the treaty is extended until June 23, with the threat that there will be no further extensions. What choicc docs Germany have? Sign or prepare for civil war. Sign or prepare for invasion. Sign or prepare to starve. Late in the day of June 23, Paris receives word that Germany will sign.

The signing date is June 28 in the Hall of Mirrors of the Palace of Versailles. The spot where France had been humiliated fifty years ago is the same spot where Germany will now be humiliated!

No German of importance will agree to sign for Germany … no high ranking official and certainly no one from the military. Only low-ranking officials are sent to Paris, and, still the night before, they cannot agree which of them will sign. Finally, two lower-ranking officials agree.

The signing is a spectacle that further disgraces Germany. With trembling hands, the two representatives sign document after document.

When it is over, the world celebrates … all except Germany!

It is a stupid ending to a stupid war.

President Wilson will leave for home this evening. He will now have to convince the United States Congress to accept the treaty and, with it, his proposed League of Nations.

CHAPTER 19

The Versailles Treaty is now completed, and I am on my way home, at long last, home to Susanna, home to my country that has not been devastated by war.

Now, at last, I have some peace and time, time to think, and there is so much to think about. My thoughts are rambling. But I think about that treaty.

Yes, we Americans lost thousands of men fighting with our allies. Yet, as Wilson was often told during the negotiations, especially by that ass, Clemenceau, American losses cannot be compared to what France, Belgium, and Britain had lost. He's right but try telling that to the young mother who lost her husband or to the poor mother who had depended on her slain son for survival. After all, it wasn't America's war.

What has been gained by it all? Nothing! Absolutely nothing! That's my conclusion. We haven't learned a damn thing!

And what awaits the world now? I am afraid for it. This agreement that we forced Germany to sign is asinine. No one even bothered to listen to anything their diplomats had to say. We have stripped Germany of much of her land, her coal wealth, and her means of producing the money needed to pay the insurmountable debt that is yet to be assessed! And with this Treaty, we have stripped Germany of her dignity. Instead of making her a partner with us, we have only embittered her. As I had feared before this Paris Peace sham started, we have won the war, but we have lost the peace.

Germany's age-old animosity with France will continue. I fear we have only planted the seeds for another war. Time will tell.

IT'S AMAZING HOW THE MIND WORKS AND CAN SORT THINGS OUT during sleep. I awaken one morning with thoughts of an old Greek myth. I know that myths are not just silly imaginative stories with no meaning, but they are stories that seek to make sense out of the big questions in the big story of life. This morning, I awaken thinking about the old Greek myth about Pandora and her role in horrible events.

I intentionally seek out my friend, Dieter. I figure if anyone can help me put some pieces together, he can. After all, he teaches the classics at Columbia University.

"Well," Dieter begins, "the story of Pandora starts with Prometheus, a Greek whose name means 'forethought'. Prometheus was always looking forward to seeing what was ahead, in the future. He had a brother named Epimetheus, whose name means 'looking backward'.

"Prometheus wanted to give mankind the gift of fire to keep warm and to provide a form of protection. But Zeus said, 'No', because he thought that fire was only meant for the gods and that man could not manage it. But Prometheus disobeyed Zeus and gave fire to mankind anyway.

"Prometheus was then punished by Zeus who tied him to a rock, and an eagle came every day to devour his liver. It was excruciating. But during the night Prometheus grew a new liver.

And so, every day, day in and day out, again and again, Prometheus was tortured by that eagle that was sent from Zeus.

"Zeus was not satisfied only to punish Prometheus; he also wanted to punish mankind as well, for having received the gift of fire. And here is where Pandora enters the picture. Zeus created Pandora, a very beautiful woman. Her name means 'all gifts', and she received from the other gods and goddesses such great gifts as wisdom and beauty and peace and generosity and kindness and health. All wonderful gifts!

"When Epimetheus saw her, he was smitten by her great beauty. And even though Prometheus in his foresightedness had warned his brother not to marry her, Epimetheus couldn't help himself. Lacking foresight, he married Pandora.

"As a wedding gift, Zeus gave her a jar and warned her not to open it. But Pandora, being very curious, eventually could not resist the urge. When she opened the jar, horrible things immediately came flying out of that jar … things like hatred, greed, pain, disease, poverty, war, and death … all of which were released onto mankind. Pandora immediately shut the lid back up on that jar, but it was too late. Everything had already escaped … except for one thing. That one thing was hope.

"And ever since that time, human beings have had to endure all the miseries and the brokenness that were unleashed from Pandora's jar. But there was still hope."

Dieter, after telling the story said to me, "Heinrich, that's a heavy story, something that we all need to think about."

I think about it … long and hard. First, the story of Prometheus and mankind somewhat reminds me of the familiar story about Adam and Eve in the Bible. They have been given virtually anything and everything … it is all theirs, freely to use for good. But at one point, God draws the line and says, "This far and no farther." They are also given the freedom to disobey as well. And then it's as if they "opened the jar". They ate the poisonous fruit and released misery and death and all the other calamities into the world.

What does all this have to say for me today? I have experienced my share of the pain and the misery; I have seen the destructive power of men. I have also seen the beauty and the kindness and the compassion and the love of mankind as well.

I can't help but wonder, is it wrong to be curious, curious about the contents of the jar, curious about eating the fruit? Is it wrong to search for knowledge of what is good and what is evil?

No, I think not. I can still recall all the marvelous things I saw at the Saint Louis World's Fair back in 1904. I have been privileged to live in such an age of progress. I have seen Man's progress from horsepower to steam power to internal combustion. I have seen cures and therapies for many diseases. I have seen farm productivity increase a hundred-fold.

But I have also seen something else … man's progress is so capable of going wrong, like a train running off the track. Prometheus in his foresight saw what would happen and tried to warn his brother. Epimetheus saw in Pandora her beauty, her wisdom, her grace, and peace, and all the other great things that could come. I don't blame Epimetheus. Lacking foresight, he did what looked right. But he hadn't heeded his brother's wisdom!

He saw only the promise of Pandora, and she wondered about the contents of the jar. As Eve, also had wondered about what she was missing, what God was not allowing. They felt the warning was not a word of wisdom. They felt that they were being cheated.

Is that what this is all about? The misery and death and hurt and pain and killing and mistrust? Why the strongman impoverishes the weak man? Why the man of great knowledge uses it for evil, even unintentionally? Why the whole damn world is broken? I think of Amelia, of Friedrich, of Papa's inability to manage his anger, of my wife's brilliance being stymied and constrained simply because she is a woman. And I think of Eric and Franz … who died for nothing … Robert and Joey and their wives … and I think of Clara and all her heartbreak and losses.

And then there's this damnable treaty that is supposed to end all wars. That's a joke! I know that it's only an armistice; it stops the fighting for now … but does it stop war? Can we stop war? Will Germany passively accept these terms that have been laid upon her? Will she accept the sole responsibility for all of this?

I think about the wisdom of the Greeks and the wisdom of the Bible. Different stories but both are true to life. And I wonder why mankind never learns. How many times have we been through this? And how many more times will we have to go through this before we finally get it right?

But maybe … just maybe … I am now coming closer to an answer … or at least, perhaps a tentative conclusion. Man is just not capable of handling power. As Susanna reminded me in her last letter, quoting Lord Acton. "Power tends to corrupt, and absolute power corrupts absolutely."

But might it not be even more dreadful than that?

A sense of melancholy stays with me for the next two days until we dock in New York City. Arriving in New York reminds me of what it was like when I arrived almost fifty years ago. This time, though, I don't have to endure an immigration center. I am welcomed home.

I catch the fastest train home and arrive back in the arms of my beloved Susanna. It has been such a long time, too long. So much has happened to me and in me. In this screwed-up world, Susanna has become my refuge. As I hold her in my arms, the emotional dam within me breaks, and I begin to weep uncontrollably. They are tears of joy … and tears of pain … and tears of hopelessness. Joy, to be in the arms of my beloved wife … pain because the world is so broken … hopelessness because mankind still hasn't learned a damn thing!

LIFE HAS CHANGED.

Some of it is good. With the war over, the suspicion of Americans of German descent seems to have come to an end. I am offered my job back by the University but I don't take it.

Secondly, America has reaped unbelievably huge financial benefits from this long, destructive war. The U.S. has now become the leading financially sound nation on earth. The nations of Europe are broke.

Karl and his family have especially benefited financially from the war. With an average of 1,000 horses or mules a day being exported by the U.S. for the war effort, Karl and everyone else who bred horses benefited substantially from the high price the government was paying. That and the high prices he's received for his grain have enabled him to buy even more land for his ever-growing family. That, of course, means that Susanna and I have also benefited since we receive the agreed-upon share of the farms' profits. Somehow, it doesn't seem right that we have benefitted from the world's pain and destruction in this *Great War*, as it is now being called.

Yes, we now are referring to it as the *Great War*. It was fought on such a huge scale, and with such powerful technology and weaponry, that it's thought there can never be another one like it. My cynicism from what I have seen causes me to wonder about that.

Americans of German ancestry refer to themselves less frequently as "German-Americans." More often we prefer to speak of ourselves simply as "Americans." This transition has been one positive result of the war. Many thousands of immigrants are leaving the chaos of Europe and Germany and are arriving in the United States through Ellis Island, desiring to be American citizens.

During the war, the Missouri State legislature passed a law to require that only English be spoken in our church's school. For a while, that decision was being contested in the courts. But realistically, we are all pretty much moving in that direction. English is becoming our language.

However, I have to say that the English translations for many of our German hymns fail to convey the original meaning. Susanna and I attend worship services only twice a month when the German language is still being used. While we know that change has to happen, we also regret relinquishing so much of our German heritage.

There has been a change in attitude toward our government within the German-American community. There's residual resentment toward the harassment and suspicion that many endured. The *American Protection League* was a very negative force, especially in our area, in that many felt that they were under constant suspicion. Of course, I attribute most of that to Augie Gaebler, who was extreme in his zeal.

But then there was the *Trading with the Enemy Act* that prompted our government to go overboard in its effort to prevent support for Germany. The Busch brewing family in St. Louis lost very valuable property in Germany that had been handed down for generations.

All of this has left a bad taste in the mouth of many people. Yet, truth be told, there were some Americans of German descent who were strongly pro-German during the war. Efforts were arising from within our country to undermine America.

Though it's not perfect, America is a great nation to which I owe allegiance. American author Mark Twain said it this way, "Loyalty to the country always. Loyalty to the government when it deserves it." I only wish that had been the attitude of the leaders in Germany back in early 1914. Untold horrors might have been avoided.

Our government did suppress the accurate reporting on the effects of the Spanish Flu. Our military training camps and their overcrowded conditions did serve to spread this disease unnecessarily. Clara's grandson was tragically a casualty of overcrowding the transport ship, along with so many thousands more.

The losses have also been devastating, especially for our family. Clara and her family have lost both Eric and Franz. I am bitter, and my anger toward Augie has now turned to hatred. But I have no recourse. I must bear the secret alone, but thankfully Susanna is with me to help get me through.

So, this is how it ends. For Augie it was just a payback of some kind … a cancer oozing out of a misguided sense of loyalty to his father.

Clara will eventually go to her grave not knowing the details. She will be better off that way.

But for me, when I die, I will carry the hatred with me. Nothing will have been resolved; there will be no conclusion. I will pass away with this injustice lingering in my heart and soul.

And then there's the dark stain of the war that I also carry. There are untold millions of dead men and women, soldiers, and civilians, including innocent children. There's the massive destruction of cities and villages, poverty, rape, pillaging, starvation, and disease. Widows and orphans … mothers and wives who receive back home their physically and emotionally wounded sons and husbands. A generation of young women will never be able to marry because so many millions of young men are dead and gone.

I have seen so much, and it has stained my soul, the innards of who I am! I am scarred. And I wasn't even present in the trenches or running across No Man's Land and into the teeth of machine gunfire. Even so, my sleep is interrupted with dreams of war, the cries of the wounded, the hopelessness of the POWs, the desperate pleas of soldiers to go home when there are no homes left to which they can go. Am I having my own kind of shell shock? Can't be. I wasn't there in the trenches hearing the relentless explosions of artillery hour after hour. But whatever it is that I am suffering from, it is ghastly.

On July 10, 1919, two days after President Wilson arrived home from Paris, he presents to the fractured United States Senate the terms of the Versailles Treaty which includes the League of Nations. He urges them saying, "Dare we reject it and break the heart of the world?"

He faces an uphill battle. He runs into major resistance not only from the Republicans but also from many Democrats.

He is not the same man he had been before. When he speaks, he often loses his train of thought, and he frequently loses his temper even over little details. He looks worn out. He has become obstinate.

Amendments and modifications and six-week-long hearings drag on in the Senate. But Wilson is unwilling to compromise.

On September 2, he sets off on a whistle-stop train trip across America to present his vision to the American people. Speaking two, sometimes three times a day, he seeks to sell the Treaty and the League to America. Meanwhile, in Washington, resistance grows, and even his own Secretary of State, Robert Lansing, agrees that there were serious blunders made at Paris. In response, Wilson lashes out at those who oppose it, "Disloyalty!" There will be no compromise. "We have got to adopt it or reject it."

As Wilson's trip continues, his physician, Dr. Grayson, notices with alarm that Wilson is looking pale. He has headaches that are steadily growing worse. He has fits of coughing and must sleep propped up by pillows, and he seldom gets more than two hours of sleep.

At 2:00 AM, on September 26, in Pueblo, Colorado, the President awakens gasping for air and his face twitching. He tells his secretary, "I have never been in a condition like this, and I just feel as if I'm going to pieces."

The remainder of the speaking tour is canceled, and the train heads back to Washington. On October 2, Wilson suffers a massive stroke.

Subsequently, he recuperates to some extent, but he still refuses to compromise. Eventually, even though a slightly modified version of the treaty receives the majority vote of the Senate, it does not receive the necessary two-thirds majority. Neither the Treaty nor the League of Nations is ratified by the United States.

But all the while I cannot but wonder what is going on with President Wilson? Is it exhaustion and high blood pressure only, or are these aftereffects of the Spanish Flu?

My diligence in Europe paid off in that the Graves Registration Service has agreed to have the bodies of Eric and Franz immediately exhumed and reburied next to one another at the Suresnes American Cemetery not far from Paris. Robert and Joey have received letters to that effect with the invitation to go to France to visit their son's graves at any time.

Maybe this will bring a sense of closure to their still-open wounds. Most especially their wives, Magdalena and Louisa, need to bring their deep grief to some kind of conclusion or, at least, acceptance. Susanna's and my attempts to help them have not succeeded in the least.

On October 18, 1919, they leave by rail to head to New York to sail to France. Clara was invited to go as well, but she feels she's too old to make the trip. They will not arrive back until Thanksgiving time.

CHAPTER 20

Augie Gaebler has proudly flown an oversized flag of the United States. He's a true patriot. And now that the war's over, it is his "day in the sun".

In early July, the newspaper in Cape Girardeau featured an interview with Augie as an example of a true patriot of German descent. And now, even in Cape Girardeau, he is well known and highly regarded by many folks in town.

When he walks into a local bar, someone will buy him a drink. Here is a solid citizen who did the right thing on the home front. He stood tall as a true blue American!

One day, Augie is in a bar in Cape Girardeau and is offered a free drink … and then another … and another. Augie's just like his old man … can't hold his liquor. It's not long before he begins bragging about what he calls his accomplishments during the war. He is especially proud of his diligence on the County Exemption Board. A major function of this board was to examine whether a claim for exemption from military service was legitimate. Did the draftee have a just reason why he should not be conscripted in the war? Augie proudly declares his ability to sniff out those who were legitimate from those who were not.

And then, as the liquor continues to loosen his tongue and

dull his awareness, he goes so far as to particularly speak of two cousins. "They claimed they were needed on the family farm for the war effort, but I knew that they were just making excuses. And so, I lobbied hard to push the board into rejecting their request." Stopping a moment for emphasis, he glibly concludes, "It was too bad, but they didn't make it home."

There was something about the way he related that story that was unsettling to those who heard him tell it … something about his tone of voice and body language. It left them wondering whether Augie saw that decision as a tragedy or as an accomplishment. Had he honorably sent them off to fight, or had he sent them off with the hope that they would be casualties?

There are no more free drinks that day for Augie. The party breaks up, and everyone left him sitting there at the bar … alone. A little while later, the barkeeper strongly suggests that Augie go on home.

It didn't take long before the bar incident with Augie was related to me. And then a couple of days later, Clara heard it as well.

Clara is beyond devastated, an emotional wreck. Susanna and I take her into our home, with the hope of nursing her back to health and sanity.

She is numb … lifeless. She has no more fight left in her. She weeps, she cries out, she moans and writhes on her bed … covering herself with multiple blankets … not to stay warm but, I think, somehow to disappear. She just lays there. She doesn't move. She won't eat. She won't talk. Nothing.

Susanna and I try. But we feel helpless; we are helpless. We continually express our concern, our love, a listening ear, our desire to help her, to do anything.

Early one morning, while I am still in bed, I hear the latch on the front door closing. Knowing that Susanna lies next to me, I get up and, as I go into the next room, notice that Clara is not in her room. But I see lying on her unkempt bed, a piece of paper with Clara's writing:

Oh God, why am I alive? Why have you left me here? Why didn't I die back then ... when old man Gaebler attacked me? Why ... why didn't he just rape me then ... get it over with ... even kill me! And then, I wouldn't have to face, I wouldn't be alive now ... to have seen the results of my living. The pain inflicted on the world because of me.

Oh God why, why have I had to live through one tragedy after another? Nothing makes sense. Nothing about my life makes any sense at all. It's all hopeless; it is all meaningless. I am a plague. I have plagued my family. Papa died because of me because I wouldn't go along with his plan to marry that old man Papa had picked for me. My loving husband, Gus, died, then my husband, Joseph, died. They were both good men, loving husbands, and fathers. Too good for me, I didn't deserve them. Everyone who touches me dies. Why couldn't I have died instead?

All I have left to show for my life are my sons, Robert and Joey. And now, because of me, their sons have been taken. My secret shame from so long ago ... shame we tried to hide ... like a demon, its tentacles have wound their way to the surface ... again. My grandsons, both dead at their prime of life. And for what? Nothing makes sense. It's all nothingness. Nietzsche called it nihilism, nothingness, and that's what it is ... Life makes no sense.

Oh God, what can I do, where can I go? I don't want to live any longer. Take Me Home! Take me from this, this cesspool of sickening people, this world of hatred and brokenness ... war and betrayal, Take Me Home. I ... I don't want to live here any longer. Please, God, take me today. O Lord, I'm going to die today!

Oh, Jesus, I am so sorry. I have failed you too. I have not been faithful unto death, and now I am choosing death because there's nothing of life left in me. Oh, Jesus, I am so sorry. The load is too great. I am so sorry that I have failed you. I am broken. Lord, I believe, but you're hard to believe in. I cannot trust you Lord ... You have let me down. Forgive my lack of faith.

I don't know if it's you or the devil who has done this to me. But it doesn't matter ... nothing matters anymore.

And so, I pray, if it is possible, may I wake up after I die today, yes wake up and see you. O dear Lord, please forgive me.

My God, she's going to kill herself! "Susanna, wake up! It's Clara … she's in trouble. Help!" I run out of the house and head straight to the barn. I instinctively know that's where she's headed … to the back of the barn where she and I had met back in those old days … those times after August Gaebler's abusive attack. The only thing different now is that the barn is now old and rickety. But there's still the hayloft!

That's where I find her. There she is on the edge of the hayloft. One end of a rope is tied tightly around a rafter, and she has tied the other end around her neck. The rope is quite taut, and Clara is standing on the edge of the loft, her toes hanging over the side, her hands covering her eyes. It would take her only stepping off and she'd be gone. Thank God she's hesitating!

Inside I am in a panic, but I try to speak calmly, "Clara, it's me … Heinrich. I want to come up there to talk to you. You stay there … don't move until I get there?"

Keeping her hands over her eyes, "No, Heinrich, you have rescued me too many times, and now it's too late. I don't want to be rescued again. My life is not … everything I touch and everyone who touches me regrets it … they die. Heinrich, I'm like poison."

Susanna arrives by now. And she slowly ascends the ladder up to the loft.

I continue, "Clara, your life has been devastated by Gaebler.

He has hurt you over and over … even from his grave … more times than I can even begin to imagine as he has haunted your dreams and played havoc on your mind."

"Yes, he has always been there … lurking in my memory with his leering expression, calling me a 'sweet little thing' … even sometimes when Gus or Joseph touched me … they touched me out of love and pleasure … a sacred touch … but sometimes it brought back that horrible touch of those sick lecherous hands of Gaebler! Not often, thankfully, but sometimes … and when it happened, I couldn't…". Her body now being wracked with sobbing, she cries out, "I had to reject even my husband from having me in love!" I'm afraid she'll lose her balance or accidentally step off. And if she does, Susanna, who has now reached her, won't be able to grab and hold her.

"Clara," I call out emphatically. "Look at me! Open your eyes and look at me!" She does, and I continue, "Clara, who is the poison? Who has taken away your life … time and again … without remorse? Clara, Gaebler is the poison, and you cannot allow him to hurt you again … not anymore."

She opens her eyes and stares down at me, slowly, blinking her eyes and thinking. But I continue, "We are not going to stand by and let you kill yourself. Susanna and I are both here. We want to help you come down and then let us take care of you. Ok?"

Out of the corner of her eye, she sees Susanna who has now come close. Clara looks at her and smiles through her tears and pain.

Susanna gently assures her, "Clara, don't move. We'll get you down … trust us. Just don't move."

By this time, I am making my way up the steps to them. As Susanna continues to talk to Clara, I am able to reach up and, with not a little effort, untie the knot. We both embrace Clara, enfolding her in our arms.

She'll have a long process ahead. Will she be able to heal … again?

I am reminded of the question that Peter once asked Jesus, "How many times must I forgive my brother … seven times?" How many times will it be for Clara? But I don't like the answer Jesus gave Peter, "Not seven but seven times seven."

SUSANNA AND I TALK ABOUT WHAT WILL HAPPEN WHEN THE report gets back to Karl about the underhandedness of Augie in sending Clara's grandsons into the war.

Susanna, suggests, "Karl may have already heard but he hasn't put two and two together yet and figured out the connection."

I counter, "Yes, but when he does … and eventually he will put it together … there's no telling what he'll do."

So, I decide that I must tell Karl the whole story, from the very beginning. I walk over to his place and ask him to come with me out to his new barn so that we can talk privately. When we're settled in a couple of old chairs, I begin, "Karl, what I'm about to tell you … well, I hoped I could have taken with me to my grave. But there have been some things happen that make me realize that you need to hear this story."

He looks at me very warily as if he's been, somehow, betrayed. I quickly continue, "Karl, this all happened when you were still a baby, just a few months after we arrived. You probably don't know but back in those days, when we were needing money, Clara got a job watching August Gaebler's four children. This was after his wife had died in childbirth, along with the baby."

Karl says, "So that's what's happened to his wife. I always kind of wondered but never bothered to inquire much about it."

"Yes well, anyway your sister Clara was a cute little fourteen-year-old, but very naive, and to make a long story short, one day old man Gaebler came home drunk and tried to rape her.

A look of shock and anger falls over Karl's face and body as he clenches his fists … his eyes burning with hatred. "My God, what happened? Did he, do it?"

"No, thankfully one of August's daughters came into the house, and when she saw the ruckus going on, she screamed. As Augie turned to look at her, in that split second, Clara was able to squirm away and run home. She'd been attacked. Her dress was torn where he had tried to tear it off, and he had … what's the word, intruded … hands feeling a place where he had no business."

"Poor Clara," exclaimed Karl, "was she violated?

"Well, no … well no, she wasn't … I mean she was still a virgin. I want to be clear about that but yes, she was violated, attacked."

"And then, what happened."

"Well, a few nights later Papa and I pulled masks over our faces and waited for August to come out of the bar …. drunk as he usually was … and when he got to the top of that ravine, we tackled him. Papa beat the crap out of him, and it wrenched August's shoulder. He had a bad shoulder for the rest of his life."

"Good, served him right." In catching on to our plan, Karl says, "That was pretty shrewd ... wearing those masks and, since he was drunk, he couldn't possibly positively identify you. And besides, how is he going to explain it without giving away his crime … molesting a pretty young girl!"

"Yes, but he knew that it was Papa and me. We always knew that he knew. But you're right, he was drunk, and he couldn't try to lodge any complaint because he knew that the whole truth would then come out."

I take a deep breath and continue, "Well, Papa, Mama, and I decided to keep it all secret. But that was not a smart thing to do. We didn't want to get off to a bad start with the folks around here. But we didn't consider how keeping it a secret was affecting Clara. Clara came up with the idea that she was somehow at fault. She thought we were keeping it a secret because we were ashamed of her. And so, she had to keep all her struggle and feelings and an unfair sense of shame and guilt inside. It tore her up for a long time."

"OK, I appreciate knowing all this, but why is this important today?"

"Well, August Gaebler Sr. hated our family from that day on, and he passed on that hatred to his children, especially to his son Augie Jr."

"Well, I knew there was a problem, but I never knew why." With a tone of resentment, he continues, "It was a secret from me, too, I guess."

"Yes, but Karl, here's the problem today. Augie Jr. weaseled his way onto the County Exemption Board that determined whose requests for exemption from the war were valid. And a few days back, he was drunk in a bar, and he started bragging about how he managed to make sure that two cousins were sent to war, even though they had claimed to be farmers as their reason for being exempt. He said he knew that they were lying. The others on the board didn't know anything different, so they accepted his word."

This news hit Karl like a lightning bolt. Rage filled his eyes and flowed through his entire body. He jumped to his feet and looked me straight in the eye and asked, "Are you telling me that Augie intentionally singled out Eric and Franz so that they would have to go? That son of a bitch! As God is my witness, that man will die; I'm gonna kill him."

For several minutes, Karl paces, repeatedly clenching his fists, spouting whatever expletives come to his mind … as he absorbs this. His face is beet red, and, in his fury, wants to strike out. He looks at a pole of the barn but, at the last second thinks better of hitting it. He paces … his face shows rage and resolve

… he's pounding his clenched right hand into his open left hand. I let him pace and listen with my head bowed calmly as he yells out curse after curse, expletive after expletive. I don't blame him. I just let him rant … just like I had with Papa.

Finally, he looks at me and angrily asks, "Why wasn't I told this years ago? Why was it kept a secret?"

"It shouldn't have been kept a secret. I know that now. Clara has had to carry this with her for her whole life, ever since that day. It almost broke off her relationship with Gus, even before they were married … it was the secret … not what happened, but the secret … and how it had affected … infected … Clara."

"And now this S.O.B. has gotten his revenge, and man did he ever! He's got the blood of our nephews on his hands." Karl stops and thinks … and wonders, "Heinrich, do you think Augie even knows why it is that he hates us so much."

"Probably not. His old man explained it by saying that he slipped down that hill and rolled into the Creek, and that's where he hurt his shoulder. I think Augie Jr. hated us simply because he knew his father hated us. I doubt if he even knows the reason why. He just did. Pretty sick family."

Karl declares, "I'm going to go after him and kill him."

"No, Karl this is the reason I came over to tell you. I knew that soon you would hear the report about Augie's bragging, and you would put it all together. I wanted you to know the whole story. Yes, I want him dead too, but if you or I did that, the Gaeblers' would only win again. We'd be found guilty, and he would hold it over us even from his own grave."

"Well, what do you suggest … just let it be? I can't do that; this will never stand!" And through clenched teeth, he seethes. "There's no justice in that … and what about Clara? Will she ever see justice?"

"Well, there's something else, Karl. Yesterday morning, Clara tried to kill herself."

Karl abruptly turns and yells, "What?"

“She feels responsible for all the suffering and the death that has afflicted our family, and now, she feels responsible for the deaths of her grandsons. She says she can’t live with that shame.”

Karl retorts, “Well, that’s stupid … she shouldn't feel that way … it's Augie who's responsible.”

“I know that, but she keeps blaming herself. She's my first concern. I don't want to do anything rash that would somehow boomerang back on her or add to her sense of guilt and shame. She's very fragile right now, close to going off the edge I'm afraid. If she goes through with it, then Augie wins again.”

“Well then, what do you suggest we do?”

“I have an idea. But it's hard for me to accept even my own idea … and I expect it will be hard for you to accept it too.” I pause and then continue, “I suggest for now … and I mean just for now, until Clara gets stronger, let's just have a sit-down… just you and me with Augie … you know, kind of a heart to heart … at Brun’s Bar this Saturday night. Let's just tell him that we know and that we’re onto him and that we're watching him, and he needs to watch himself.”

“That ought to put the fear of the Lord in him for sure. But I don't know … what if he ups and runs away. I wanna kill that S.O.B.”

“I understand, but let's work on his mind. Make him suffer some. Make him afraid. Get him to mentally suffer the way he's made us suffer, especially Clara. If he runs, he won't get far.”

Reluctantly Karl agrees. “But just for now,” he concludes.

Karl and I arrive at Brun’s Bar around 4:30 PM. As expected, there’s Augie, sitting alone in his usual corner. Karl and I go over and surprise him as we sit on either side of him. Augie is immediately confused … agitated. I start, “Augie, it’s time that we have a talk. We've been hearing what your drunken mouth spewed out a few days back … about how you made sure that two cousins didn't get their exemptions as farmers."

Augie's breathing staggers, he coughs nervously, and his eyes and face become immediately tense, afraid.

Karl continues, "Yep, Augie, it didn't take a lot of brains to figure out who you were referring to … Heinrich's and my nephews. Isn't that about right?"

Augie tries to get up and leave, but we firmly push him back into his chair.

I continue, "I knew about it already before I shipped out back two years ago. A friend of mine, Bill, on your County Exemption Board, told me what a fireball patriot you are … the kind of patriot that would make sure that men didn't try to weasel out of their responsibility."

Karl ups the stakes, "Yep, I don't know if it's a crime against the United States, but it's certainly a crime against humanity. You certainly committed a crime against humanity, against the humanity of the Mendorf family, that's our family, Augie … the family that your no-good drunken father taught you to hate."

Scared and sweating, Augie tries to speak but he has a dry mouth, like cotton. "What's wrong, Augie … the cat got your tongue? Well, my brother Heinrich here is going to explain to you why your old man taught you to hate us. This may be news to you."

"Yep, Augie, when you were just a lad, you may remember that my sister Clara used to takc care of you and your sisters after your Mama died. Little Clara was a cute innocent young teenager until your father came home drunk and tried to rape her. It's that simple. He tried to rape a young lady … she was a virgin, Augie … our sister. Thankfully, she got away at the last minute. But he hurt her, Augie … your disgusting father hurt our sister!"

Karl jumps back in, "Yep, Augie, that's the kind of father you had. Wanted to put it to that little teenage virgin." Karl lets that sink in for a few seconds, and then Karl continues, "I know you probably know that we're right. Deep down, you knew the kind of old man you had. I'm sure you're not surprised by any of what we've been saying."

Augie is blinking uncontrollably, and tears are forming … he's scared … tears of fright, not compassion. He tries to get up again, and we put him back to where he needs to be. Karl even presses his huge heavy boot down on top of Augie's right foot.

"Augie, you feel trapped? Well, too bad, that's how your father made our sister Clara feel that day."

I resume the account, "A few nights later, my Papa and I happened to bump into your father up on top of that ravine, and your Papa had an accident and rolled down that hill and ended up in the creek. Somehow, most of his clothes came off. You know that gimpy shoulder he had until his dying day? Well, that was another accident when Papa tried to rescue him from drowning in that creek."

"And Augie, we just didn't want you to have to go to your grave without knowing the truth, the truth about your good-for-nothing drunk of a father … the one you have wanted to please so much by continuing his hatred. But now, you know this when you go to your grave. And believe us, you will go to your grave!"

Karl and I release our grip at that time and scoot our chairs back. Augie gets up and shoots out of the bar like a bullet out of a gun. Karl and I go home, satisfied with ourselves. It has proved to be a nice brother-to-brother experience for the two of us. After all we Mendorfs' take care of our own.

On Monday morning, Augie was found with a rope around his neck … hanging from the front tree of his yard.

As much as Karl and I enjoyed our brothers' night out on that Saturday, I never had the guts to ask Karl if he knew anything about how Augie died. The doctor said it looked to him like it was a suicide, but he couldn't be sure.

I comment to Susanna that I'm just glad that Robert and Joey and their wives are in France visiting their sons' graves during all this. They might well have strung Augie up!

THE DAY AFTER AUGIE'S DEATH, HE WAS BURIED IN HIS backyard cemetery next to his father and mother and the sister who had died at birth so many years before.

An effort was made to find his remaining sisters since Augie himself had never married.

Meanwhile, the livestock that Augie left behind needed to be cared for and sold for whatever price they would bring, and the money held until Augie's next of kin could be located. Word went out through Brun's Bar that there would be a small auction held out at Augie's place to dispense with his animals.

Some ten local farmers gathered. Karl was there and brought home several chickens that afternoon. To me, it seemed improper and out of place for Karl to have reaped some of the benefits from Augie's death. But Karl is Karl.

Augie's house had not been entered, except for a quick entry the day he was found dead to make sure there were no pets left behind or other matters that needed immediate attention. The house was then shut up tight and padlocks attached to the front and back doors, the keys held by the owner of Brun's Bar who also serves as our community's Marshall.

It took some phone calls and letters, but eventually, through estranged relatives living not far from our area, our minister was able to find and send word to one of Augie's sisters, Elisabeth, living in St. Louis.

Meanwhile, a few days ago, two men from the Secret Service showed up and began asking questions about Augie. This came as a total surprise. Their presence made Karl and me uneasy because we were worried that they might find out about our soured relationship with Augie and might think wc had something to do with his death. But why this high level of attention from our government?

They got a warrant to search his house and got the keys from Brun's. Other agents arrived, and, yesterday, they spent the entire day going through his house, barn, and other buildings. What were they looking for?

At the end of the day, they loaded boxes into a truck and left. This morning, several locals gathered at Brun's and went out to Augie's place to see what they could, hoping to find answers to this strange development. They came back reporting that they had looked in through the windows and saw that the boards covering interior walls had been removed. In addition, many of the floorboards had also been pried up and furniture moved. In the barn, they found a small empty interior room. Near as they could tell, the trampled straw and marks in the dirt left behind suggest that these agents had spent a long time in the barn, as well.

YESTERDAY, ELISABETH GAEBLER DROVE INTO TOWN! SHE WENT to the General Store to get acclimated to the town and find information about her brother, Augie. Susanna's brother, George, is the store owner. He meets her, and they discuss for a few minutes some of the details about Augie and his death and burial.

When George brought up the peculiar visit by the law enforcement, she responds that she knows nothing about the reason these law enforcement agents have ransacked the house and barn. She told George that they had visited her for information about her brother. She had told them that she and her brother were estranged and hadn't seen each other in many years. Before leaving, they did tell her that she should not sell the property until they had finished their investigation. When she asked them what this was about, she was told that it was at this time confidential.

She then asked George if he or anyone knew what happened to Clara Mendorf. George replies, "You've asked the right person. She's my sister-in-law, the widow of my brother, Joseph."

Relieved to discover that Clara is still living close by, she drove out to see her. They talked late into the night and Elisabeth spent the night.

Today, I watch as Elisabeth prepares to leave. She and Clara hug one another for a long time. Both are in tears. Elisabeth gets in her car and drives slowly away. Clara goes back inside her house.

A short time later, Clara comes over to see me. She needs to talk. She has so much to report.

Without wasting any time, Clara begins, "Elisabeth ran away from home when she was fifteen years old and spent all her life in St. Louis working as a housemaid for a string of wealthy families."

I ask, "Why did she run away?"

"Because she could no longer tolerate the conditions in her home. Her father was a drunk and was mean and the drunker he got, the meaner he was. He demanded unflinching loyalty and agreement, and, if you didn't agree, he would take off his belt and use it."

"Even on his daughters?"

"Yes, but Augie, Jr. especially was on the receiving end of his father's rage. Being his only son, the old man demanded that Junior knuckle under his authority and toe the line. He could survive the ordeal only by immediate obedience."

"Or else?"

“Elisabeth said, ‘He was mean and cruel to us all, but ruthless if Augie Jr. stepped out of line.”

“Am I supposed to feel sorry for Augie, Jr.?”

“Heinrich, I can’t tell you how you should feel. But Heinrich, Elisabeth remembers that day when she happened in on her father attacking me. She didn’t know what it all meant. She remembered only seeing my tears and hearing my cries as I wrenched myself free and ran out, clutching my dress.”

“Did you tell her that she had saved you?”

“Yes, and she was so happy she had.” Clara breaks into tears, “But mostly, she remembered her father’s anger, as that day was seared in her memory with his belt.” Crying still more, she says, “Heinrich, he beat her … a belt … what did she do?”

“Good Lord, no wonder she remembers!”

Through her sniffing and irregular breath, Clara continues, “And she was told never again to talk to me.”

We sit in silence for a minute.

Clara resumes, “She didn’t understand what had happened that day until a few years later when she was able to piece it together.”

Clara continues to relate how, unlike Junior, who never quit trying to please his tyrant of a father, Elisabeth just feigned respect and withdrew into herself.

“The day came when Elisabeth came home one afternoon and found her oldest sister, Lydia, lying in bed sobbing and curled up tightly. When Elisabeth asked her about what was wrong, Lydia clenched her eyes closed and shook her head, and muttered, ‘I can’t talk about it. I won’t talk about it’.”

Clara continues, “A few nights later, after August had gone off to the bar, Lydia disappeared, leaving a note for Elisabeth and her other sister, Hildegard, that read, “I love you. Be careful.”

The next day, August discovered his oldest daughter was gone and her horse missing. In a rage, he set off in search of her. Two days later, he came home, alone but drunk.

Somberly Clara continues, with tears forming in her eyes and running down her cheeks, "Sometime later, her other sister, Hildegard, began to act despondent and sullen. Elisabeth never knew exactly what had happened but only conjectured. By this time, she did know one thing for sure. She understood the craziness of her father, of her family. By this time, she figured out what had happened to me that day."

After a brief silence, I ask, "What did Elisabeth do?"

"She took her first chance to run off … ran away to St. Louis. She lived in fear for many years until the day she received word from one of the distant relatives that August was dead. She was so relieved. Heinrich, she was happy to hear that her own father was dead!"

Disgusted by this, I say, "That is so sad, heartbreaking … that this kind of thing happens. It's sick … just sickening … with your own daughter!?"

We sit in silence for a time.

Eventually, Clara resumes, "But poor Augie stayed … probably never quit trying … trying to earn his father's love."

"But still, that doesn't justi . . ."

Abruptly interrupting me, Clara says, "I know it doesn't, but maybe it does explain it … a little."

I'm thinking, "Well, maybe … but so what?"

"Heinrich, I told her everything. I told her about that horrible day. I confirmed what she had figured out. Heinrich, she said that after that day when she saw me, she wanted to talk to me, to have fun with me again, but she couldn't because of her father. She was afraid."

Looking down with her eyes closed and tears seeping out, Clara haltingly whispers almost to herself, "She told me that she never really ever had a fun day again. Her father took away her childhood."

Clara relates that Elisabeth also knew that her father bore animosity toward our family. She mentioned how the German flag of Bismarck's Unification was posted on the inside wall of their house and that her father forbade speaking any language other than German in the home.

"Did you tell her about Robert and Franz?", I query.

"Yes," Clara replies with tears in her eyes."

"What did she say?"

"She came over to me and hugged me and held onto me … we held on to each other … while we both cried. She said, 'Clara, I am so sorry for my family. It was sick. Maybe now it will die with this generation … as it should'."

We sit in silence for a long minute.

"Heinrich," Clara continues, "This is strange. Elisabeth was surprised to hear about how pro-American Augie had become. She herself had been torn with questions of loyalty during the war, as many of us were. Augie's extreme patriotism shocked her."

"Hmm," I reply, "that is strange, isn't it?"

CHAPTER 21

Robert and Joey and their wives, Magdalena and Louisa, arrived back in town yesterday, and today, we are all together as a family as we celebrate Thanksgiving, 1919. It's not what anyone would call a celebration, but it is an important time for our family to be together again.

The whole family has gathered, including Karl and Emma and their seven children. Plus, our children, Henry and Christina, and their families also have come. Only the children seem to have much of an appetite.

We want to hear a report of the trip to France from Joey and Robert and their wives. The trip was emotionally very difficult for all of them. And as they each have a part in sharing their stories, many tears are shed as they relate the impact of seeing the white crosses inscribed with their sons' names marking their graves. And to be able to see their respective sons buried next to one another seems so fitting for them, cousins who had grown up together. But it was hard.

They had nothing but praise for the way they were treated by our Army. There is still a lot of confusion and chaos in France, but the military took very special care of them. Seeing their sons' graves and hearing about the plans for this and other cemeteries in France to honor our American soldiers who died in the *Great War* has given them a sense of closure. They are so proud of their sons who were willing to give their all for their country! They will be honored for years to come for their service.

After our dinner, Clara, Susanna, Karl, and I gather with Joey and Robert and their wives alone. This is a meeting that four of us have been dreading … having to tell Clara's sons and daughters-in-law the truth that has come to light while they were gone. But rather than their finding out from others, this is something we must do.

As we tell the story of Augie's treachery, it is initially met with shock and anger. When I first mention how I knew that Augie had intentionally targeted them, Louisa cries out, "God, please no!" and Magdalena buries her face into her hands and breaks down in tears. Robert and Joey both sit there, stunned, as if not comprehending what I said. But as it settles in, expressions of sheer hatred creep over their faces. Joey slams his fist down on the table and shouts, "I will kill that son of a bitch! God help me, if it's the last thing I do, I will kill that bastard!"

Karl quickly pipes in, "That won't be necessary. He's already dead."

Joey yells out with a venomous expression, "What?"

Karl responds, "Looks like he killed himself, found him hung. He knew he was a goner. Apparently took the coward's way out."

I am struck by Karl's choice of words … "looks like" and "apparently". I can't help but wonder if Karl knows something he's not telling.

Karl continues, "Yep, saved you the trouble. Guess he couldn't live with himself … especially when Heinrich and I had a heart-to-heart with him and told him we were on to him. Told him you would be coming home soon, too. Guess he didn't want to wait around for that. So, there he was … found the next day … hanging in his front yard tree."

Again, I'm reading between the lines. What is Karl saying?

The whole despicable story of Augie's deceitfulness serves to rekindle the pain but now, with the added dimension of its premeditation. Now the wounds have a specific source. It isn't now the anonymous war, but it's the deliberate plan of Augie.

Louisa composes herself enough to ask, "Why? Why would he do such a thing? What did our boys ever do to him?"

Clara breaks down in anguish and cries out, "It wasn't your boys! It's me! It's all me!" All four immediately turn to look at her with stunned confused faces. Joey shakes his head and blinks and looks at her and asks, "Mama, what are you talking about? What did you ever do to Augie?"

Completely crumbling emotionally, Clara tries to tell the story, but she can't get it out. She is so distraught, beyond her ability to function. Susanna goes to her and gathers her in her arms. My son, Henry, comes in the room to join us, mainly to be there and to keep a watchful eye on his Aunt Clara.

I'm the one who has to tell the story. I begin, "Years ago, when your mother was just a young teenager, when we were still brand new to this country, Augie's father tried to rape your mother." From that point on, I tell the whole sick story … about their grandfather's revenge and the settled hatred of the Gaeblers' just waiting to somehow get even. During this whole time, they all sit there engrossed by the account and stupefied by the family hatred that had passed from father to son.

When I finally finish, I ask if there are any questions that I can try to answer. And Robert says, "Not at this time, but I'm sure there will be. I … I just … I just have to let this soak in." He breaks down and cries and reaches over and hugs his wife, they both cry together.

Joey and Louisa also embrace in tears. Louisa is trembling with heavy breathing and sobbing. Joey tries to comfort her.

Susanna continues to sit next to Clara with her arm still around her.

The room is quiet except for the sobs and sniffing. I sit with my head down, fighting back tears. I'm chastising myself, asking how I could have done this differently so there wouldn't be so much pain. But I see no other option.

I look over at Karl, and he's sitting there with his head down. Every few seconds he squirms uncomfortably in his chair. I figure he is not used to such intense emotion and doesn't know what to do or how to respond.

After a few long minutes, Robert comes over to Clara and says, "Mama, let me hug you." He takes her hands and helps her stand and hugs her tightly and breaks down and cries with her. "Mama, it's not your fault. Don't ever say that again. It's not your fault."

Clara breaks down again and says, "Joey … and Robert … Magdalena and Louisa … I am so sorry. I am so sorry." Joey comes over and hugs her too, saying, "Mama, it's not our fault. We'll get through this together. I know we will."

There's nothing more that can be said tonight. But I know there will be a lot to be said in the future. The closure that they found in France at their sons' graves has now been ripped open once again.

Soon, we go to our homes. Susanna and I insist that Clara come to our house for the night.

THERE'S AN ARTICLE IN THE DECEMBER 10 ST. LOUIS newspaper. The Secret Service has unveiled a plot that during the *Great War*, horses being shipped to Europe for the Allies had mysteriously died while awaiting transport from St. Louis. One shipment of over one hundred horses had originated in the southern parts of Missouri and Illinois and western parts of Kentucky and Tennessee. They had been gathered at Cape

Girardeau and shipped by rail to St. Louis. When they arrived, some had died and many were dying and were put out of their misery. August Gaebler, Jr. has been named posthumously as the perpetrator. Chemicals that would cause anthrax and glanders along with syringes were found in his house and barn. There were also incriminating letters and documents found. He had most likely slipped into the horse corral at night and began injecting them with poisonous bacteria. The article also mentions how Augie had used his position as a member of the American Protective League and service on the County Exemption Board as cover.

That S.O.B. was a saboteur!

Two days later, the newspaper in Cape Girardeau issued an apology for its earlier article that had honored August Gaebler, Jr. The editor admits that he, as well as all of us, had been duped.

Clara said, "But this won't bring my grandsons back."

Karl's chickens have mysteriously gotten sick, and many have died. No matter what Karl has tried, they still die.

Karl blames it all on those chickens he bought from Augie's place that day at the auction. He says that it wasn't long before those chickens got sick and were the first to die. And then the others followed. He speaks of it as Augie's revenge. That seems far-fetched to me. But Karl is Karl.

Today Karl mentions that two of his children have gotten sick. They have the classic symptoms of the flu. The "Spanish Lady" continues to live even now. But bull-headed unreasonable Karl now blames this on Augie's chickens. He says that the demons have jumped from the chickens to his family. But I ask, "How can a person get sick from a chicken?"

This is just the beginning. In the days that follow, the sickness continues to spread in his family. It is bad. On February 6, 1920, his twenty-four-year-old son dies. Three days later, his twenty-one-year-old son and seventeen-year-old daughter die the same day!

But still, the Spanish Lady lives on in Karl's household. On February 12, his nine-year-old son dies. And then, it stops, and it looks like the others will all live through this tragedy. But no, a week later, on February 19, his youngest, his lovely four-year-old daughter dies.

And having killed five children within thirteen days – almost two years after it all began - the Spanish Flu finally dies out in Karl's house. Emma is distraught, having endured the sickness of her children and having lost five of her seven loved ones. Susanna, Clara, and I have pitched in as best we can … especially to be present and helpful for Emma.

Karl is furious, understandably so. But to continue blaming all this on a curse from Augie. It defies all logic. But I'm not going to argue with him. It's a terrible tragedy.

It is a sad, sad sight to see the now five heaps of new dirt mounded up over the graves of these five children whose young lives have been snuffed out by this horrific flu.

We can only hope that the flu is now gone.

CHAPTER 22

On this cold winter night, as Susanna and I sit reading, I begin to feel chilled and suddenly I'm very tired. I tell Susanna that I'm not feeling well, and I want to go to bed. She looks at me with a sense of loving worry and inquires, "Tell me, how do you feel? Do you think it's maybe the flu?"

"God, I hope not. I just want to go to bed. I'll see how I feel tomorrow."

With her caring and concerned expression, she says good night. "I love you, but we better not kiss … just in case."

When I get into bed. I soon realize that I'm running a fever. I feel awful, and then the pressure of diarrhea. I've got to go outside to the privy … hope I get there in time.

Getting back into bed I feel worse. It feels like my head is going to blow off. Fever, sweat, and chills. Exhausted, I fall asleep … into a deep sleep.

And then I find myself in a different place. How did I get here? Where is here? It's surreal … a familiar place, but also a very different place. I'm in that valley again, the battlefield, the valley of the dry bones. And there I see my nephew Franz standing there, safe behind the line tending horses, and he's waving at me with an expression of joy. I wave back. But then out of the blue, he's gone … disappears … obliterated by a stray artillery shell. He's gone, nothing left, nothing left to bury. He's vanished, like a vapor. I smell the air. It's the smell of death … burnt powder … rotting flesh. I see a rat come out of its hole and start eating a dead man's flesh. Suddenly, a soldier's hand swoops that rat up, breaks its neck, and starts eating it … desperate to survive. And then, I see my own fork, lifting a piece of that dead rat into my own mouth.

In my restlessness, Susanna comes and awakens me … to wipe my fevered face and chest with a cool rag. She tells me that Clara has gone to town … to Henry's house … to tell him that I'm sick with the flu. I open my eyes, but it hurts just to open them, and I fall back into sleep … back into this phantom world.

The earth shakes as an artillery shell shatters a tree near me, splinters and debris crashing down on me. And then they come! An army of monstrous tigers streaking across the field, their teeth bared, picking up men and throwing them to their death, their teeth cutting them in two, decapitating them, maiming others, and leaving them in the agony and hopelessness of dying. The cries of pain, the crying for their mamas, for their sweethearts, for their wives. Young strong naive men in their prime, being cut off. They had marched off joyfully, confidently singing "the Yanks are coming," and now they cry, "the Yanks are dying." They had never imagined in their worst days this … sudden death, defenseless … even to the proudest and the mightiest among them.

There's Wilson, our American president. He has such grandiose notions, strutting around with all the answers, so proud of his plan to end the war … to end all war forever. After all, he says, "Man is basically good. Just give him a chance." He's an educated and learned man … former president of Princeton University … former governor of New Jersey. "Listen to me," he proudly proclaims. And they laugh at him; they mock him.

An onslaught of vipers arises, snakes of all sizes spewing

their venom as they dig into this mighty elephant, our President! With a final hoarse scream of agony, the elephant dies. The vultures move in; it's their turn. They ravage the corpse of his dead dream and pick him clean.

I'm back in that valley of bones, nothing but bones, bones of my friends, my nephews … even my unnamed Bavarian relatives who had fought for the Germans.

I am awakened again … back to the real world. By Susanna. She has brought me some medicine from Henry. She says, "Heinrich, here are two pills and a cup of water; put these in your mouth and swallow them." Her cool hands feel so wonderful on my fever-wracked body. I want to say but am unable to express to her, "Don't leave me, please; stay with me. Help me through this."

Then, I'm back in that cavern of sleep … on the battlefield watching in terror as bayonets creep over the dead and dying … making sure that there will never fight again. I cry out. "God Almighty, why? Where are you? Don't you care?"

J. P. Morgan and his friends sit smiling as they rake in the profits. The ledger sheet looks good. Wall Street is thriving. From the sale of new and improved arms and munitions. "You scumbag … all of you are scumbags … making your fortunes on the backs of this generation … who will never enjoy life, the pleasure of a woman, the planting of new life! You scumbag, you have taken away their dream!"

And there's August … it's a nightmare … throwing Clara to the floor, ripping off her clothes and raping her. There's no Elisabeth, running in to distract him. Not this time. Clara lies there helpless. "You sweet little thing … thing … thing … thing." This selfish fiend … sick monster! He doesn't care. The love of power … power makes right. My sister is left like a limp discarded rag, never to be whole again.

And now, Papa, out for revenge … for the family honor! Gaebler's crime must be punished. He holds August down as he struggles to get free … wrenching his shoulder. And there, I see myself, taking my bayonet, and castrating him … like a bull calf turned into a steer … for what he did … and I enjoy it! I enjoy doing it. This is MY revenge!

I am awakened from my dream again … this time by Clara with more medicine. Clara, thank God she's still alive! But then horrors, I can see that she is no longer whole. She's missing half her heart. August's scalpel of lust and power has removed half of her heart. Now, she's weak, frail, and fragile. "Don't break her, please God, don't break her!"

My hand is covered with blood, dripping with the blood of that bastard, August, for raping my sister, for raping my family. I am glad that my hands are dripping his blood. I have gotten my revenge. But I am still not satisfied. August's debt has not been paid, not yet. It will never be completely paid. I'll not let it be.

Clara is wandering around in No-Man's Land. She trips and falls, and there she finds the remains of her grandson, Franz. But there's not much left. She finds his head and holds it to her breast, begging him to nurse … to return to life. But he doesn't; he can't. She digs a hole in the muddy remains of the field, repeatedly cutting her hand on the shards of shrapnel. The hole completed, with tortured hands, she lays Franz's severed head into the hole and covers it over with the mud – mud soaked with blood, shrapnel, and her tears.

She crawls on her hands and knees as she wanders off plaintively calling out for Eric. As she moves on, her voice slowly fades.

And there is Augie, August Jr., just like his father. Laughing, smiling, bragging. Carrying home by their hair, the heads of Eric and Franz … prizes to show his father … his loyalty … to make his father proud … to finally gain his father's approval!

I'm driving along Augie's lane and see him … or what's left of him … hanging by a rope, dead! I smile as I see the vultures beginning to shred his rotting flesh. I had told him the sins of his father and how he cut out half of Clara's heart. Perhaps, he could no longer live with himself, not any longer. Or maybe Karl did it. And if Karl did it, then I'm proud of him. That's the end of this sick and evil family. I'm glad they're gone.

I look again at the dripping blood - the blood of August's testicles in my hands, and I smile. I have neutered him. He can never hurt Clara again. This is for Clara.

Clara awakens me again … back to reality … and wipes my face with a cool rag. "How bad is it," I ask. "How sick am I?"

"Heinrich you're sick and I'll take care of you. Just let me take care of you as you have always taken care of me." Sweet Clara, with only half her heart remaining. But it's the kindhearted half.

I'm back in the valley of the bones, the very dry bones, surrounded by death and decay, the now dried blood on my own hands beginning to smell as it begins to rot - decomposing body matter.

And then there's the roar of a Lion, the majestic roar of the King. It overpowers even the thunder of the cannon. "Son of man, can these bones live?" I cover my ears … the sound is deafening … but it reverberates within my head. "Son of man, can these bones live?"

I conclude, as I look around, there is no way! Here is the final result of heaven's gift of fire … after Pandora opens the jar and releases the plagues. Here I see the remains of naive lovely innocent naked Eve after she eats the apple and releases this alien Power.

I'm back in 1904 at the world's fair, all the great accomplishments, the breakthroughs, the inventions, the endeavors, and the achievements of mankind. Even the Liberty Bell from Philadelphia. Liberty? Freedom? Who am I kidding? We're all slaves!

Lord Acton was right … and wrong … he didn't go far enough. It's not power that corrupts, but it's our corruption that cannot handle any of the gifts that we've been given! We have corrupted power and everything else our hands have touched.

"Papa, wake up, Papa wake up! It's Henry, your son, Papa."

I can barely open my heavy eyes, let alone lift my pounding head. It hurts too much. I am so cold. "Cover me up, Henry. I'm freezing!" He puts a heavy blanket over me, and I'm in that deep sleep once again.

Back at the battlefield, it's in the dead of winter. Frozen corpses of horses, men in the trenches freezing to death.

Again, the roar of the Lion, "Son of man, can these bones live again?" And I don't know. I don't see how. Look at what we've done to ourselves?

Brilliant stupid President Wilson thought he could do it. Thought he could fix the world. So sure, that he had all the answers. Then he turned; he changed, and he became the problem. They had hoped in him; they had trusted that he would not let them down, that he would be compassionate, as well as just, fair. But he changed and became the greatest fraud on earth!

The Lion again beckons, "Son of man can these bones live?"

"God, I don't know. You have measured us with the plumb line, and we are all out of plumb. Our wall that we have proudly built for protection, for success, for domination … cannot stand. We have our Tower of Babel. Tear it down, God, tear it down! You build us one … a wall that will stand."

I'm being disturbed again. "Leave me alone. Let me be." It's not Henry. Oh, at last, it's Susanna. "Here, let me wipe your face and body with a cool rag. Heinrich, my love, here is water, take this medicine. I am praying for you, Heinrich. You will be okay. I know you will."

I whimper, "Thank you, Susanna, my incredible wife, thank you for taking care of me. I love you."

"I love you too, Heinrich." And then she's gone.

Again, I'm back in my dream. That Lion again, "Son of man, can these bones live?"

"God, they're so dry, bleached out. I don't see how."

Again, the Lion, "Son of Man, hear the word of the Lord. Say to these bones, 'I will cause breath to enter you and you shall live. I will lay sinew upon you, cause flesh to come upon you, cover you with skin and put breath in you, and you will live'."

I cry out to the Lion, "How can I know? How can I know that there is hope? I put trust in Man … to be able to bring peace … wholeness … to have ultimate answers … all I see in Man is more of the same … more sophisticated, to be sure … but still only more of the same. Meaninglessness … nothingness … death."

And I hear a sound coming from the bones … a rattling sound … bones coming together … sinews and skin … and finally breath … the Lion's breath … and the army arises … allies and enemies … united … one army arises … an exceedingly great army.

From a distance, I hear once again the deafening roar of the Lion. I look to see where the voice had come from. And as I look, I see a hill and, on that hill, a cross, and on that cross, a bloody and tortured body hanging … dead. Is this somehow the answer? But how? What does it mean?

I feel cold water on my forehead. "Heinrich, can you hear me? It's Clara."

"Papa. Can you hear me? Wake up, Papa; it's Henry."

"Papa, it's Christina. I love you, Papa. Wake up."

I open my eyes and through the blurry scales of sickness over my eyes, I make out three smiling faces: Clara, Henry, Christina. Christina hugs me and says, "O Papa, you're alive. You're going to make it; you'll be all right. Thank God, you're alive."

Henry lifts my heavy head and shoulders, and Clara hands him a cup of cool water, refreshing water from the spring, "Here Papa, drink this. You need lots of water. Your body is worn out; it's been through hell."

I look and see the relieved expression of Clara … her face worn out by worry and anxiety. "Heinrich, welcome back." I can tell she wants to throw herself at me like in days of old, but she restrains herself, lest she hurt me.

"Where's Susanna? I just saw her. She said she was praying for me, and she knows I'll be all right. Where's your Mama … where's Susanna?"

Tears immediately form in all their eyes, and I know. Henry and Christina look away. It's Clara … resilient strong Clara … who kneels and looks me straight in the eyes, with her tears dripping onto my face, confirms what I now know, "Heinrich, Susanna died … the flu … came down with it two days after you. She died three days later. Her last words were, 'Tell Heinrich, I love him'."

"No, she came to me … not long ago … I saw her … talked with her … she cooled my burning forehead … told me to take the medicine … told me she was praying for me …told me I'd be all right… told me that she loved me. She was fine … she wasn't sick!"

"You're right, Heinrich. She's not sick … not any longer."

I CAN'T BELIEVE SUSANNA'S GONE. SOMETIMES, SHE COMES TO me in the middle of the night … she says, "I'm fine. All is well." This gives me comfort, but it also hurts. I want her here, physically present … next to me in bed, so I can touch her, cuddle her … inhale her presence … taste her lips … feel her skin, hold her in my arms, caress her. But as the days and now weeks pass, she's not coming to me so often.

Those around seem to have been able to move on with their lives … even Henry and Christina are getting back to their normal routine. It's time to move on. But not for me. It has just begun to sink in. I don't know what normal even looks like.

Even Karl seems to have moved on … planning his crop and getting the equipment ready. But his wife, Emma, I can tell, is still struggling over the deaths of her children. Clara tries to help both Emma and me. Sweet, wonderful, caring Clara! She knows grief first-hand and is there, present, for us both.

As I walk through the cemetery and now sit at my dear Susanna's grave, there is so much going on … the gut-wrenching grief … the emptiness. I spend hours there … every day … week after week, it seems.

Eventually, Clara and I realize that we're the last of that founding generation. After all, Karl doesn't remember those early days. I move into Clara's house so we can take care of one another until the end … when first one and then the other of us is placed into the ground of the family cemetery next to our loved ones.

We spend a lot of time remembering … through many tears … laughter … joys and sorrows. We remember back to that day … when news came about our oldest brother, Friedrich. That's when it began, it seems. We retell and sort of relive the events and circumstances that have brought us here. In my old age, I can now freely cry real tears, and no longer be embarrassed. We're together … again … Clara and me … brother and sister … like at the beginning … until the end.

DURING THE SUBSEQUENT MONTHS TOGETHER, CLARA AND I reflect not only on our respective journeys through life, but also on our respective journeys of faith. They are so very different. It's hard to believe that two people could live through the same history and in the same family and yet have such different perspectives on God and what faith means.

Clara now kiddingly calls me "Doubting Thomas", for I have been like that particular follower of Jesus who, when he heard that Jesus had been raised from the dead, said, "Unless I see for myself and touch him, I will never believe." But of course! Dead people don't come back to life. When you're dead, you're dead!

On the other hand, I refer to Clara as, "Steadfast Mary", who, when Mary was told that she would be the mother of the Savior, said, "Ok, whatever you say, Lord. I'm a virgin, but that's not a problem! I have no husband, but You'll figure it out. No room? God's still in charge."

I can recall only that one time that Clara doubted. This evening after dinner, we're sitting in our comfortable chairs. She's reading another book and I'm skimming through the newspaper. I ask, "Clara, remember that day when you stood on the edge of the loft," I pause, "in the barn?"

Putting down her reading she replies, "You mean the day I was ready to hang myself". Seeing me nod, she says, "Of course I do." Pausing for a short time, she continues, "Yeah, that was a tough time." Tears suddenly appearing, she says, "I miss Franz and Eric so much still. They were such endearing and respectful young men, so easy to love." She wipes her eyes with her handkerchief, looks down and bites her bottom lip, blinking back tears, "I have never really been able to forgive that … monster who did that to them … to us … to me."

In a gentle voice, I inquire, "Clara, thinking back to that day in the barn, do you think you would have …" I pause, hesitating to say the word.

"Jumped?" she adds. "I've wondered about that a lot since. I don't know. I wanted to die. I really did. I didn't want to live any longer." Again, pausing briefly, "That was my lowest point when my faith was weakest, I think."

I venture, "But as I recall, in your note you wrote that morning before you went out to the barn … your prayer to God, you still believed. At least that's how I remember it."

Clara responds, "Yes, I still knew He was there. But where was He? That's hell, to know that He's there, but life doesn't make sense. I thought He had turned his back on me. To believe in God when He failed me! Heinrich, I was angry at God."

"You don't need to tell me!" I respond.

She continues, "But as I stood there, my hands over my face, my eyes closed." Gently rubbing her neck with her hand, she says, "I can still imagine and feel that rough rope around my neck. In my mind, I saw Eric and Franz, and I thought, if I jump, I won't see them anymore. And I wanted to continue to look at them in my memory. But if I jumped there would be no more memory."

As we continue this conversation, I realize what I had always thought. She has always had an implicit trust, belief in God, even when it seemed that God had deserted her. And even that day, when she says her faith was weak, she believed in God. She was angry with God and felt cut off from Him, but she still knew … she still believed! I wouldn't call that weak faith. Struggling to understand, yes … angry with God, definitely … feeling let down, sure … but weak? Not in my opinion.

As our conversation continues, she explains how she has found strength in the suffering of Jesus. "I think of Jesus, in agony on the cross, and think, if my Savior could suffer like that for me, then I can endure this." She pauses and closes her eyes as she considers, "It's been hard at times ... so hard."

Pausing for more reflection, she goes on, "But I have to be honest. I know I shouldn't feel this way, and God forgive me, but when I heard that Augie hanged himself, it was a relief. I remember saying out loud, 'May you burn in hell, you sack of *Scheisse*'."

"I don't blame you for that. I was overjoyed when I heard it."

"But Heinrich, I just have to believe and keep trusting that Jesus died for this hatred of mine, too. I hate Augie and his father, and I can't help it. I can't stop. Jesus' grace is the only hope I have. I go to church and see the picture of Jesus on the cross hanging there above the altar, and I can't help but think that He did that for me. So why can't I … at least, stop hating them. Besides they're gone."

We sit quietly for a long minute, when Clara asks, "Heinrich, I want to ask, and you may not want to answer … but do you feel certain that Augie killed himself … or maybe someone else did that? The doctor said he couldn't be sure."

"Clara, I have wondered the same thing. A lot of people couldn't stand him after what he did to your grandsons came out. But please know that I had nothing to do with it."

"You think maybe Karl and maybe one or two of his boys?"

"I don't know; I don't know what to think. But I'm not going to ask him. I don't want to know. I just assume that Augie hanged himself, especially if he knew the authorities were after him, too."

She smiles, lowers her head, and after a little a while says, "It's time for me to get some sleep."

"Good night, Clara, and thank you for our talk tonight."

She looks sternly at me but with a smile on her face, "Tonight we've talked about me. Tomorrow, Doubting Thomas, you're going to tell me about your doubts and how you got it figured out."

I smile and head off to my room.

As I lay in bed, I try to piece my thoughts together in an orderly way so that it makes sense. I know Clara wants to know. She'll be asking tomorrow.

THE NEXT DAY, AFTER LUNCH, CLARA AND I SIT IN OUR comfortable chairs, each enjoying a cool beer.

Clara starts it off, "Heinrich, as I recall, you began having some pretty major questions about God early on in your life."

"Yes, it was just at the time when I found out that Amelia had died. Or maybe even before ... maybe when we heard that

Friedrich had been killed in battle. I questioned why God took away my brother and my girlfriend, and maybe why He didn't stop Papa from leaving Bavaria. That's when it started for me."

Clara seeks to understand, "You had the notion that, if you believe in God that He should be doing good things for you?"

"Yes, kinda silly, looking back on it now and all I've been through … but that was basically how I saw it. Also, we were living in a great age, a great time to be alive. An age of knowledge, inventions, and breakthroughs … an era of human progress. If something was broken, then mankind could fix it. If it's a mystery, then Man will discover its meaning. Man can do it all … all by himself. And, let's face it, many incredible things were accomplished."

Clara remarks, "Yes, even some brilliant minds were saying that Man doesn't need God, that God is only a crutch. And then, too, some distinguished German Bible scholars were casting doubt on some essential truths of the Bible."

"Yes," I say. "I was proud to be German. German education, scientific and industrial know-how … what we were contributing to the world. All this progress! Who was I to second guess what was being accomplished? I went along with it."

Clara asks, "Then you began to rethink it?"

"Yes," I continue, "it was even before the war when I began to wonder. I didn't like the conclusions that some of our so-called brilliant thinkers were coming to. It was disturbing. Life according to them had no meaning. Life just was. It had no purpose. They were using the word 'nihilism' to describe life. There are no real values and morals. Ultimately, life and the world are senseless, meaningless. There is no hope!"

Clara remarks, "Life as a godless existence. Nietzsche succinctly said it, 'God is dead'."

"Yes, and then I went to France," I continue, "and I saw what I now realize is the inevitable result of Man's hope in Man when he has no objective truth and values. Man cannot handle his own accomplishments. He cannot handle his own knowledge. He cannot responsibly handle his own power!"

"That's an interesting insight," remarks Clara.

"Well, I wasn't on the front lines nor in the trenches. But I didn't have to be. I saw enough. I met a British soldier who, in 1916, had fought at the Somme. He expressed his lost hope in God this way, 'We are your ghosts in this game played by monkeys organized by lunatics.' What a sense of futility! The whole war was just that … futile, meaningless … and for what?"

Clara replies, "Wow, what a sad and depressing view!" She shares her struggle, "I had always been so proud of my German heritage. But Germany provoked this war and then invaded and overran Belgium. Belgium was neutral! It was no contest. And what the Kaiser's army did to Belgium and its people was unprecedented, horrible! I was embarrassed … ashamed of being German!"

Agreeing with her, I respond, "Oh, I know what you mean. I had tried to defend mankind, kept saying that the innate goodness of Man would prevail. But the war was a huge turning point for me. I saw what Man can do when he loses his moral compass."

Clara asks, "During that time, what were your thoughts about God?"

"I was struggling. I had lost hope in God, and now I had also lost hope in Man." I pause, looking down, "But nihilism was not the answer for me. That is not an answer!"

"I am so sorry, Heinrich. That had to be so, so disheartening … depressing."

I resume, "Yes, the Paris Peace so-called 'Agreement' only made me more depressed about it all. Instead of bringing healing, it was all about revenge! It was such a waste, a missed opportunity."

Clara recalls, "Heinrich, when you came home, you were not the same person you had been when you left. You had changed."

"Yes, I did come home different. I came home angry. I was cynical. What had we done and what had we failed to do? My hope in mankind was gone. I was still angry at God … and I came home angry at Man."

In the silence that follows, I stop and think and then say, "Clara, I can honestly understand why a person who has been through so much, seen so much, experienced such a sense of hopelessness … why a person can conclude that there is no God. I think it makes life easier not to have to endure those big questions that faith expects to find answers to."

Seeking clarity, Clara asks, "You mean, like what those men in combat endured and what those poor people of France and Belgium faced?"

"Yes, I wasn't on the line or in the trenches, but even so, I struggled. I can't begin to imagine what it would have been like for a naïve optimistic young man who thought it would be an adventure … who maybe even thought that God was on their side."

We both fall into a period of silence and reflection.

Soon, tears come to my eyes, "Thank God for Susanna. She didn't try to explain or reason with me. We talked about this so often … about my disillusionment and my faith struggle. She just accepted me and listened … and loved me. She did not get anxious about my questions. She said she had many of the same questions, but still, she just knew that God was not dead."

Clara responds, "Yes, she was a rock. She held this family together. She was always there,"

Closing my eyes and leaning back, I say nothing for a while. And then, looking at Clara, with tears pooling in my eyes, I say, "I miss her." Pausing again before continuing, "and I only wish that she could have known where I've finally arrived with all my questions."

We both again sit quietly for a time, and Clara says, "That damnable flu. It took so many."

"Yes, the flu. What a plague, a modern-day plague! So many in our own family … just gone." I stop and think before resuming, "But Clara, for me, in that deep strange sleep, I began to see and experience things that shook me to my core and yet, comforted me, too. I found answers!

"What I found was not pretty. But it was truth. I discovered an ugly truth about myself, that I too am capable of horrible evil. Clara, recall what I had told you about how in that dream-state I had gotten revenge on August? Well, I enjoyed the feel of August's blood flowing over my hands. But I still wasn't satisfied. I wanted more revenge. I still wasn't satisfied!"

Clara interjects, "Heinrich, I understand. That's me, too, honestly, at times. I still struggle, too."

"Clara, in France, I saw men … wounded, some dying … some turned away from God into hopelessness and despair. And I saw others who were experiencing the same thing turn to God for comfort and peace. I couldn't understand that.

"But in my dream, I found some answers. I heard that penetrating yet peaceful voice of God. I saw that it came from the cross! I can't explain it logically. Here is Jesus … in misery … on that horrible cruel cross! And here is the voice of God calling from a broken dying man? It's like here is God Himself stepping out of the trenches, running across No-Man's Land and into the face of certain death. That's the last place I'd expect to find God. On a battlefield? A God who suffers? Never! But yes! A God who comes into the middle of our suffering and who Himself suffers and dies. I'd heard that all my life … in church. It was what we were taught … but it was more of an idea, a theory, I guess.

"But now, I have begun to comprehend it. Those men who were dying … even in their suffering, they could turn to God and find comfort and even hope. How? I think it's because they knew their God is a God who Himself suffered and died and was with them in their suffering and death."

Feeling the tears in my eyes, I look at Clara, as I smile and excitedly continue, "And Clara, that's where He wants me to find Him, to know Him! There on the cross, hanging there, that's God Himself, His way of reclaiming this world … reclaiming me! And I knew, just knew, that here is God! This is where He wants to be found! He doesn't fight the world! He loves it! He suffers for it, dies for it!"

In the silence that follows, Clara reaches and takes my hand in her hands, "Heinrich, what can I say but 'Wow! Thank you for telling me'."

Looking into her eyes, I continue, "And now something else makes sense. After he died, he didn't stay dead. I used to think, 'well, dead is dead'. But God raised him! Jesus died, and he came back to life. And here I now find hope.

"Again, I can't explain it logically. But I do know that it's not just a fairy tale! It happened to Jesus, and it is God's promise to you and me. After death, there is life and resurrection, somehow. Yes, there are more questions. But this enables me to sit at Susanna's grave and not be completely lost.

"But it's more than that. This is not just some psychological explanation for dealing with the pain of life. It's real. I saw it. It gave those young men comfort even as they died. What power! To face agonizing death in hope and peace. That's all the proof I need." I pause and think about Susanna and conclude, "I'm sure it gave Susanna hope and peace."

Clara responds, "Yes, Heinrich, I know Susanna had that hope and peace … she died in peace … I was there with her. What a beautiful person … so much love." Pausing for a few seconds, Clara continues, "And I'm sure it gave my grandsons, Eric and Franz, peace when they … when they died." She closes her eyes to stop the tears.

I look down, concentrating on how to explain it. "I still have many questions … especially about undeserved suffering, like what I saw in France. And then there's the issue of evil. I know it's real. I ask 'why' an awful lot. And I remember that even Jesus asked 'why' as he died on the cross. But he still trusted. But now, I don't need to have all the answers before I believe. I can have faith and still not have to have understanding. Of, course, I like it when I do understand, and that helps my faith as well. The voice of God that called me from the cross … that's the final word … where I find hope."

I look up at Clara, her smiling face now streaming with tears. She doesn't say anything. Her smile says it all.

I venture, "But Clara, I think God wants us to make a difference in this world."

Clara nods silently.

I continue, "The world is still so broken. I fear for the future. But what has God done for its brokenness? He entered it. He experienced it firsthand, took it on Himself. And I think He wants us to be engaged in bringing healing, even if it means that we, too, have to sacrifice and endure hardship."

I venture, "Clara, you may think I'm kind of crazy." I stop to think how to express it, and then go on, "I think that God wants us to also be willing to suffer, too. That suffering is not in itself evil."

Surprised, Clara responds, "Why, Heinrich? Why would God want that?"

"I don't really know why, but I do know that those young men who were suffering so much, died with faith in Jesus, and even as they were dying, they had peace. And that made such a deep impression … and there were so many others. I mean, such faith … such peace … even in their horrible suffering! I even saw one man who was horrendously burned by a flame thrower, but he was able to die in peace. The man's peace in suffering spoke to me!"

I explain even more personally, "Clara, take yourself, for example. Your faith has always inspired me, but never as much as when you went through the hard times, the pain, and loss.

Even at those times … especially at those times, you still looked to God."

"But Heinrich," Clara disputes, "there were so many times when I was at my wit's end. You know that."

"Okay, you may have been fighting with God sometimes, but you still believed! Your faith was incredible. I couldn't understand it, but I was amazed." I pause to choose my words, "It maybe sounds strange but it's true, Clara. It moved me because of your hard times and sorrow. You still had faith … and hope, even then. You had faith still when I had given up on God!"

In tears and burying her face in her hands, Clara cries, "O thank you, Heinrich, I've never thought of it like that! I always saw it as my failure." Pausing and considering, "Maybe my struggles and the tragedies that didn't make sense … maybe they did have meaning!"

"Yes, Clara, it's hard for you to see how real your faith is. But I see it.

"And Clara, I feel in myself, that my journey … all the questioning and cynicism … well, I wouldn't trade it for the world because it is my journey. It's a mystery, but it's true."

"Heinrich", Clara says, "it is a wonderful journey. I can't help but think that Susanna knows how it ends."

I smile at that thought as tears flow down my face. Sheepishly, I say, "Thank you, Clara. I hope so."

Clara and I sit quietly as we collect ourselves, our emotions, and our thoughts. We are both worn out.

Our conversation for this day has come to an end.

TIME MARCHES ON.

Clara and I are spending our days together. We started the journey together and so shall we complete it. We are brother and sister nearing the end of our days.

We speak often of the journey … from a perfect world's idealism to shattered dreams' realism … from simple faith to complex paradox … from an insistence on finding answers to a willingness to let the big questions just be.

We can live with the enigma of our hidden God Who owes us no answers yet has bound Himself to our broken world. A God who showed Himself on the cross and invites us to find Him there … living by faith and promise, not necessarily knowledge and proof.

We speak freely of our questions, discussing and exploring them without fear … asking them in faith … no longer needing answers. We have faith that seeks understanding yet doesn't have to have it. We seek wholeness but are content with the pieces.

We miss our loved ones … still shedding many tears … but finding joy in our memories, comfort in our love, and hope in God's grace.

September 25, 1922

CLARA DIED YESTERDAY. WE BURIED HER IN OUR FAMILY cemetery today … between Gus and Joseph. I alone am left from those first days, and I am now an old man. I sit and close my eyes, remembering all those whose remains lie here. I gaze at the spot where I too will soon lie … next to Susanna. I am at peace. Though filled with lingering questions, I look forward to that ultimate promise of hope … the resurrection … a new creation … no more war, no more hatred, no more sickness. When the Lion will dwell with Man!

THE END

AN APPENDIX

Excerpt from Albert Schweitzer's
Nobel Peace Prize Lecture
The Problem of Peace
November 4, 1954

The statesmen who were responsible for shaping the world of today through the negotiations which followed each of these two wars found the cards stacked against them.... They were obliged to regard themselves as the executors of the will of the conquering peoples. They could not aspire to establishing relations between peoples on a just and proper basis; all their efforts were taken up by the necessity of preventing the most unreasonable of the demands made by the victors from becoming reality; they had, moreover, to convince the conquering nations to compromise with each other whenever their respective views and interests conflicted....

The First World War, then, had its origins in the conditions which prevailed in eastern and southeastern Europe. The new order created after both world wars bears in its turn the seeds of a future conflict.

Any new postwar structure is bound to contain the seeds of conflict unless it takes account of historical fact and is designed to provide a just and objective solution to problems in the light of that fact. Only such a solution can be really permanent.

ACKNOWLEDGMENTS

I could not have written this without help and encouragement. I especially thank my wife, Janine, whose store of knowledge from having read much historical fiction enables her to give valuable suggestions. Mostly, though, I thank her for her encouragement.

I thank Greg Stout, a published author, and friend, for giving me the courage to try and advice and assistance along the way.

I thank the good people of Trinity Lutheran Church - Egypt Mills, MO for encouraging me and bearing with me as I meandered my way to this book.

I also thank Michael Hahn who shared with me copies of letters of an ancestor who fought and died in the Civil War. Portions of this soldier's letters to his mother have been quoted exactly as written.

I also thank the many friends who agreed to read it, critique it, and encourage me along the way.

If it seems to have a message to us today and if it causes you to think, then it's been worth it.

ABOUT THE AUTHOR

Barry L. Pfanstiel has been a Lutheran Minister for forty-seven years. He received his BA from Concordia Senior College, Ft. Wayne, IN and his Master of Divinity degree from Concordia Seminary, St. Louis. Since then, he has served churches in DeWitt, AR, McMinnville, TN, Humble, TX and Cape Girardeau, MO. He retired in 2014 and has continued to serve part-time in Egypt Mills, MO and in Scott City, MO.

Barry and his wife, Janine, were married in 1971 and have twin daughters, Lindsey and Rachel, and one granddaughter, Bailey.

This is his first book. He got the initial idea two years ago when he was looking at a tombstone in a church cemetery marking graves of five siblings who died within two weeks of each other in 1920 of the Spanish Flu … two years after it had first begun killing. He thought, "There has to be story here." And this is what eventually became of that thought.

Made in the USA
Columbia, SC
26 April 2022